The Dog and its Day

By the same author

World 2.0:
A History from Enlightenment to Terrorism and Beyond

~

The Cuban Missile Crisis:
How Close We Really Came to Nuclear War

~

9/11:
102 Minutes That Changed World History

The Dog
and its Day

J.C. Peters

Odyssea Publishing
New York / Amsterdam

Published by Odyssea Publishing.
Layout by Merijn de Haen
Cover design by Teddi Black

ISBN: 9789082506310

If you have a question about the book, want to read more from the author, or stay informed about upcoming books, go to jellepeters.com or send an email to info@jellepeters.com.

Dedicated to Frederick F.

Prologue

On June 5, 1968, shortly after midnight, Senator Robert F. Kennedy entered the packed Embassy Room ballroom of the Ambassador Hotel in Los Angeles through the swinging doors from the kitchen area, to give a boisterous, energetic crowd of supporters what it had craved for all evening: a victory speech for winning the California Democratic presidential primary against Senator Eugene McCarthy.

After the speech, Kennedy was to go out through the crowd, to another reception on a lower level. But while he was speaking, campaign aides Fred Dutton and William Barry decided the Senator should instead meet with the writing press in the Colonial Room, on the other side of the small kitchen behind the ballroom. So when Kennedy started out after concluding his speech, Barry moved up to him and said: "No, it's been changed. We're going this way."

Dutton and Barry began clearing a path for the Senator to enter the kitchen area through the swinging doors on the far left of the stage. But assistant maître d'hôtel Karl Uecker, who had overheard Dutton and Barry, instead took Kennedy—by now boxed in by an enthusiastic crowd of supporters—through a back exit directly behind the stage. By taking this shortcut, however, Kennedy was suddenly ahead of his aides and personal bodyguards (the Secret Service did not provide protection for presidential candidates at the time) as Uecker led him by the wrist to the Colonial Room.

In the middle of the kitchen, the corridor was narrowed by a large ice cube making machine on the right and two stainless steel serving tables on the left. As they moved through the small, crowded kitchen, Kennedy stopped to shake hands and speak with the kitchen help. After a few moments, Karl Uecker took hold of the Senator's arm again to help him move towards the Colonial Room, which was now only about 30 feet away. They walked another few paces before Kennedy stopped again, shaking hands with hotel waiters Martin Patrusky to his left, Vincent di Pierro to his right and student Robin Casden, who was trying to get out of his path. Another few steps and Kennedy turned to his left to shake hands with kitchen porter Jesus Perez and busboy Juan Romero.

At the end of the ice machine, college student and campaign worker Lisa Urso stood by the tray stacker. She felt a shove from behind as a short, dark young man moved in front of her, reaching across his body with his right hand and moving toward the Senator. He pulled out a snub-nosed .22 revolver and, fully extending his right arm, aimed it at Kennedy.

"Kennedy, you son of a bitch!" Sirhan Bishara Sirhan exclaimed.

Witness accounts differ as to the pace and number of shots that were fired. Some reported hearing one shot before a pause, followed by a rapid volley of several more shots, others heard two shots first, while still others did not hear any pause at all in the firing.

Some witnesses thought they heard at least ten shots being fired, but Sirhan's revolver held a maximum of only eight bullets. Kennedy himself was shot four times—one bullet hitting his jacket but not entering him—and five others were also shot. One of them, Ira Goldstein, a nineteen-year-old rookie radio reporter, was shot twice, but one bullet went through his pant leg without entering his body. Aside from the victims' wounds, there were also several bullet holes in the ceiling, kitchen floor and walls. According to the Special Unit Senator (SUS), the LAPD task force created on June 11, 1968, to carry out all aspects of the investigation, multiple impacts were caused by ricochets and otherwise altered bullet trajectory paths.

In 2004, the only known audio tape of the assassination, made by independent journalist Stanislaw Pruszynski—who at the time had not been aware his recorder was still on—was discovered in the California State Archives in Sacramento, California. Analysis of the tape led several acoustic experts to conclude that at least thirteen shots had been fired, though others believed no more than eight shots were recorded on the tape.

Thomas Noguchi, Chief Medical Examiner-Coroner for the County of Los Angeles, who performed the autopsy on Robert Kennedy, determined that stippling patterns on the Senator's body indicated he had been shot from a distance of no more than 1-2 inches and that the three bullets that hit him and the one passing through his coat had all traveled back to front, right to left, and upwards. The assassin would therefore have had to have fired from behind Kennedy's right side, nearly touching him with the muzzle of the gun. Yet all witnesses agreed that Sirhan was standing in front of Kennedy as he fired and almost all placed him at least 1-3 feet from the Senator.

1

The Barkers had just let the last of their guests out, except for Paul Skovack, Chris Mathers and Congressman Charles O'Connor, who were still in the den. Bunny Barker sighed. "I'm going to bed. Are you going to be long?"

She already knew the answer. After forty-four years of marriage, she knew late night discussions with Paul Skovack and Chris Mathers never ended quickly. She just wanted to let him know she still preferred falling to sleep together.

"No, no, just one last drink," Alan Barker said musingly.

She smiled and briefly touched her husband's arm. "Well, good night."

"Good night dear."

As Bunny walked up the stairs, the butler entered the hall. "Will you be needing us anymore this evening sir?"

"No Jackson, thank you. Tell the staff the cleanup can wait until tomorrow."

"Very good sir. Good night sir."

"Good night Jackson."

Barker strode back to the den, his cap toe Oxfords click-clacking on the hall's black and white checkered marble floor, then swooshing softly on the thick Persian rugs in the still brightly lit ball room, past the empty glasses left on the mantelpiece and Louis Seize coffee tables.

He had never cared for the kitschy decorating style his wife was so fond of—the cream-colored wallpaper with golden fleur-de-lis pattern, the impractical Roman style one-armed sofas, the white Steinway concert piano—but he did care deeply for his wife. One of the few things he cared for.

The only room safe from Bunny's relentless redecorating efforts was the den. There, one wall was taken up entirely by a titanic bookcase, housing books from floor to ceiling and equipped with a rolling library ladder for easy access to the upper shelves. The fireplace, embedded in the opposing wall, was encased by a Victorian-era mantelpiece; a lion's head, shot by Barker himself, hanging above it. To its left stood a glass display case that held the revolver used by Confederate General James Longstreet during the Civil War. To its right, a liquor cabinet that had once belonged to President Theodore Roosevelt, fully stocked with the finest hard liquor. Finally, on the far end, an antique mahogany desk, massive and unyielding, quietly guarded the masculine integrity of this one room that still belonged to the man in the house.

The den was where Alan Barker came home, where he pondered and planned, rested and regrouped. It was where he had his best ideas and was able to see clearest, undisturbed by the many ad hoc demands heaped on him on a daily basis.

He took a right, finding Jackson clearing some cocktail glasses that had been left on the pedestal table used by Alexander Hamilton's bust. His favorite one.

"What did I say Jackson," Barker said with a smile as he passed the old servant, "leave it until tomorrow."

"I know sir. But I know how much you like Mr. Hamilton's bust and I couldn't just let these filthy glasses stand there."

"Alright, suit yourself," Barker said, walking on without looking

12

back.

He entered the den and walked to the bar. "Alright, anyone up for a refill?"

"I'm good Alan, thanks," Skovack said.

"I could do with another glass of that excellent Macallan Lalique," O'Connor said, holding up his glass.

"Count me in as well," Mathers held up his glass.

After pouring the drinks and handing O'Connor and Mathers their glasses, Barker sunk into one of the comfortable chairs with a sigh of fatigue, weight and old age. "Well, if ever a fundraiser was useless as hell, it was this one. Drump will never win, sure as sermons on Sundays."

"Oh, I don't know," O'Connor said, stroking the edge of his glass. "It's early days. He might still pull it off."

Barker chuckled derisively. "Oh come on Charles, the fundraiser is over, no need to sugarcoat the horse manure anymore. He's a buffoon and we all know it."

"Well, at least he's our buffoon," O'Connor said, taking a sip from the $30,000 a bottle Macallan he could never afford himself.

"You think?" Barker snickered. "Because he flip-flops more often than a sixteen-year-old gymnast. One day he's pro-choice, the next he's pro-life. First he's in favor of a whole bunch of limitations on gun rights, now he is against any limitations. We can't trust a guy like that to do the right thing."

The right thing. For those who knew Alan Barker there was no doubt as to what that meant. But, as his life-long friend and business partner Paul Skovack also knew, Barker was not the kind of man to complain about things he had no control over. He wondered where he was going with this. "I agree," Skovack said, "but at the same time it seems like a fait accompli, Alan. Ronald Drump is the Republican presidential nominee and that's that. Meaning the next President of the United States is either going to be him or Valery Clayton."

"No. Never her," Congressman O'Connor said with the conviction of a man who perhaps had had one Macallan Lalique too much already. "Anybody but her. This country can't survive another eight years of failed liberal policies."

"It sure as hell can't," Barker agreed, though, contrary to Congressman O'Connor, who had been a tea party favorite for years, his own thinking was far more practical than it was ideological. He was concerned about the 22 active coal mines Barker & Skovack Industries owned and operated in the U.S., mines Senator Clayton had vowed to close if she would be elected the 45th President of the United States. He was concerned about the increased fiscal scrutiny of multinational corporations Senator Clayton had promised, which would make it much harder to continue evading taxes on foreign business activities, nowadays accounting for more than half of B & S Industries' revenue. And he was thinking of the two, possibly three Supreme Court Justices the next president would likely get to nominate and which could swing the court in a decidedly liberal, anti-business direction for the next thirty years.

"But if you don't think Drump will win," O'Connor said, turning his glass in his hands, "and on top of everything else you don't trust him, then why did you organize tonight's fundraiser? And how much did B & S Industries itself pledge tonight?"

"Ten million," Barker said quietly, looking down at the melting ice cubes in his Baccarat tumbler. "But what choice do we really have?"

Another remark that breathed the kind of resignation and defeatism Skovack found very uncharacteristic for his friend. On the contrary, his signature remark for the past three decades, as they had aggressively expanded their mining empire, had been a combative "we'll see about that", and many African and South American dictator had heard it at his peril.

"This is the hand we've been dealt," Barker continued, "a couple of deuces pretending to be aces, running against the queen of the night and some jack."

"Of course two deuces are actually slightly favored against a queen and a jack in a heads-up Texas Hold'em game," Chris Mathers remarked, a smug smile lounging in the corner of his mouth. He was the long-time Chief Security Officer at B & S Industries and was often abroad to 'deal' with certain problems at the company's mines, most of them in Africa and South America. But whenever he was back at the head office, he and Barker would play heads-up Texas no limit Hold'em at least twice a week. They had been doing it for years. Mathers was the only one who wouldn't let Barker win (aside from Skovack, but he was a terrible player) and one of the few people Barker simply couldn't read—perhaps because there was nothing to read. He had this cold, dead stare Barker used to joke he had probably learned at some CIA introductory 'psychology for spooks' course.

Barker grinned. "Well, no analogy is perfect Chris."

"I wouldn't call Mike Vance a deuce though," O'Connor said, referring to the VP on the Republican ticket.

"You're right," Barker conceded, "in fact, he'd have a much better chance to defeat Clayton."

"That's exactly what I was thinking the other day."

"Yeah, very sensible man that," Barker mused, giving Skovack the kind of look he had been giving him ever since their days at Colombia University, when they were still chasing girls at frat parties and college bars, and later on, in tense negotiations with the United Mine Workers and greedy, corrupt politicians. 'Pay attention and follow my lead', it meant.

"I always thought so," Skovack said.

"You, eh, know him quite well, don't you?" Barker casually asked O'Connor.

O'Connor nodded. "We've been best friends since college. I even introduced him to his wife."

"You think he'd be a good president?" Barker asked.

"Honestly, I think he could be a second Ronald Reagan," O'Connor said without hesitation. "He is a true conservative and has served as Congressman for more than a decade without being corrupted by the Washington political establishment."

"And as governor of Indiana, he was also one of the strongest supporters of the coal industry, right?" Barker added.

"Oh yeah, he loves the coal industry, *loves* it!" O'Connor said, emphasizing the word 'loves' the way only drunk people can. "Absolutely *hates* the EPA." He took another swig, before continuing: "I wouldn't be so sure about Ronald Drump, though. Mike told me last week that Drump had said the Chinese and the Europeans are getting too far ahead in alternative energy, and that the only way to catch up would be to heavily subsidize alternative energy here in the States as well, and to retrain coal miners as solar panel producers."

O'Connor scoffed. "I mean, can you believe that? Back in May he gave this whole speech about wanting to bring the coal industry back to America again. Talking about how he was going to bring back coal mining jobs to Ohio and North Dakota, remember that?" He took another swig. "Subsidizing alternative energy instead of letting the market do its work," he mumbled in his glass. "Now that is one thing Mike Vance would *never* do."

Barker shot another look at Skovack. "So, do you think Vance wants to be president himself somewhere down the line?"

By now, Congressman O'Connor was far too imbibed to read

anything substantial in the question. "Of course he does. Even before his first House race he was talking about running for president one day."

"Is that right?"

"He lost that race, by the way, and the one after that. But he just kept coming back until he won. Hell of a guy."

"Well," Barker said, after a moment of silence, shooting Skovack a quick glance before overtly looking at his wrist watch, "It's getting late."

"Yeah," Skovack said, standing up, "I think I'll call it a night as well. Tomorrow is another day."

Barker and Mathers got up too.

O'Connor, who had been sinking deeper and deeper into his chair for the past 30 minutes or so, had just enough sense of propriety left to understand the party was over. "Yes… yes, I think I will be leaving as well," he said, struggling to get up without having to put down his drink.

"Here Charles, let me help you," Barker said, gently taking his glass while gesturing Skovack and Mathers to stay behind. "I'll show you out."

"That is mighty kind of you sir," O'Connor said, in an awkward attempt to sound both British and South-Carolinian, while standing next to his chair as if he was riding the subway.

Barker took the Congressman by the elbow and guided him across the ballroom and into the hall, where he placed a short call to the reception desk to hail a cab. As they waited for the elevator, O'Connor loudly proclaimed what a wonderful fundraiser it had been, how Barker should certainly not forget to thank his wife for a most pleasant evening, that the whiskey had been "fan—taaast—tic" and more of the kind of talk from a man who should find a bed or a couch before the floor finds him.

A few minutes later Barker returned.

"What was that all about?" Skovack asked right away. "Those questions about Vance and if he wanted to be president? What were you playing at?"

Barker closed the door, but said nothing.

"You want to pull the $10 million donation? Just because of what that drunken idiot said? I mean, come on. We don't know Drump will be bad for the coal industry. You said it yourself, he flip-flops all the time. So even if he tells Vance he wants to get rid of the mines, nobody knows what he'll think a year from now. Besides, he's a business man, he knows better than to bite the hand that feeds him."

"It's not just the mines," Barker said, walking to the bar. "I mean, yes, that's a big piece of it, but a Drump presidency could also be disastrous for our overseas interests, the geopolitical stability and the long-term course of the nation." He reached into the ice bucket, grabbed a couple of cubes and dropped them in his glass.

"So what are you saying? That because Drump is unreliable and potentially even dangerous, you want to consider backing 'Venomous Valery' instead?" Skovack asked, using Drump's favorite epithet for his opponent.

Barker scoffed. "Of course not. She has already said she wants to close all remaining coal mines in the U.S. and she will never back down from that. And any Supreme Court justices she'll nominate will be anti-business, pro-environment, anti-gun and pro-abortion."

A deep, v-shaped wrinkle formed between Skovack's eyes. "I'm confused. Are you saying you want to sit this one out? Because I have to tell you, when it comes down to it, I still prefer Drump over Clayton."

Barker crossed his arms. "I want Vance."

Skovack looked at Mathers, but the one-time CIA operative didn't move a muscle, either because he was uninterested or because he already knew where this was going. "Yeah, well, me too Alan, but unfortunately he is not on the top of the ticket," Skovack said, a smile of disbelief around his mouth.

Barker gave the rolling library ladder a push, he always liked walking around and doing things with his hands when having discussions like this. "You know, Valery Clayton must be the most unpopular Democratic presidential nominee in modern political history," he scoffed, pacing the room. "I mean, moderates don't trust her, the liberals positively hate her... against almost any other opponent she wouldn't have stood a chance, because the liberals would have stayed at home and moderates would have either done the same or voted for the Republican candidate. The only way for her to win would be if the other candidate was so ridiculously unqualified, so erratic, so dangerous, that everybody with half a brain would have no choice but to vote for the candidate who promises *not* to start a 21st century version of Nazi Germany."

"So, what, you want to politely ask Ronald Drump to move over, offer him money to step down—what?" Skovack still didn't get it and by now was getting slightly annoyed with this kind of wishful thinking.

"I think we should get rid of him," Barker said bluntly.

Skovack opened his mouth to say something, then closed it again, realizing he was neither as surprised nor as dismissive of the idea as he would like to give himself credit for. The thought hadn't crossed his mind before, but now that Barker had put it out there, he could hardly deny its logic. Still, murdering a presidential candidate... it certainly went further than anything else they had ever done. The most high-profile politician they had eliminated was that Nigerian Minister of Justice opposed to the privatization of the Nigerian Coal Corporation, which was going to give B & S Industries an important foothold in the Nigerian coal industry. What was his name again? Those African names... he remembered the incident well, it was just a few months after 9/11. Jesus, was it fifteen years already?

The last time they had decided someone had to go was that South African agitator who had been stirring things up among the miners at the Witbank colliery, Bwala Galala or something. What was that, about three years ago? Still, that too was a far stretch from killing a U.S. presidential candidate. A very far stretch. And would Vance even become the presidential candidate if Drump was gone?

"Would Vance automatically go to the top of the ticket?" he asked.

Barker smiled. "No, not automatically. If, for whatever reason, Drump would no longer be an option, the Republican National Committee would vote on a new candidate. But the existing VP candidate would have a strong shot at moving to the top of the ticket—especially if Drump were to be eliminated close to the end of the campaign and the VP candidate was a popular conservative bulwark like Mike Vance."

"You really have thought this through, haven't you," Skovack said, sounding impressed if not yet convinced.

"You know me, I don't like going off half-cocked," Barker replied.

Skovack sighed. "I could use another drink."

"Of course. Same?" Barker asked, pointing at his own glass.

"Please."

"How about you Chris?"

"I'll take a cold beer if you have one."

"I sure do," Barker said, pulling a beer from the mini fridge next to the liquor cabinet. "Heineken, right?" Barker grinned.

"You know it," Mathers said, taking the beer.

"What do you think of all this?" Skovack asked Mathers. The head of security shrugged. It wasn't the first time he had been present at conversations like this and it probably wouldn't be the last. He had never concerned himself with the politics of it all. He served the man, the organization, nothing else.

Realizing this, Skovack rephrased, "I mean, is it doable?"

Mathers put his beer on the dark oak coffee table. "Sure. You can get to anyone, it's just a matter of resources. The difficulty is getting away with it. But if we hire an outsider, exposure to B & S would be minimal. Would be expensive, though."

Skovack waved the last words away. "Money is not the problem, and if we withdraw it in cash from a couple of friendly offshore accounts before depositing it into a numbered account in the Emirates, the money will be untraceable."

"And tonight's fundraiser, together with our $10 million donation to the Drump campaign, will create a perfect cover story in the highly unlikely event we should ever need one," Barker added. "We have been Republicans all our lives and B & S Industries has given money to the Republican cause for the last 30 years. No one will ever suspect we were even remotely involved in this. It will look like an attack from the extreme left." Then, to Mathers: "Do you want to hire the same guy who did the job of that marxist community organizer from South Africa a couple of years ago?"

"He is the best," Mathers said evenly.

"You should ask him to make it look like an attack from the extreme left, like anti-fascists or Greenpeace or something, or maybe a deranged lone nutcase. I'm sure it's easy enough to leave a faded green army jacket with one of those nuclear disarmament signs sewn on at the crime scene."

"You don't think that'd be a little too obvious?" Skovack mocked.

"You know what I mean. Something to corroborate the already obvious, that the bullet came from the left."

Barker looked Skovack straight in the eye. "Then, we agree?"

Skovack hesitated, but it wasn't a real hesitation. The die had been cast a long time ago. He slowly nodded.

Taking it as his cue, Mathers said, "Good, I'll make the necessary arrangements and get back to you soon." He emptied his beer, put it on the table and got up. "I'll let myself out," he said, gesturing a short goodbye to the other two as he walked to the door. And with that it was done.

2

Wednesday, August 3, 2016,

Manhattan, New York City

Conrad Richter looked down on Manhattan as the plane made its descent. He had been away for five months, not the longest stretch, but still long enough for the familiar vista below him to be tinged with a sense of estrangement. New York was the only place he would ever call home, and yet he had not stayed there for more than one month at a time since he had left for the Marines, almost exactly 30 years ago.

He leaned back in his seat. Pre-law at Hunter College… the only connection he still felt to that kid was the part that didn't want to be a pre-law at Hunter College, that had wanted to be more than just another lawyer in the city, walking around in a suit and tie all day long until he could finally take it off at dinner, like his father. The part that had had just the vaguest notion that life should be different.

Wanting to join the Marines had not come out of the blue, though. To Conrad, it was the other way of life. There was his father's way, a lawyer's life, and then there was his grandfather's way.

His father, Joe Richer, had been the first Richter to go to college. Drafted for Vietnam in 1963, he had enrolled at Hunter College after returning from the war, backed by benefits from the Vietnam G.I. Bill. After getting his law degree and passing the New York bar exam, he had started as a junior associate at Tripp, Stanwyck & Menken, working 60 hours a week in pursuit of a better life, while somehow still finding time to marry and start a family as well. Twelve years later, he had made partner and moved his family from Williamsburg, Brooklyn, to a spacious apartment in Midtown Manhattan, on Fifth Avenue, between 63rd and 64th Street. Walking through that big, empty apartment and seeing Central Park from what would be his room, Conrad had realized for the first time just how successful his father really was.

Joe Richter never forgot where he came from, but he would have liked to. Like the once unpopular teenager who finally secures a seat at the cool kids table, he was never able to completely shake off the Cinderella syndrome—the fear that everything would return back to normal once the clock struck twelve. The visits to his father back in Williamsburg had grown increasingly infrequent. To Conrad's father, going back to Brooklyn was like going back in time, which was about the last thing he wanted.

For Conrad, however, the opposite was true. He loved visiting his grandfather and went there at least twice a week. As far as he was concerned, the better life was back in Brooklyn.

Hans Richter had fought as a Marine in the Pacific during World War ii. He had lost both his legs at the battle for Mount Yaedake, on Okinawa, and for more than twenty years had not spoken a word about it to anyone. But when he had held his first, and what would turn out to be only grandson in his arms, something in the Marine part of his brain had cracked open and started telling the stories—locked away but never forgotten—to the little bundle in his arms. With his deep voice and lively eyes, Hans Richter had conjured up images of heroic Marines storming the beaches of tiny islands, of holding fast against wave after wave of 'yellow monkeys', of charging 'Jap' bunkers under heavy fire, pushing flamethrowers into their small openings and burn everyone of those 'yellow cowards' inside, of hand-to-hand combat with bayonets, and sometimes with nothing more than fists.

For Hans, it was—for lack of a better word—therapy. For little Conrad, it was a big show of sound and a myriad of facial expressions. And while Conrad's father was working his socks off at Tripp, Stanwyck & Menken, hoping to one day get his own name on the door, and his mother was mostly occupying herself with her two daughters and a part-time job as a Kodak technician, grandpa Richter nursed young Conrad on stories taking place at exotic sounding, deadly places like Guadalcanal, Peleliu, Iwo Jima and Okinawa, telling and re-telling (and maybe here and there slightly embellishing) tales of valor about the Marines in the Pacific. By the time Conrad was old enough to actually understand them, they were as polished as Hollywood blockbuster movies.

How could a lawyer's life ever compete with a Marine's life? To an outsider, any comparison between a successful lawyer with an apartment on Fifth Avenue and a house in the Hamptons, and a washed out, legless Marine withering away in Brooklyn, might seem ludicrous. To a boy reared on stories of valor and glory in far away places, the comparison was equally ridiculous. How could rich, boring and repetitive ever compete with exciting, glorious and adventurous?

Conrad Richter joined the Marines in January 1986. Three years after Grenada, three years before Panama and four before Operation Desert Shield. But the Marine Corps he knew through and through—or rather Hans Richter's gung-ho island-hopping Marine Corps, led by men like Lieutenant Colonel Chesty Puller, who once replied to a messenger informing him they were completely surrounded: "*Those poor bastards. They've got us right where we want 'em. We can shoot in every direction now*"—that Marine Corps no longer existed, or if it did, it was mostly reduced to waiting for the next war. In August 1987, desperate for action, he put in for a transfer to the Navy SEALS, the elite soldiers of Naval Special Warfare Command, but was shortly thereafter contacted and subsequently recruited by the Central Intelligence Agency's Special Activities Division (SAD), for its Special Operations Group (SOG), to carry out the kind of tactical paramilitary operations the United States deemed of vital interest but did not wish to be associated with.

In December 1988, Richter was sent to Angola as a Specialized Skills Officer, attached to the group of CIA operatives liaising with Jonas Savimbi's UNITA rebels, who had been entangled in a civil war with the communist Popular Movement for the Liberation of Angola (MPLA) since 1975, after first having fought and defeated Portugal together in the war of independence. The MPLA was heavily backed by the Soviet Union and its allies, notably Cuba, while UNITA received military support from South Africa and— from the 1980s—the United States.

The Angola CIA station was authorized to carry out covert, paramilitary activities against the MPLA and its allies without having to ask for specific mission authorization, so as to maintain 'plausible deniability'. Likewise, the Angola station authorized its Paramilitary Operations Officers and Specialized Skills Officers teams to carry out so-called 'wet jobs' against the MPLA without having to ask for specific authorization. Consequently, in the spring of 1989, Conrad Richter and Paramilitary Operations Officer Chris Mathers formed a kill team specifically aimed at eliminating MPLA officers and Soviet and Cuban liaisons. They were somewhat of an odd couple—Richter being tall, blond and shaped like a triathlete, while Mathers measured a scant 5'5 and had an already retreating hair line, almost comically offset by dark, bushy eyebrows—but that did not stop them from being highly effective.

Authorization for covert military operations was suspended in

April 1991, at the beginning of peace negotiations between UNITA and MLPA, leading to the Bicesse Accords of May 31, 1991, which laid out a transition to multi-party democracy from the previous single-party rule under the MLPA. Elections were held in September 1992, but after Savimbi failed to receive an outright majority in the first round of the presidential elections, the fighting resumed.

Although the U.N. had declared the elections free and fair and the Bush administration faced increasing pressure to urge Savimbi to participate in the run-off election, the suspension of covert paramilitary operations was nevertheless lifted. The Clayton administration would soon take a different approach with Savimbi, though, culminating in Executive Order 12865, issued in September 1993, which prohibited all arms sales to UNITA.

The Clayton administration would also mark the beginning of a new era for the CIA. Between 1992-94, the CIA budget was cut by 24 percent, fulfilling a campaign pledge of President Clayton to cut the central intelligence budget by $7 billion during his first term in office. During the Cold War, roughly half of the Central Intelligence Agency's resources had been targeted at the Soviet Union, but Clayton had vowed to *"make the economic security of our nation a primary goal of our foreign policy"* and therefore shifted the CIA's focus towards the area of economic intelligence. During the Cold War, economic intelligence had accounted for only 10 percent of the CIA's activities, but under the Clayton administration it grew to 40 percent.

Richter left the CIA in the spring of 1993.

3

The two men were sitting in front of the lawn at Bryant Park, between Fifth and Sixth Avenues, with the pink granite fountain at the park's western gateway to their back. Ten feet away, a mother was helping her two-year-old daughter navigate nature's carpet for the first time, a proud father carefully filming the moment. Fashionable girlfriends, corporate executives and lowly data analysts were toying with low-fat lunches, sitting at one of the park's many, signature pine-green round tables. Hipsters were squatting on the grass, hobos were hanging in chairs or resting their unwashed heads on one of the signature pine-green round tables. On the other side of the lawn, the bronze statue of William Cullen Bryant was sternly overlooking it all.

"How'd it go?" Mathers asked, looking at the giggling kid.

"Well, you know," Richter said, looking at Mathers with cold, cerulean eyes, a cynical smile lingering in the corner of his mouth, "he went."

"No problems?"

"None. Got him when he was closing the drapes for the night, while his wife was in the shower."

"Good." Mathers took a sip from his espresso. "I have a new assignment for you. High profile."

"Ok…" Richter said, a hint of curiosity in his voice.

"It's also stateside."

Richter waited until two suits had strolled by. "You know I don't do domestic."

"I know and you're right not to. But this is a big one. Could set you up for life."

"Retire? Why would I? I just hit 50, I'm the best I've ever been. Besides, I love my life." Richter shook his head. "Sounds more like what you're about to ask me will not just set me up for life but also make me a target for life."

"I wouldn't go that far. Maybe just for a couple of years," Mathers grinned.

"That's what I thought."

"Well, want to hear it or not?"

"What does it pay?" Richter asked.

Mathers downed the last of his espresso. "That's the easy part. Money is no object. Just name your price."

"Wow, that desperate huh?"

Mather shrugged. "It's a high-value target, comes with a high-value contract."

"Jesus, the suspense is killing me," Richter sneered, "out with it already."

Mathers pulled out his iPhone, accessed it with his fingerprint and showed Richter the screen.

"Him?" Richter whistled softly. "No wonder you were so slow to mention it."

"Can it be done?" Mathers asked.

"What did you tell your masters?"

"That you can get to anyone depending on the resources."

"Spoken like a true operations officer," Richter sneered. He fished a pack of Luckies out of his pocket and banged out a cigarette. "I don't get it, though," he continued, putting the cigarette in his mouth while feeling for his lighter in the other pocket, "why him? I mean, why not Clayton? What does B & S have to gain? Assuming they are the ones who put out the contract."

"You can't smoke here," Mathers said.

Richter lit up. "What are you talking about? We're in a public park."

Mathers chuckled. "You know my friend, a lot has changed in New York since the '80s. You don't have to worry about getting shot on the corner of 42nd Street and 7th Avenue anymore, Williamsburg has gone from mob hangout to hipster clubhouse and smoking in public parks is prohibited."

Richter leaned back. "Get out of here, I know this city like the back of my hand." He blew out the smoke in little circles.

"Oh yeah?" Mathers teased, "when was the last time you were here for a whole month in a row?"

"I don't know, somewhere before the Clayton administration I guess," he snickered. Then, turning to Mathers, "Which brings me back to the issue at hand, why not her? I mean, her husband really fucked us over back in '93." He took another drag. "Besides, I rather like Drump. He's nice to vets and he's always talking about rebuilding the military."

"You think he might hire you back into the agency again?" Mathers mocked.

"Well, no, but still…"

"I thought you weren't political."

"I'm not, but taking out a presidential candidate… pfff. My grandfather would spin in his grave."

"Look, if it makes you feel any better, they want to take him out because they think he'll never win, that Clayton would never be elected if she were running against Vance or whoever else the Republican National Committee would elect in his place."

A devilish little smile curled around Richter's lips. "Son of a bitch, now that's what I call higher politics. So they think that with him out of the way, Mike Vance would become the next President of the United States." He shook his head a couple of times. "Damn, that is some devious shit."

"There's more," Mathers said. "It can't look like a professional hit. It has to look like an accident, or an amateurish attack by some extremist, left wing, Islamic, take your pick. In other words, it has to look like it was done by someone who had a real beef with him. Could even be a Mexican for all I care. But it cannot look like the work of a hired gun."

Richter squashed the cigarette butt with his shoe. "You do realize what you're asking, right? I mean, this is not going to be even remotely similar to anything we did in Angola, or any other job I've done since then. This man is protected by a small army of Secret Service agents, any venue he visits is thoroughly checked in advance multiple times. There are bomb-sniffing dogs, security checks of every person allowed close enough to snipe him from a mile away. And locations where security measures can't be that elaborate—spontaneous appearances, surprise drop-ins, that sort of thing—will be kept secret until the last possible moment. I mean, I suppose it's possible to get his itinerary, but by the time events are listed it'll be too late to make the necessary preparations."

Mathers gesticulated nonchalantly. "It's difficult, I know."

Richter shook his head. "No, I don't think you do. Getting yourself into a position where you could take a shot—just one shot—and get away, will already be close to impossible. But somehow making it look amateurish… I mean, that effectively rules out a long range, high-powered rifle shot, because no amateur would be able to do that. Amateurs use handguns, AR-15s, crudely made bombs, a grenade if they can get their hands on it. But you can forget about planting a bomb, even a crude one, because they will be sniffed out, and all of the other stuff is short-range, meaning you could never get out after."

"Jesus, when did you become such a pessimist," Mathers joked.

But Richter didn't laugh. "Since I decided I want to stay alive and out of prison my friend."

Both men were silent for a while.

"You know what you need?" Mathers said after a few minutes.

"You mean other than the $10 million I would want for this job?" Richter replied bluntly.

"Agreed, and yes, other than that."

"Okay, what?"

"A Sirhan Sirhan."

"A what?"

"Actually it's not a what, it's a who," Mathers said, as Richter banged out another cigarette.

"Sir, I'm sorry, but you are not allowed to smoke here," a park security officer said, towering over the two men.

Richter looked up. "Oh I'm sorry officer. Frankly, I already thought so, but my friend here said smoking was allowed in Bryant Park from sunrise to sunset."

"Ah, no sir," the officer replied, now looking at Mathers. "Smoking is prohibited in all New York public parks at all times."

Mathers looked up, his lips pressed together, gesturing he got the message. "Alright, officer, thank you for telling us," he managed to say, as Richter put the cigarette back into the package with a gentle smile.

"No problem sir. Have a nice day," the officer said, tapping his cap.

As the security officer strolled on, Mathers gave Richter a dirty look. "Anyway, like I said, it's a who. Sirhan Sirhan was the guy who shot Robert Kennedy."

"Oh yeah, I remember that. Well, I mean, not personally, I was like two years old or something, but yeah, in the kitchen of some hotel, right?"

"Happened on the day I was born," Mathers nodded. "Anyway, he was the guy who did it, but there were a lot of people who thought he'd been set up, and that he wasn't the only shooter."

"What do you mean set up, like a patsy?"

Mathers shrugged. "Why not?"

Richter stared ahead, processing the thought. "Not just making it look like it was an amateur, but use an actual amateur," he mused. "I help him get in, get him a gun, and he does the actual shooting." He nodded a few times. "Yeah, that might work."

"Nothing can lead back to us though," Mathers said, "you understand what I'm saying?"

"Yeah, I understand…" Richter said, still sounding far away.

"So… could you?" Mathers asked.

"Hmmm?"

"Pull it off."

Richter tilted his head a bit and shot Mathers a short, intense glance, then nodded. "Two million up front. The rest on completion."

"Agreed."

4

Thursday, August 4, 2016,

Upper West Side, Manhattan, New York City

On the subway from Bryant Park back to his small apartment on the Upper West Side, Conrad Richter started mulling the two questions that lay at the heart of every new job: where, and how?

Every professional has his preferred methods and Richter was no exception—his weapon of choice had been the USMC M40A1 sniper rifle ever since his days as a Marine sniper scout—but this job would be like no other in the more than 25 years he had been doing this kind of work. The sniper rifle was out, because it couldn't look like a professional hit, but how in the hell could he take out a target protected by the Secret Service without using a long-range rifle? A hit from up close was out too, for obvious reasons, unless he could find some schmuck to do it, like Mathers suggested. But even if he did, he could never completely rely on an amateur to take out the target.

As for the 'where', Drump would of course make plenty of public appearances in the coming months, but not all of them would be equally suitable. For one, he needed to know the location weeks in advance in order to make the necessary preparations. He could probably get his hands on the candidate's itinerary, but campaign schedules frequently changed, because of fresh polling data, tweaks in campaign strategies, unexpected developments. No, he needed an event where the candidate was sure to show up and that would not, could not, change.

He got out at Times Square Station and walked up the stairs to the platform for the 1,2 and 3 lines heading Uptown. As he waited for one of the express trains on the damp, sweltering subway platform—an inescapable torture during the summer months—the first version of a timetable began to take shape in Richter's mind.

He figured he would need to know at least a month in advance where the candidate would make his appearance. That would give him enough time to scout the venue, plant the weapon—or weapons—acquire the necessary credentials to get in and plan his escape. Today was August 4. If he could get access to the itinerary within the next two weeks, that would give mid-September as the earliest possible time. Six weeks. That might be cutting it a little close for the gunsmith, though, who, as he knew from past experience, was as much of a perfectionist as he was himself, and would perhaps need more time manufacturing the specific weapons he had in mind. And then there was the question of the amateur, the lone wolf. He had no doubt such a person could be found, but that too would take some time, as would recruiting and training him to carry out the diversionary attack. So, all things considered, early to mid-October was probably more realistic.

By the time he got off at 96th Street, Richter's mind was fully committed to the job at hand. Back at his apartment, he sat himself at the twenty-year-old Ikea table, opened his laptop, lit up a cigarette and began researching Bond Arms derringers. He didn't get up again until hours later, to buy some fruit and eggs at Barzini's. By then, the radiance of the laptop's screen was the only light left in the apartment.

In the days that followed, he began reading up on Drump, watching his debate performances and rallies on YouTube, noting what kind of rallies he had held so far, their locations, how they were set up, how far back the crowd was held, what he did after speaking— did he leave right away or linger and take his time to meet his supporters? He did not bother too much with the security, knowing it would be top notch, but he did take notice of a little incident during a rally at Dayton Ohio, on March 12, when a 22-year-old left-wing extremist, later identified as Thomas Caravaggio, had jumped the bike racks and tried to get on stage, in an apparently planned attempt to, well, get on stage. There was video footage from multiple angles but one wide shot was especially interesting, as it showed the attacker from the beginning of his attempt. The interesting part was that he was able to climb the fence at all, even though there was a Secret Service agent positioned not three feet away from him. But it still took that agent 1.5 second to react, and 5 full seconds before the first agent was close enough to Drump to physically shield him. As for the protester, he succeeded in touching the stage, but that was as far as he got. Still, the crowd was less than 20 feet away from the candidate. A determined fanatic could certainly get one or two shots in before being overwhelmed—provided he could get a gun inside the secured area.

Caravaggio would have been perfect for the job. Of course, now that he was known there could be no question of using him. But it did set Richter on the trail of what kind of person he was probably looking for. A man between the ages of 20-45, probably white, above average intelligence, a left-wing activist with a history of protesting, anti-racist, anti-fascist, pro-environment, that sort of thing. Someone with a penchant for drama, who needed the moral high ground to feel better about himself and showed strong feelings about it.

Not so long ago, such a person might have taken quite a long time to find, requiring infiltration of left-wing extremist groups by attending their gatherings and protests and slowly building a group of friends there, who, in turn, could help further widen the network of possibles by introducing their friends. But in the social media age, most people eagerly displayed every little thing about themselves and shared everything about everybody else they were in contact with, providing the kind of information treasure trove intelligence agencies the world over could only dream of before the advent of the internet.

Just by mining Facebook, Twitter and LinkedIn, combined with specific searches on Google, Richter was able to scan dozens of possible candidates over the span of just a few days. He bought a simple software program that allowed him to filter Twitter account searches for things like location, age, sex and most recent activity, together with specific keywords such as 'racism' and 'anti-fascist'. One keyword that proved particularly interesting was 'black lives matter', as Richter found out that white people actively supporting this movement were far more likely to be actively involved with the more extreme left-wing organizations as well.

After this first selection round, he went through the tweets of the remaining candidates to get a quick handle on their level of political involvement and the sort of things they said about Ronald Drump. Obviously, anything they said about the Republican presidential candidate was negative, but he was not so much interested in comments that aimed to counter the candidate's political positions or went above and beyond in creative name-calling and ridiculing him and his supporters. Rather, he was looking for remarks that conveyed a willingness to take action, tweets like "*Drump pro-white, anti-rest, r we really going to allow this man in* WHouse *#StopDrumpNow*", and "*Drump 21st century Hitler, must not happen again! #StopDrumpNow #Drumpism*". He then used another little program to match the most promising Twitter candidates to their LinkedIn and Facebook profiles. Almost all of them had a Facebook presence and about 70 percent also had a LinkedIn profile. The LinkedIn profiles were particularly useful, as they provided a clear overview of the candidate's educational level and career history, and he was specifically looking for well-educated people, who, in his experience, were more easily frustrated about the state of the world and their place in it, and ultimately more willing to act on the logical conclusions—however extreme—that followed from their convictions.

For the ones that were left, Richter did a search on both Facebook and Google, to find out who their friends were, who they admired, what magazine and newspaper articles they liked, what videos, photos, locations and activities, what blog posts they had written, what photos they had taken, what videos they had made. The amount of information was overwhelming, but it did provide him with a number of highly interesting candidates.

One of the most promising subjects was the head of the Anti-Fascist League, one Peter Veldman, thirty-one years old, a Dutch national who had come to the United States in the summer of 2009 to pursue a Ph.D. in history at the University of Cornell, but had dropped out a few years later and had somehow managed to stay in New York. Veldman was only moderately active on Facebook, but he wrote a very honest, personal blog on his website that entertained Richter for an entire Tuesday evening and convinced him that the Dutchman could be the perfect candidate. Veldman's last blog post also put him on the trail of an event the candidate would most definitely not cancel, thus giving him a date and a venue to fix his timetable on.

5

Saturday, August 13, 2016,

(en route to) Las Vegas, Nevada

On Saturday, August 13, at 7:29 a.m., Richter took American Airlines flight 1263 out of JFK to Las Vegas, Nevada, which would arrive at McCarran International Airport at 10:06 a.m. local time. He had no luggage other than his backpack and would be taking the 9:59 p.m. AA return flight that same evening, which would touch down at JFK the following morning, at 6:01 a.m. Eastern Time.

In his inside jacket pocket he had tickets for the 2016 World Hip Hop Dance Championship, which was to take place tonight, at 6:30 p.m. PDT, at the Thomas & Mack Center, on the campus of the University of Nevada. He would have preferred going to a Runnin' Rebels game, but the regular basketball season had ended months ago. In fact, other than the hip hop championship final, there were no events at all at the Thomas & Mack Center in the coming weeks.

On the plane, looking out the window, his thoughts drifted back to three days in Paris during the summer of 1990, the only time he and Mathers had ventured outside Angola to take out a prominent MPLA member.

The target, General Lúcio Santos, had been the Minister of Defense and the mastermind behind the successful reorganization of the MPLA's military structure, which had significantly enhanced its military strike capability. There had been rumors he would soon be appointed the new military commander of the MPLA, but UNITA had discreetly requested the CIA's assistance in preventing this, prompting the CIA station chief to discreetly inform Richter and Mathers that the agency regarded it highly unfortunate that Lúcio Santos was still alive, though he had stopped short of giving any sort of actual directive.

The two CIA operatives had subsequently collected intel on the general, but soon discovered he was possibly the most boring workaholic in all of Angola and would not be an easy man to get at. Generally, routines are a professional killer's best friend. They can be probed, tested, prepared and planned for. But in the case of General Santos there really hadn't been much to go on. If he wasn't working at the heavily guarded Ministry of Defense, he was being driven to his heavily guarded house in his heavily escorted, heavily armored car, where he stayed until the next morning, until it was time to go back to the heavily guarded Ministry of Defense. There was no mistress, no gambling, there were no parties, no late night dinners in the city, nothing.

But just when they had started to become desperate, they had gotten word that General Santos was leaving for a two-week vacation in Paris with Mrs. Santos. After properly thanking God for wives and their eternal love of Paris, Richter and Mathers had gotten on the first available flight from Lubango to Johannesburg, arriving there just in time to catch a connecting flight to the City of Light.

If routines are a professional killer's best friend, then the voyage abroad is his unexpected booty call. Away from home—often also the home of his rivals and enemies—the target is generally more at ease. Whether the trip is work-related or purely recreational, it will almost certainly involve shopping, visits to tourist attractions and lunches and dinners at popular restaurants. With the exception of extremely high-profile targets, the security detail is usually trimmed down, routines are more lax and impulsive movements hard to avoid. And then there is the wife. If she accompanies her husband (contracts are almost always taken out on men, though there are of course exceptions) on his trip, she will probably want some R&R with him as well.

Back in Luanda, a Soviet T-34 tank couldn't have dragged General Santos to a restaurant with his wife, but there he was, on the terrace of café *Le Bouquet d'Alésia*, right next to the sidewalk of Avenue du Général Leclerc, sitting next to Mrs. Santos in a light-grey suit on that warm August night in 1990. The table behind the romantic couple was occupied by four bulky Angolan security guards, but honestly, what could they have done against a guy, driving up on one of the hundreds of scooters zooming by, pulling a Glock 17 and double tapping General Santos in front of his wife. Nothing.

At the same time, though, Paris wasn't Luanda, and an open, military-style execution of a foreign general on French soil would not sit well with one of the United States' more… sensitive European allies. 'Stealth' and 'plausible deniability' thus being the operative words, Richter and Mathers had opted for a CIA-developed weapon that could be deployed unnoticed and obfuscated the cause of death. The weapon, a modified Colt 1911, could fire a small, frozen dart of liquefied, slow-working poison at high speed, piercing clothing, breaking the victim's skin and entering the body without leaving any trace, except for a tiny red dot. The dart would subsequently melt inside the victim, releasing the poison. On their second day in the French capital, an operative from the Paris station had brought it over to their cheap shithole of a hotel in Rue Barbes.

The next evening, they followed General Santos, his wife and their four-men security detail—two in the car with Mr. and Mrs. Santos, two following in a second car—on a scooter to café *Le Bouquet d'Alésia*. Being an impromptu event, Richter and Mathers had had no time to scout the place, but as they passed the café where the two cars carrying Mr. and Mrs. Santos and their bodyguards stopped, Richter quickly spotted the construction site next to the café, where work on a new movie theater had apparently just begun. After doubling back, Mathers parked the scooter in front of the construction site's half-open gate and Richter quickly sneaked through.

With the exception of the gate, the entire fence was covered with sheets of fern-green cloth, obstructing view of the site from the sidewalk. Richter walked to the right edge and made a small hole in the cloth of the first section of the fence, just beyond the outer left wall of the café. Peeking through, he saw Santos and his wife sitting at the third table in the second row, the four security guards sitting right behind them. He got on his stomach and carefully made a second hole, this one large enough for the barrel and front sight of the gun.

As he looked past the front sight, he could make out General Santos' light-grey pant legs, beige socks and chestnut-brown leather shoes, flanked by the legs of the cheap wicker chair he was sitting on. Close to, but not directly in his line of fire were the hind legs of Mrs. Santos' wicker chair and the blood-red pumps of the twenty-something girl sitting alone at the table next to the four security guards. It would not be an easy shot, and unlike with regular bullets, the shot from this gun would be deadly no matter what body part was hit. Two inches to the left and he would hit the ankle of the girl, sealing her fate. But Richter had never been one to hesitate once all the pieces were in position and pulling the trigger was the logical next step.

Confident he had the lower part of Santos' left calf in his sights and with his finger on the trigger, he slowly exhaled. But just as he squeezed the trigger, Mrs. Santos got up, pushing her chair back a bit. The frozen dart shattered against the left hind leg of Mrs. Santos' chair without making a sound, at least none Richter could hear through all the street noise. He quickly pulled back the gun and retreated behind the wall of the café, cursing his bad luck. After waiting a few seconds, he peeked through the upper hole to assess the situation.

When he did, he saw that Mrs. Santos' chair was empty but the General hadn't moved, nor had the four bodyguards. Realizing he had to act before Mrs. Santos returned, Richter quickly pulled an insulated container the size of a ballpoint pen from his left inside jacket pocket, unscrewed the cap and carefully took out the last dart. He slid the dart into the modified chamber, got on his stomach again, pushed the barrel through the hole and took aim. Mrs. Santos moving her chair had further narrowed his line of fire, which was now less than three inches. But there was no time for doubt. He aligned the front and rear sight with the lower part of Santos' left calf again, moved his finger to the trigger, slowly breathed out and fired.

"Ouch!" General Santos gripped his calf and looked down.

His most devoted body guard got up right away. "Everything okay sir?" he asked, sounding alarmed.

Santos looked back over his shoulder with a pain-stricken face. "Yes, yes, I'm alright," he tried to laugh through his pain. "Those damn mosquitos. They're everywhere."

Fifty-six hours later, General Lúcio Santos had died of heart failure, brought on by pulmonary edema, in Percy military hospital in Clamart, near Paris.

"Sir? Would you like some coffee or tea?" the flight attendant asked.

Richter looked away from the window. "Eh, no, thank you," he said, looking at his watch. It was 10:30 a.m. New York time.

Exiting McCarran at Terminal 1 about three hours later, he decided to proceed to the Thomas & Mack Center on foot, seeing it was just a little over a mile. Studying the Google satellite images he had concluded that the area southwest of the Center—with its vast parking space, and beyond that McCarran International Airport—was too open to be used as an escape route; walking along Paradise Road confirmed that conclusion. Passing the Center, he continued on Paradise road, turning left on Flamingo Road, towards Las Vegas Boulevard. It would be easy enough to get lost in the crowd here, especially in the evening, but he doubted he could bridge the two miles or so if he had to escape on foot in a hurry. The campus of the University of Nevada, to the Center's northeast, seemed more promising, and after enjoying an excellent Southwest Steak Cobb salad at Café Americano, he made his way back to the Thomas & Mack Center to check it out.

Walking around the Center and taking the university entrance as his starting point, he proceeded to the classroom building complex directly behind the Center and from there walked to the Marjorie Barrick Museum, which had a parking lot behind it. After studying the different routes leading to and from the parking lot, he decided that if something went wrong, his best bet would be to try and get out by car from there. Of course, it was unlikely he would be able to even exit the Center should things go south, but it would be careless not to plan for the possibility.

An hour before the concert started, he entered the Center amid a crowd of devoted hip hop fans, somewhat standing out in his simple blue jeans and black Under Armor T-shirt amid a wide variety of baggy pants, saggy pants, Factorie trackies, oversized T-shirts and expensive sneakers. But after buying an official Hip Hop International snapback at one of the many merchandise stands, the difference was negligible. Well, almost.

As the crowd filed past the food and beverage outlets and into the arena, Richter walked through the entire, elliptical-shaped corridor, to get a better sense of the layout of the building. It made him think of the many scenes from *Star Trek: Voyager* in which chatting crew members were making their way around the disk-shaped front of the starship U.S.S. Voyager. Taking pictures of everything, he checked out the toilets—towel dispensers, garbage cans, walls, light fixtures—the First Aid station and the smoking area. He filmed a security guard walking around and opening one of the 'staff only' doors, moving quickly to hold the door and pop his phone in for a moment as the chubby guard continued on his course. He did not try to move into any of the restricted areas, though he would have especially liked to explore the one on the upper level and get a head start on possible firing locations. But there was no need to run the risk of attracting unnecessary attention. He would be back at a later date to plant the weapons and prepare a secure route to the optimum vantage point. For now, he just needed information, so that he could properly prepare things for that later visit.

After he was satisfied he had collected enough information, he took his seat inside the arena, snapped some more pictures and watched the first five minutes of the Hip Hop Championship Final, before deciding he would rather wait for his return flight at McCarran Airport.

6

If anybody ever wanted to kill the head of the American Anti-Fascist League it would be a walk in the park, or rather, a trip to the Belgian café on Amsterdam Avenue, because Peter Veldman was there at least three nights a week, writing. He would come in around nine in the evening—ruffled hair, army-green tweed jacket, shoulder-strapped shoddy leather briefcase—climb on the barstool at the far left end of the bar, his favorite spot, and order a Trappist, his favorite specialty beer. If the spot was taken, he would take the one on the other end of the bar and if that too was occupied, he would look helplessly for a while before picking a seat somewhere in the middle. On those unfortunate nights he would do very little writing though.

The briefcase was stuffed with photocopied book pages and thumbed, letter-sized sheets, filled with handwritten notes. Most of the time they stayed in the briefcase while Veldman feverishly wrote in his Moleskine notebook with an antique fountain pen, but every now and then they would be taken out, leafed through, checked and re-checked, before being stuffed back randomly into one of the briefcase compartments.

The sloppy, unorganized manner in which Veldman kept his papers stood in stark contrast to his meticulous way of working at the New York Public Library's Map Division, on Fifth Avenue and 42nd Street, where he was responsible for maintaining the library's vast collection of antique maps. When a request was made for a specific map—usually by scholars or historical fiction writers—he would put on disposable rubber surgical gloves, access the restricted area and carefully pull the requested map out of storage. For most maps, wearing gloves was, in fact, not required, but Veldman always put them on anyway, feeling it added to the status and significance of the maps (and that of their caretaker, for that matter). Assistant Conservator at the Map Division of the New York Public Library. It sounded a lot more significant than it was, but the job was steady, the pay was okay, and it allowed him plenty of time for writing.

On this particular Monday night Veldman's favorite spot was free, but a guy in a dark-blue suit, white shirt and tie was sitting on the bar stool directly next to it, hugging what looked like a double whiskey. With all the other seats available, it would be a little awkward to take his usual spot, but the urge to sit where he always sat was stronger than the desire to avoid a moment of uneasiness, so he walked past the guy, planted his briefcase in the corner and climbed on.

The guy in the suit briefly lifted his head and sized up his new neighbor with his peripherals, before returning to his whiskey.

"The usual?" the barkeeper asked.

"Yeah, thanks Martin," Veldman said, taking his notebook from his right side pocket and the antique fountain pen from inside his jacket. He opened the notebook, unscrewed the pen's cap and read the last few phrases he had written.

"What are you writing?" the guy next to him asked.

Veldman hesitated. He wasn't in the mood for a conversation, at least not with what looked to be a guy in his late forties drinking double whiskeys. "Ehh... a book about collaborators," he said curtly, quickly looking down at his notebook again and keeping his pen as close as possible to the paper without actually writing.

"Hmmm," the guy nodded.

"Here you go Peter." The barkeeper put the Trappist in front of him.

"Thanks." Veldman looked up for a moment, then quickly returned to his notebook.

"Funny word that," the man next to him said.

Peter looked up. "I'm sorry?"

"Collaborator," the man said, still looking at his whiskey. "I mean, you can say you are collaborating with someone on a project or something, but when someone is labeled 'a collaborator', without any additional information, it often means he is a traitor, right?" For the first time the man looked directly at him, his cold, deep blue eyes penetrating him without blinking.

"I guess so, yes," Peter replied, a little undone by the stranger's expressionless eyes.

"But a collaborator is a special kind of traitor," the man continued. "Someone who is working with a foreign enemy that has invaded his country. It's different from a defector, who changes his allegiance to a more equally matched enemy."

He scoffed. "Of course he's still a traitor, it's just a nicer word for it, something counter-intelligence spooks use so traitors won't feel too bad about themselves."

He brought up his glass. "But then what do you call a guy who stays in his government job after the government is taken over by an evil administration?"

"What do you mean?" Veldman asked, for the first time genuinely interested.

48

"Like, say you're a policeman in Germany in 1932. You have a wife, two young kids and a steady job in an economy strangled by the Great Depression. Then the Nazis come to power and suddenly you have to make sure Jews don't sit on park benches, don't go to Arian restaurants and wear a yellow star with the word 'Jew' on it. And you know that's just the beginning. But what are you going to do? Are you going to quit your job? You have a family to feed. Besides, you'll probably be drafted in the army as soon as you're unemployed, where you'll have to fight to conquer other countries and force them to deport their Jews. So you decide to stay and make sure Jews don't sit on park benches, don't go to Arian restaurants and wear their yellow star." He paused for a moment, then looked at Veldman. "What do you call such a person?"

"Eh… an accomplice?"

The stranger sighed. "Yeah, I guess you're probably right." He downed his whiskey and signaled the barkeeper for another one. "So, a book about collaborators. What, like collaborators through the ages or something?"

"No it… eh… it's actually a book about only one collaborator," Veldman said.

In fact, it was about his grandfather.

Growing up, Peter didn't know anything about his grandfather other than that he had died just before the end of the war. He had never given it much thought, until stumbling on an article in the May 2012 issue of a Dutch history magazine about the founder of the Dutch ss, Henk Feldman. It was the photograph that had first grabbed his attention, because the man in the picture, looking so seriously into the camera, dressed in the black uniform of the ss and wearing the hat with the *ss-totenkopf*, bore a striking resemblance to his own father. And then there was the name, Feldman.

Veldman. The name, the photograph, it just seemed too much of a coincidence.

Pretending to be just a curious reader, he had e-mailed the author of the article, writing he had really liked the piece but wondered whether Feldman perhaps had German ancestry, since the name sounded so German. A few hours later he received a reply. The author wrote that Feldman had been born in 1910 as Henk Veldman, but that his father, a sergeant in the Dutch Army, had changed the family name to Feldman after World War I broke out, to make it sound more German.

He had stared at the e-mail for hours, simply unable, physically, to move and continue doing other things. At 3:00 in the morning he had finally called his father, back in Holland (where it was 9:00 a.m.), and asked him whether he had changed his name back to Veldman somewhere after the war. The silence on the other end of the line was the longest in his life. It was also an answer of sorts. After what had seemed like an eternity, his father had said—just because something needed to be said—"So, you know." Then Peter had hung up.

One might wonder what it really mattered that his grandfather had been a collaborator. So what that he had been a member of the ss and had fought at Stalingrad, that he had killed Dutch civilians as reprisal for the killing of Dutch collaborators by the resistance? They were acts committed by another person, long before he himself had even been born. The war had ended almost 70 years ago. And yet, even if he hadn't known about it all those years, he felt the shame had still carried over, like a hidden hereditary disease.

The fact that he had only learned about it at twenty-seven made things even worse. He was Dutch, and had always been proud to be Dutch. At school, he had loved Dutch history, the stories about the Eighty Years' war against the Spanish, when the Dutch won their independence and founded the Dutch Republic, about Michiel de Ruyter sailing up the River Thames and destroying the English fleet during the Anglo-Dutch wars of the 17th century, about the Dutch colonial empire, the founding of New Amsterdam—the very city where he now lived—and the Dutch resistance against the German occupation during World War II. But suddenly he could no longer be proud of his country's past. Worse, he felt ostracized. Even though nobody knew who he was, he found the shame to be simply unbearable.

The ensuing ripple effect had upended his entire life in the course of just a few months. He could no longer find the motivation to continue his Ph.D studies at Cornell University about early Jewish settlements in New Amsterdam. It seemed pointless, even a little cruel in light of what he now knew. All he was interested in was finding out more about his grandfather, an interest that quickly grew into an all-consuming obsession. A few months later his girlfriend broke up with him, and with that last tether to his old life cut, things rapidly deteriorated further. Wallowing in self-pity, he tried to find solace in all the wrong places, and for a few weeks, Peter Veldman seemed to be on the fast-track to the kind of bottom from which there was no return.

But then he caught a break. One of his professors at Cornell took pity and got him the job at the Map Division of the New York Public Library, a job that paid reasonably well, was uneventful and quiet, demanded little and left ample room for writing and research. It stopped the downward spiral and allowed him to re-build his life.

But the real affliction Peter Veldman was suffering from was not his obsession with his grandfather, it was his firm belief that somehow, through his actions, the past could be cleared, balanced out. That there were things he could do, should do—writing an unsparing biography about his grandfather with the very fountain pen his father said had once belonged to him, running the Anti-Fascist League, protesting against any form of discrimination any chance he got—to wash away the past.

He kept a weekly blog on his website about the progress on the book, the things he had discovered. It read like the work of a split personality, with emotional and personal remarks interspersing the otherwise detached, academic writing style of a serious historian. When Conrad Richter found the blog, he knew he had found his man.

He abruptly stuck out his hand. "Don Jensen by the way."

"Peter Veldman. Pleased to meet you Don."

"Likewise, Peter."

"So what did he do? The collaborator, I mean. He must be special in some way to deserve having a whole book dedicated to him."

It was never an easy question to answer. "He… eh… was Dutch. He founded the Dutch ss during World War ii, after Germany occupied the Netherlands."

"The ss, those were the guys that killed all the Jews, right?"

Veldman nodded. "Among other things."

"So why him?" Richter asked, already knowing the answer, but needing him to say it.

Peter screwed the cap back on the white gold Cartier fountain pen. "Because he was my grandfather."

7

Sunday, August 21, 2016, 2:00 p.m.,
Zurich, Switzerland

Dieter Zimmerman liked to be alone. It was not that he disliked people, just that he never felt the need to entertain or be entertained by them. He simply preferred reading over talking. When still in his teens, he had married a sweet, shapely girl who loved to talk and have sex almost as much as he loved to read and think. It didn't last. She soon remarried and got a string of kids, but Dieter decided married life was not for him.

For the past 36 years he had lived at the same address in Zurich, on the corner of the Kämbelgasse and the Wühre, overlooking the Limmat River. Every morning, he would walk along the Western bank of the Limmat, cross the Münsterbrücke and stroll on Limmatquai to Café Odeon—known for its one-time clientele of (in)famous writers, scientists and politicians, among them Lenin and Mussolini—for a coffee and brioche with his morning paper. The ritual would repeat itself at the end of the day, only this time with a glass of Campari and a good book. Some of the waiters and other regulars had known him for years—or seen him, at least—but none of them knew anything about him. All they saw was a bespectacled older man with grey hair and a friendly face, always dressed in the same charcoal-grey suit and black tie. None of them knew that the nice, slightly unworldly older man sipping his Campari was a renowned ballistics expert. And of the select group of people who did know, only a handful knew he was also a master gunsmith, one with a very select clientele of expert assassins.

From time to time, they would visit him at his home—he had never seen much sense in trying to hide his address from professional assassins—and ask him to manufacture a firearm for a specific purpose. Some brought schematics, others only described what they were looking for. Sometimes he would ask questions, but never more than he needed to know to fulfill the client's wishes. What was the likely distance to target, would the target be moving, would there be time for multiple shots? Some of them he had known for years. In a way, they were the closest thing to friends he had, even if they never spoke one word outside what was required for the job. And although 99 percent of their lives was completely alien to him, in that one percent they were completely aligned.

The man he knew as Hans Kruger was one of his oldest, still active, clients. He remembered the first weapon he had made for him, an exact copy of an M40A1 sniper rifle, outfitted with the Unertl 10x fixed-power scope and the McMillan A1 fiberglass stock. It had to be an exact copy of the sniper rifle used by the United States Marine Corps, a modified version of a Remington 700 bolt-action rifle, right down to the stock and trigger guard. It hadn't taken Zimmerman long to realize the man was a former Marine himself and wanted to remain loyal to the gun that had turned him into a deadly accurate marksman. It was the same for many snipers.

His musings were interrupted by the sound of the doorbell. Dieter looked at his watch. 2:00 p.m. exactly. He walked to the door and opened it.

"Ah, Herr Kruger, welcome. Please, come in."

"Herr Zimmerman," Conrad Richter nodded. "Pleasure to see you again."

"Likewise, Herr Kruger. Likewise. Would you follow me upstairs to my office please?"

The two men walked the stairs and Richter followed the short man into his rather spacious office.

"Can I offer you something to drink? An espresso? Cold lemonade, or perhaps something stronger?"

Richter pointed his head toward the far right corner. "Espresso, of course," he grinned.

Dieter smiled. "Of course." The little gunsmith walked over to the chrome-plated, manual espresso machine and started working the La Pavoni as he if he were a barista at an Italian café in the 1950s.

"And what can I do for you this time, Herr Kruger?"

"That is a slightly more difficult question Dieter," Richter said. "I mean, I know what I need, but I'm not sure you can make it."

Dieter looked back over his shoulder, his smile broadened. "Ah, a challenge. You know nothing pleases me more. Tell me."

The American rubbed his thumb over his lips. "Well, in short, I need something that can fire a small, poisonous dart over a range of up to 100 yards," he said, just as Zimmerman switched on the coffee grinder.

"What was that, Herr Kruger!?" Zimmerman shouted. Richter could have shouted back, but decided to wait until the grinding was done.

At last the little receptacle was filled and silence returned. "I am sorry Herr Kruger, but you know that using freshly ground beans really enhances the taste."

"You get no argument from me Dieter."

Zimmerman tamped the ground coffee, let out the steam from the espresso machine's boiler and clicked the portafilter in its place. Next, he put a tiny cup underneath the tap and worked the lever, pushing it down with what seemed to be all his weight.

"You know, I almost can't tell whether you are reboring the barrel of an old Winchester rifle or making me an espresso," Richter joked, looking on as Zimmerman hunched over the lever to push the water through the portafilter.

"I assure you," Dieter groaned through his smile, "reboring a Winchester barrel is much easier than making the perfect espresso."

After he was done, he took a few seconds to regain his strength. "No sugar, correct?"

"Correct."

"A purist. Like myself," Zimmerman laughed, as he put the cup in front of Richter.

He walked around his massive, antique desk and sat down in the black faux leather office chair, which immediately started descending with a loud 'swooosh'. "So, tell me of this, eh, impossible challenge," the gunsmith said, trying to ignore his now uncomfortable height.

"New chair Dieter?" Richter said with a wry laugh.

"Yes indeed," Zimmerman smiled apologetically. "You see, the old one broke down…" while talking, he was also trying to get his hands on the handle bars he knew had to be there somewhere underneath his seat, "… and I got this one only yesterday."

"It's very nice," Richter commented, unable to completely neutralize the mocking melody in his voice, "though perhaps a bit small for such an impressively large desk."

"Well, the desk…" the renowned gunsmith said, as his right hand found a handle, "… belonged to my father, and…" he pulled the handle, another 'swoosh' sounded and he sunk even deeper away.

"Need any help?"

"No, no, I think I've got it now," Zimmerman said, still trying to smile. Another swoosh and he was back at the proper height. "Ah, that's better."

"Much better indeed," the American smiled.

"So, you were saying?" Dieter said, folding his hands on the table in an effort to look more business-like.

Richter's face turned serious. He looked at Zimmerman. "I need a weapon that can fire a small dart, a needle, over a range of up to 100 yards," he said. "The needle needs to deliver a slow-working poison that is undetectable."

"Do I understand correctly that the hit itself also has to go undetected?"

"Yes," Richter said.

"Hmmm, yes… yes…" Zimmerman mused, leaning back a bit and folding his hands over his chest.

"Ricin?" he asked after a while.

"Yes, that's what I was thinking. Takes anywhere from a few hours to a couple of days to work, cause of death often cardiac arrest, hard to detect."

"Hmmm, yes, quite right. But I'm afraid there are two problems with your suggested solution for delivery. The most obvious one—and I know you must have thought of this as well—is that the needle would remain inside the person, rendering it detectable. Unless you are thinking about using some sort of frozen dart, which has been used by your CIA in the past with some success, if I'm not mistaken."

"The thought had crossed my mind," Richter said.

Zimmerman shook his head. "Impossible. I mean, not modifying a pistol so that it could fire such a dart, that wouldn't be difficult at all. But it would never work long range. You see, the dart would quickly heat up in flight and when it has to travel a distance greater than, say, 15, 20 meters, its solid state would no longer be strong enough for it to pierce the skin upon impact. Most likely, it would shatter."

"Is there no way to enhance it?"

"Not without adding some sort of casing that would not completely disintegrate inside the target's body, no. It's a matter of physics, you see. But frankly, even if you could, the accuracy would still suffer when firing such a projectile from a long range. That is the second problem. This is not an M118 long range cartridge you would be firing Hans," discussing ballistics always brought out a more casual Dieter Zimmerman, "the material, the miniature size, the shape, I doubt you would be able to hit a target the size of a watermelon from 30 meters away, let alone 50 or a 100."

"Well, that's disappointing," Richter said, leaning back into his chair.

"I'm sorry, Herr Kruger."

Zimmerman looked at his desk, absorbed in thought. "Actually, there might be another solution," he said after a while, looking up again.

"I'm listening."

The gunsmith looked at Richter's empty espresso cup. "Would you like another espresso?" he asked, nodding encouragingly.

"Right now, I'd rather hear about your solution Dieter."

"Of course. Well, I was thinking, what about using a drone?"

"What do you mean, like what the military uses or more like a toy helicopter?"

The gunsmith waved his index finger. "Neither. I am thinking of a small drone, tiny actually, modified so that it can shoot or inject a needle."

"Wouldn't people see it?" Richter asked.

"Not if it's the size of a fly."

58

The American looked puzzled. "And this exists already?"

"It does," Zimmerman said triumphantly. "I was at the Eurosatory arms exhibition in Paris a few months back, where they demonstrated a military reconnaissance drone the size of a common housefly—it actually looked like one too—which you could control with an iPhone app from up to about 75 meters away."

"75 meters, huh? Hmmm...." Richter considered this for a moment, working out in his mind whether he could smuggle such a drone inside and stealthily maneuver it into a position behind the target.

"You sure you don't want another espresso?" Zimmerman asked. "It's no trouble really."

The American put his finger on his lips. "Shhht."

Zimmerman nodded apologetically.

After a while, Richter asked, "And you could... equip... this, eh, tiny drone with a needle or something that could deliver the poison?"

"Oh yes, I'm quite sure of it. The drone I saw in Paris was already equipped with a tiny gripper that was controlled by the app and could carry something weighing a couple grams. It would not be difficult to modify the mechanism so that it jabs and retracts instead of grips and releases."

"Okay, I'm sold," Richter said. "But how would you acquire this drone without it being traced back to you?"

The little gunsmith smiled confidently. "I sometimes use the services of someone who buys products with freshly stolen credit card numbers and then has them shipped to houses that are for sale and where the owners have already moved out. Delivery estimates are so accurate these days he often has to wait only a couple of hours at the house before the package arrives and he can sign for it. He's not cheap, but it's guaranteed to be anonymous and untraceable."

Richter nodded. "Sounds good."

"Okay, then I shall make the necessary arrangements." Zimmerman quickly wrote down a few notes.

"There's something else," the American said. "Are you familiar with those little Bond Arms pistols?"

"You mean the two-shooters? Yes."

"Is it possible to make an all-plastic version of this one?" Richter showed him pictures of the Bond Arms Backup derringer on his phone. "I took these pictures off their website. The specs information they list there is pretty elaborate, but I assume you'll want to work off the real deal."

"May I?" the gunsmith asked, gesturing at Richter's phone.

"Of course."

"Hmmm, yes. And which barrel would you prefer? The 2.5"? 4.25"? Or multiple ones?"

"I was thinking the 2.5"."

"And the caliber? .45 ACP or 9mm?"

"9mm."

"And the same barrel-switching mechanism? Cocking the hammer changes the barrel being fired?"

"Yes. As long as all the parts are plastic."

"I take it the purpose is passing a metal detector?"

"What gave it away?" Richter joked.

But Zimmerman was not amused, in fact he looked almost annoyed. "I'm only asking because I'd like to use some non-plastic, non-metal materials, which would be no problem if the sole purpose of your request to use plastic is to evade discovery by a metal detector."

"Alright, alright, no need to get upset."

"I'm not—"

"I know, I know," Richter waved him down, "I'm only messing with you. So, when do you expect you can have it all ready?"

Zimmerman looked at his calendar. "Let's see, today is August 21… I estimate ten to fourteen days before I have the drone, another few days to modify it and run some tests with the injection system… the plastic derringer I can manufacture in the meantime… shall we say… September 12?"

"September 12 it is," the American said. "10:00 a.m.?"

"Excellent."

"As to the matter of your fee, I trust you'll come up with a fair price as usual," Richter said, as he was getting up. "But Dieter?"

"Yes?"

"Get yourself a better chair, will you?"

8

"Yes, here please," Richter said.

The cab driver swerved to the right and parked the car. He pointed across the street. "*Sze café is over szere monsieur,*" the cabbie said, showing himself from his best side in hopes of a good *pourboire*. Americans were always good tippers, best not waste a good opportunity.

"Yes thanks, I know." He checked the meter. Twelve euros. He gave the man fifteen and got out. The taxi immediately sped away, in an apparent attempt to beat the traffic light, thereby almost hitting the right side of a silver-grey Peugeot who was trying to do the same. Aggressively honking their horns, both cars raced through the orange traffic light as if they were driving the French President to his new mistress.

Standing on the sidewalk in front of the *Saint-Pierre-de-Montrouge* church, Richter looked across the street at café *Le Bouquet d'Alésia*. He could hardly believe his eyes. Nothing had changed. The Belle Époque-style, chocolate-brown facade, the crimson canopy with the yellow lettering, the marble round tables, even the wicker chairs. The bakery of Dominique Sabron, the butcher, the cheese store, they were all still there. But what really freaked him out was the gaping hole to the left of the café. The movie theater—for which construction had just started back in the summer of 1990—had been demolished again, a large billboard stating a new cinema would open in January 2017. For a moment, Richter saw himself standing behind the fence again, peeking at MPLA General Lúcio Santos and his wife through the tiny hole in the fern-green cover. Jesus, had it really been 26 years already?

He crossed the street and walked to the table of the slender young female rattling away on her MacBook Air as if she was playing the lightening fast staccato finale of Rachmaninoff's No. 3 Piano Concerto. The Apple sign on the back was covered with the black-and-white logo of the *Parti pirate*. "Jackie?" Richter asked.

The girl looked up. "Mr. Greenwald?" she responded in the same tone of voice.

Richter sat down.

She landed a few more piano forte chords on her laptop before abruptly closing it, pulling her John Lennon sunglasses down a bit and looking at Richter with a boyish smirk. "You know, I hope you didn't travel all the way to Paris just for this, because I could have simply set up an encrypted private connection."

"No, I was in the neighborhood," Richter said, a little smile hanging in the corner of his mouth.

"You know Paris well, this area?" she asked. "I mean, since you asked to meet at this café?"

"It was a long time ago," Richter shrugged.

"So you do know it here. Did you live here?"

"You know, you don't sound French at all," Richter said, ignoring the question.

"*Why, becoz I ave no stupide acsant like oll sze oszer French?*" she joked.

Richter raised his eyebrows.

"I was born here in Paris, but my parents moved to New York when I was six," she explained. "I went to school right here, in the Fourteenth *Arrondissement*." She pointed behind Richter. "I lived just a few streets away, in the Rue Antoine Chantin. My father used to take me to *Le Bouquet d'Alésia* and treat me to hot chocolate."

"You don't say."

"Yeah, talk about a coincidence, huh?"

"When was this?"

"Ehmm, early 1990s?"

"Wow, small world indeed," the American chuckled. "Anyway, Marco recommended you. Said you were an expert, and discreet."

"And expensive," Jackie said, "did he mention that too?"

"Money is not an issue, but we'll get to that in a minute. First I want to know if you can and are willing to do what I need done."

She folded her hands on top of her laptop. "I can get into almost any system, depending on how much time I have."

"'Almost any system'?" Richter smiled.

A waiter presented himself at their table. Richter looked up. "I'll have a Heineken." He looked at Jackie, but she shook her head. "No, I'm good."

"Just the Heineken," he said to the waiter, who nodded and disappeared inside.

Richter leaned forward. "Two months from now, there will be a certain exclusive event in Las Vegas. I would like to attend that event, possibly with someone else."

"I'm assuming we're not talking about a boxing match?"

"No, not exactly, but there will be thousands of people. The exclusivity lies in the fact that you can't buy tickets for it, it's invitation only."

"And you want me to add your name to the list."

Richter nodded.

"When and where is it exactly?"

"Before we go any further, I want to make certain things clear," the American said. "If—"

"*Votre Heineken monsieur.*" The waiter opened the bottle and poured the beer in a glass in one smooth movement. He put down two little cups—one filled with salty peanuts, the other with fresh olives—then sped to the next table, where he elegantly served two glasses of rosé to an older couple making out as if they were two teenagers in a drive-in.

"If we go further, you will not tell anyone about this, even if you choose not to take the job. You will not enlist anyone's assistance. You will work only on a computer specifically bought for this job, which you will destroy after the job is done. Not just wipe or format, but completely destroy. Is that understood?"

For the first time, Jackie saw something other than indifference and casual arrogance in the American's ocean blue eyes. It could be that she only saw it now because the smile was gone, as was the nonchalance in the voice, but suddenly it seemed as if the eyes were completely devoid of emotion, like the eyes of a leopard; or a jackal.

The young woman nodded slowly. "I understand."

"Good. Now, as to your fee, I will pay you €50,000, expenses included, €15,000 of which I will pay you in advance and which will be yours whether you succeed or not." He looked her straight in the eye. "Do you accept the job?"

She reflected on the American's words for a few seconds. Marco usually brought her people that wanted her to steal sensitive data from competitors, customer data, distribution lists, recipes, sales cycles, proposals, that sort of thing. Once a large car dealer had even asked her to hack into the website of a competitor and raise the prices on all his cars and accessories. That hadn't been exactly legal either of course, none of it was, but this… this was something different altogether. Whatever sort of event this Mr. Greenwald wanted to get into, he was probably going to do more than just attending it. A robbery? In Vegas? That would probably mean a casino or a large sporting event or something. And the criminal investigations into that sort of thing tended to be a lot more serious than the ones looking into hacked websites of local car dealers. Then again, she could certainly use €50,000.

"I accept," Jackie said, surprising herself with how serious she sounded.

"Good." The American gave a short nod and the right corner of his mouth curled upward again. "The event I am talking about will be held on October 19, at the Thomas & Mack Center in Las Vegas, Nevada. It will be organized by the University of Nevada, which is also in charge of the invitation list, so it might be that you have to access both systems, that I don't know, neither do I know when the list will be finished, but I would be very surprised if it was any later than one month before the event." He grabbed a handful of peanuts and trickled them into his mouth.

Jackie opened her laptop to make some notes. "Getting in those systems won't be much of a problem," she mumbled, as her fingers rattled over the keyboard. "In fact, I recently came by a new zero-day vulnerability in a program commonly used by universities and academic hospitals." She popped a glistening green olive into her mouth. "I will need your passport data though, and that of anyone else you'd like to put on the list."

"Right. I will be back here on September 13. I trust by that time you will have found a way to get in and out of these systems undetected. I will get you the ID data and the rest of the payment then. Ok?"

"Sure. I mean the sooner the better, but yes, that will work. Same time, same place?"

Richter looked at the fence surrounding the construction site, some 30 feet away. "Sure, why not."

9

Thursday, August 25, 2016, 5:00 p.m.,

Rockefeller Center, New York City,

The O'Brian Factor

"Good evening, I'm Bill O'Brian, and thanks for watching. We have an O'Brian Factor special for you tonight. An exclusive interview with Republican presidential candidate Ronald A. Drump, who is joining us now from his own plane, which is cruising at 30,000 feet. Mr. Drump, welcome to the Factor. How's the weather up there, Ronald?"

"Sunny as always Bill, and thanks for having me. You know I love your show, absolutely love it."

"Thank you for kind words. So, let me just get right down to brass tacks here for a minute, Ronald. I have here in my hand the latest poll numbers and they have you trailing by ten points. In other words, you're not winning."

"Well, you shouldn't trust the polls too much Bill, I just come from an event in Flint, Michigan, and the crowds were absolutely unbelievable, unbelievable. Thousands and thousands of people who want to make America amazing again, because they hate that it's not amazing anymore, that we're not winning anymore. We're not winning against China, we're not winning against Mexico, we're not even winning against Europe anymore. Remember socialist Bernie, talking about how we should be more like Denmark. I mean Denmark, for crying out loud, it's not even a country it is so tiny."

"Actually, it is a country Ronald," O'Brian, looking up from his notes, interjected.

"Well, yes, but it's really tiny, one of the tiniest countries in the world really. The Germans even forgot to conquer it in World War II, simply forgot. But the point is, 50 years ago, nobody, not even the most hard-core socialist, would have ever dared to compare the United States to this tiny, petri dish size of a country. But they are doing it now Bill. That's what they're doing. Because we're weak. China is beating us on trade, Mexico is stealing our jobs, and Europe is enjoying our protection without paying a dime for it. But I will make us win again, Bill, I will make us win so often you will get sick of winning. Just watch me."

O'Brian slightly leaned his right elbow on the table. "Now, for the viewers at home, you're talking about NATO of course, that the United States is by far the largest contributor, while many European nations contribute very little, even though they have more to fear from the Russians than we do. And you've said similar things about South Korea and Japan, that they should acquire their own nuclear weapons?"

"I don't fear Russia and I don't fear China. We still have the greatest military in the world, in the history of the world really, even though the current administration has been hollowing out our military like a pumpkin. It's sad, very sad. But NATO, I mean, it's obsolete. It's not 1950 anymore, Germany is one of the richest countries in the world and they can't pay for their own defense? It's ridiculous."

"Are you saying Germany should acquire its own nuclear weapons as well?"

"Why not Bill?"

"Well, you know there were these two big wars during the last century and both of them were kind of started by the Germans."

"That is a long time ago, the Germans have been our allies for more than 60 years now."

"And the South Koreans? And the Japanese?"

"Well North Korea has them, the Chinese have them, why shouldn't our Asian allies have their own bombs?"

"Some say it might destabilize the world, if more countries acquire nuclear weapons."

"You know who says that? Russian and Chinese agents, who have infiltrated the extreme left and are trying to convince the hippies that we should abandon our nuclear weapons."

"You are referring to the recent article about this in the Universal Enquirer," Bill said.

"You know, I am not sure where I read it, maybe I heard it in the National Intelligence debriefing I received last week."

O'Brian's raised his left eyebrow. "Isn't everything you and Senator Clayton are told in that briefing supposed to remain a secret?"

"Well, some things are. I think."

"Was there anything in there about alien life forms still being held at Roswell?" O'Brian quipped.

"Afraid not Bill, but I promise you that when I become President I will make public everything there is to know about Roswell, because I think the American public deserve to know."

For a moment, Bill O'Brien didn't seem quite sure how to respond, a very rare thing. He looked to the side, shuffling some papers. "Well, eh, that's certainly a new one."

"Look, I'm not a politician Bill, I don't need fake secrets or fancy language to be seen as important. I'm already important. And I will probably be one of the most important presidents of the 21st century—or *the* most important—because I'm going to put a stop to this hollowing out of our values, of our greatness. I'm not going to apologize for our country, like our current president is constantly doing. I'm not going to lie about who I am and what I do, like Venomous Valery is doing, about Benghazi, about abusing the State Department to hand out favors to Clayton Foundation donors, about her private e-mail server—which the FBI called 'extremely careless' Bill, extremely careless—and I certainly wouldn't condone my wife sleeping with other guys, like Senator Clayton was condoning Richard putting it where it didn't belong. Do we really want someone like that running our country? I mean, Abraham Lincoln didn't condone slavery, did he? You're a bit of a history buff Bill, so you must know that."

"Well, when Lincoln was elected he was in fact willing to allow slavery to continue in the territories where it already existed," Bill said with his lecturing voice.

"I don't think you're right Bill. Pretty sure he abolished slavery. You know, I know a lot about history, I've probably read thousands of books about history and I am 200 percent sure Abraham Lincoln abolished slavery."

"He did, but only in 1863, when the Civil War had already been raging for two years, and even then it did not affect slaves held in states not in rebellion to the Union," O'Brien said smugly, tapping the desk with his pen to triumphantly claim his victory.

"Well, you weren't there, but it's not important. I mean it is, slavery is huge, it's tremendously important, so he deserves that memorial. In fact, every president that does something really important, that like, changes the nation, should get a huge memorial."

"Eh, yes, couldn't agree more Ronald. We'll go out for a short commercial break now, but stay tuned because there's much more when we come back."

"Much more."

10

"I've got another one for you," Richter said, his hands hugging the whiskey glass as if it was a cup of hot cocoa on a cold winter's day.

Peter Veldman's notebook lay in front of him, the elastic band still wrapped around it, the antique fountain pen on top. He hadn't written one word tonight, but the conversation with his new friend Don Jensen had certainly been stimulating. He felt strangely at ease talking to Don about his grandfather, as if he already knew everything and wasn't shocked at all about all the horrible things Henk Feldman had done during the war. And he didn't try to sweep it all under the rug either, like his other friends always tried to do—not to mention Kelly, his ex-girlfriend—offering all those fake reassurances and consolations, that it didn't matter, that it all happened so long ago, that he shouldn't feel guilty about something his grandfather had done. No, Don got it. In fact, he was the first person who really seemed to understood that it *did* matter.

"Tell me," Veldman said.

"Okay, so you push the button on your wristwatch slash time machine again and are instantly transported to 1912. You are in Vienna. It is a warm, sunny day, young boys in little sailor costumes are running through the Stadtpark, girls with pig tails and pink dresses are enjoying lollipops, fathers are reading their newspapers, mothers are preparing a picnic lunch."

"It all sounds very idyllic," Veldman grinned.

"Then, a young man, sitting on one of the park benches, catches your eye. He is trying to paint the 'idyllic'," Richter made a wide gesture, "scene in front of him. He has a narrow toothbrush mustache and an intense, almost aggressive look on his face, a dirtied cloth, a few tubes of paint and a small cup of water are lying next to him. You move a little closer and suddenly you see he bears a strong resemblance to the most notorious dictator of the 20th century, Adolf Hitler."

"I had an inkling," Veldman said. "And of course your question is whether I would kill him, knowing what he will become."

"Have you ever killed a man?" Richter quietly asked.

"What do you think?" Veldman replied with playful cynicism. "Have you?"

Richter nodded.

"Really?" It suddenly occurred to Peter he knew almost nothing about Don Jensen, what he did, where he came from, where he lived, nothing. And here he said that he had killed someone. Or was he just playing, to make the question about killing Hitler seem more real, more interesting? He looked pretty serious, though.

"Who?——When?" Veldman asked.

"I can't say too much about it, really," Richter said. "It was in the service of my government, let's keep it at that."

"Wow."

"Look, it's no joke. Taking a life—a real, human life—is something you can't come back from. It will change you, no matter who you are, and you will never forget that moment for the rest of your life. In fact, the closer you have to be to do it, the more personal the act and the deeper it will be seared into your brain. You understand?"

72

Veldman nodded, but at the same time was unable to subdue his admittedly ridiculous, boyish admiration for what in his eyes was one of the most manly things a man could do.

"Shooting a man with a gun is easier than sticking a knife in him," Richter continued, "the full force of your body behind it, his contorted, pain-stricken face not more than a few inches away from your own. And killing a man with your bare hands, literally wringing the life out of him, your hands so tightly wound around his neck you feel his head might explode, well…." his voice trailed off as he lifted his glass and took a swig of his whiskey.

"It's nothing to be proud of, trust me. Even though most people couldn't do it under most circumstances."

He looked at Veldman with mild derision. "Frankly, I don't think you could do it either."

He waved to the bartender. "Another round for both of us Martin."

"Coming right up."

"My grandfather could," Veldman blurted out, not knowing where that came from all of a sudden.

Richter stared at him for a while. "Yeah, I suppose he could Peter."

Both were silent for a while.

Then Veldman, still staring ahead, said softly, "You know what, I think I could do it."

Richter shrugged.

"No, I'm serious," Veldman insisted. "If it was really him, and I was there in that park, knowing what we now know, I *would* kill him. I know you don't believe me, and why would you—to be honest, I have never even hit someone—but I can feel this anger inside me that is so potent, so violent, so frustrated about everything that has happened and is happening, that I really could tear that son of a bitch apart with my bare hands if necessary."

Richter looked at him. "You're wrong", he said. "I do believe you."

11

Leaving Brett Kendrick's hipster TriBeCa loft on Worth Street, Peter Veldman started mumbling to himself the things he should have said but hadn't, because—yes, why exactly? Because Brett was his last connection to Kelly. Because without Brett he would never go to any parties and he would actually miss hating having to go to them. Did that even make sense?

Everybody at that party had been excruciatingly perfect and extremely satisfied with their pleasant, Greenpeace way of life. The T-shirts were conspicuously inconspicuous—one guy was wearing an industrial-grey shirt with a faded Che Guevara on it—the designer jeans expertly torn, the hairstyles outdoorsy, the number of beards significantly above average, the tattoos deep and heartfelt, the jewelry spiritual. And of course everybody had causes, the Black Rhino, the Sumatran Elephant, the Amur Leopard. Can't be a true hipster without a cause. And how politically correct they all were! Making the world egalitarian, peaceful, inclusive and environmental friendly one piece of organic, vegetarian sushi at the time. Of course, they were all talk.

They had all agreed Ronald Drump was a 'fascist thug'—as the guy in the Che Guevara T-shirt had called him—but that didn't mean they were actually going to do anything about it. When he had put forward the Hitler in 1912 hypothesis, none of them had opted for killing him, not even Che Guevara guy. Instead, the discussion quickly focused on the concept of predetermination and the danger of convicting people before they have committed a crime, even if it were possible to foresee that crime, as was the case in the 2002 movie *Minority Report*, which everybody agreed portrayed a prototypical fascist police state, in which the individual's right to better himself was sacrificed for the greater good of safer streets. Following the same reasoning, they had subsequently agreed to leave twenty-three-year-old Adolf Hitler alive, thus paradoxically allowing the rise of one fascist state to prevent the emergence of another, future one.

Veldman couldn't believe his ears, but he hadn't said anything as the semi-artistic, semi-intellectual, affluent hipsters had congratulated themselves on their own moral superiority. He couldn't help but thinking it was much like those meetings of the Judean resistance movement *People's Front of Judea* (not to be confused with the *Judean People's Front*) in the Monty Python satire *Life of Brian*, which also never led to any actual resistance.

He realized these were the kind of people who always found an excuse *not* to go to war. And in the unlikely event they had to, their dads would keep them out. They lamented the fate of the poor and disenfranchised, admired and co-opted their raw, uncompromising style and adorned themselves with expensive versions of their clothes, but they would never give up the luxury of moral superiority, would never put themselves in the position of having to do morally questionable things for the greater good. Instead, they would have others do so, benefit from the results and then criticize them from their shiny city on the hill.

He hated them, no, loathed them. How could you wear a T-shirt with an imprint of Che Guevara and then demur when given a chance to kill young Hitler? The Marxist revolutionary himself certainly wouldn't have hesitated! Not for a second. If he'd had a gun, he would have shot him right between the eyes. If he'd had a knife, he would have stuck it in his heart. If he'd nothing, he would have wrung the little Austrian's neck until every last drop of fascist poison lay spilled at his feet. Men like Guevara, men like his grandfather, for that matter, never hesitated. They lived and died for their cause. They couldn't live with themselves otherwise.

Still angry but with a clear head, Veldman entered the Subway station on Chambers Street, taking the local 1 train Uptown a few minutes later.

12

Friday, September 2, 2016, 9:00 p.m.,

Manistee National Forest, Brethren, Michigan

The giant white truck stood out like a sore thumb between the quiet, tall trees of the forest and the ruggedly charming wooden cabin it was parked in front of. The rest of the driveway circle was occupied by four black Suburbans, a shoddy van and a Porsche Carrera with New York plates. At the cabin's front door, two men dressed in dark-blue suit, white shirt and tie—one sand-colored, the other silver-grey with black stripes—were standing guard. Two more were at the back door, while several others were walking around the premises.

The homely, cosy interior had been invaded by thick black wires, robust studio lights and professional cameras that had penetrated everywhere, except for one little area right in front of the fireplace, flanked by two comfortable chairs. In one chair, DNN news anchor Chris Anderson was getting some last minute touch-ups from a make-up artist. In the other, Senator Valery Clayton was being fitted with a microphone. Meanwhile, the three cameramen were making some last minute adjustments, to ensure the lighting from their respective angles would be just right. Sound was tested, and Mr. Anderson and Mrs. Clayton were talking through a few last points.

A few minutes later, everything and everybody was ready.

"Ready to go in 5... 4... 3"

2... 1

"Good evening and welcome to this special edition of Chris Anderson 720 Degrees. Tonight, we are coming to you live from Brethren, Michigan, for an exclusive interview with Senator Valery Clayton."

Anderson briefly gestured to Mrs. Clayton. "Senator Clayton, welcome. Or perhaps I should thank you for having me, since we are in your cabin."

Senator Clayton let out a clear chuckle. "You are most welcome Chris, and thank you for having me as well. Yes, this, uh, cabin has been in our family for generations and I have many happy childhood memories coming here in the summer and taking a breather from busy Chicago. Michigan is such a beautiful state, really, I come here as often as I can."

"The latest poll numbers also show that you are neck and neck with Mr. Drump in Michigan, whereas nationally you are up ten points. Do you think that has anything to do with Mr. Drump's promise to bring back blue-collar jobs here and slap extra tariffs on American companies moving production facilities abroad to cut costs?"

"Look, people are hurt, because during the past few decades jobs have indeed disappeared from Michigan and other places in the Midwest, but building walls, punishing companies and slapping tariffs on other countries are not real solutions, they will only make things worse. Those other countries will simply retaliate and bar our goods as well. That will not make America amazing, as my opponent keeps saying, it will make us the opposite: less competitive, less innovative, less relevant. We have to focus on winning the global competition for the good manufacturing jobs, because they are the future."

"You've been frequently saying that on the campaign trail, that we need to win the competition for the 'good manufacturing jobs', but what are they exactly?"

"With new, high-tech technology, there is a need for new, high-quality manufacturing, and I have a plan for the United States to stay competitive... to, eh, win the competition for these high-quality manufacturing jobs, through education incentives, tax deductions for companies who pay for their employees' education, and by heavily investing in innovation and technology."

"Wouldn't it just be easier to build that wall at the Mexican border and deport the eleven million illegal immigrants already here?" Anderson smiled, asking the question many white, working-class voters were asking themselves at their dinner tables.

Senator Clayton smiled back the way a realpolitiker, hardened by decades of political experience, intrigues and power plays would smile at a sixty-five-year-old redneck who has seen his world deteriorate but cannot understand why. "It certainly sounds easier, I'll give you that. Build a wall, ban all Chinese products, ban all Muslims, let the Europeans protect themselves, give South Korea and Japan their own nuclear weapons. But that's not how it works in the real world. It's bar banter."

"How about Mr. Drump's remark, the other day, that you condoned your husband's behavior while he was in the White House. Would you classify that as bar banter as well?"

Senator Clayton hesitated. Her short, blond, waving hair was just as tightly styled as a moment before, her navy-blue Chanel couture suit was just as creaseless, but for the slightest moment, Mrs. Clayton seemed hurt, vulnerable. "You know, I have gotten this question a number of times over the course of the past couple of months, and my response has always been that this sort of question doesn't dignify an answer. The presidency is probably the hardest job in the world—I have seen it up close and personal for eight years, so I know a little bit about it—and it's important that we elect someone who is really capable, who knows how to tackle the tough foreign policy issues of our time and who can get the economy back on track, not just for the rich but for all layers of society. You know, these are tough times for many people. We have real problems that require real solutions. So what does it tell you when someone who is applying for that job and all the complexity and awesome responsibility that comes with it—when that person prefers to take cheap shots instead of talking about the issues? I'll tell you one thing: that is not how the people of Michigan are going to get their jobs back."

"Thank you Senator. And with that we're going to take a quick break. Don't go anywhere, we'll be right back with Chris Anderson 720 Degrees."

13

Peter Veldman was not a fanatic, which was too bad really, because fanatics were easy. They were just waiting for the opportunity to feed that insatiable, zealous monster roaring inside of them like a caged animal. They wanted to feed it, free it and be devoured by it.

Fanatics were wonderful to work with. They didn't ask for money, prestige, or even to escape with their lives. You didn't even have to provide the grenade for them to jump on. All they wanted was live and die for the cause.

Veldman wasn't an idealist either—even if he thought of himself as one—which was maybe for the better. An idealist could be driven to extreme acts under certain circumstances, but only if he was convinced there was no other way. And unlike the fanatic, the idealist had no all-consuming desire to self-destroy, he wanted to live. Of course, over time an idealist could morph into a fanatic, but that wasn't something likely to be accomplished in a few weeks or even months.

No, Peter Veldman was neither fanatic nor idealist, but he desperately wanted to be. Perhaps, secretly, he even looked up to his grandfather, even though he said he despised him. A man who had fought at Stalingrad—even if it was on the wrong side—and had been wounded there. Who had stood for and wholeheartedly believed in something greater than himself, who had kept fighting even when others had been fleeing, and who had been killed on his way to the front, instead of running away from it. Richter knew nothing about Veldman's father, but the fact that he hadn't come up in any of their conversations over the last few weeks told him he probably didn't play a large role in his life.

No, his grandfather was the main character—in their conversations, in the more than hundred blog posts he had published on his website, in that book he was writing. It was as if by learning about his grandfather's past, Veldman had accidentally stepped into a patch of quicksand and then deliberately started struggling, instead of grabbing the tree branch hanging within reach, even though he knew struggling would only suck him deeper and tighter into the suffocating mud. Even though there was no mud.

Can you spend so much time with someone purely out of hate and guilt, or was there also admiration, at least on some level? Admiration for having fought the fight, being all you can be, taking that Luger out of its holster and actually putting a bullet between the eyes of an enemy and see the blood spurt out. It certainly was a far cry from pursuing a Ph.D. in history at Cornell. Had the accidental discovery about his grandfather's exploits shifted the limelight from a desired career in academics, studying history, to one driven by actual change, *making* history? If that was the case, then every blog post, every book page he wrote was a confirmation, a confession even, that indeed he was not his grandfather, that he was not someone who followed through on his beliefs, but preferred to spend his days as the eternal observer of a distant past, a stuffy professor Henry Jones instead of the firebrand son Indiana.

Richter took his glass and whirled it around. He always loved the sound of clattering ice cubes bumping around, but they had almost disappeared already. Time. That was his main problem.

Did Veldman crave action? Was he just looking for a cause to sink his teeth in? Could he be persuaded to act, to do something dramatic, be a lone wolf? Yes, he believed he could. But in six weeks time? Then again, that look in his eyes the other day—when they were talking about killing Hitler in Vienna and he said he would tear him apart with his bare hands if necessary—he had seen that look many times. You could always tell who were the real killers and who were only along for the ride.

In any case, he was running out of time. He would leave for Zurich next week and on September 13 meet with the hacker in Paris. If Veldman was going to be at the event on October 19, he would need to give Jackie his passport data. Of course, there was still room to develop and recruit Veldman, but still, October 19 was just six weeks away now. Considering the short time frame, the actual recruitment would have to be a crash approach, that much was clear. The best thing—

"Hi Don, how are you?"

Richter turned to his left as Veldman walked past him. "Hey Peter." He gestured to the barman. "Martin, a Trappist for my friend, and do you have some salty peanuts or something?"

"Sure."

"Well then, salty peanuts all around," he jovially waved around the largely empty bar.

"So, I saw this interesting discussion about Ronald Drump on FOS News yesterday." Richter began.

"Oh yeah?" Veldman put his leather briefcase on the floor.

"Yeah, and you know, I think for the first time FOS News really is fair and balanced, at least when it comes to Ronald Drump, because they just don't know what to do about him," he chuckled. "In fact, they may be the only news network that is treating him unbiased."

84

"What was it about?" Veldman asked. "Ah, thanks Martin." He took the beer from the bartender and took a big sip right away.

"Caitlin Shelly, you know her...?"

Peter nodded.

"Okay, so she has this talk show in which she invites talking heads to vent about the usual conservative bullet points. You know, things like how Democrats are trampling on their Second Amendment rights by not allowing AR-15s in school cafeteria, or why Christmas is increasingly referred to as 'the holidays'. And they always agree with each other, I mean it's like watching a political debate on North Korean state television."

Veldman chortled.

"Yeah. Anyway, yesterday she had this Republican senator from South Carolina, Kinsey Macmaham, and the former governor of Alaska, Clara Lacing. Both are staunch conservatives, I mean Macmaham wants to unleash World War III on ISIS and Lacing thinks global warming is a hoax and every kid should be taught how to shoot a rifle before the age of five. But they had completely opposing views on Ronald Drump, and it quickly got ugly too."

"What happened?"

"First, Macmaham—in his own effeminate way and with the kind of southern drawl that makes you think of belles and balls—called Drump a danger to America, implying that he would withdraw from NATO, which Macmaham said would invite Putin into Eastern Europe, and that he would also withdraw from Asia, which he said could cause war in the Pacific between China and Japan."

"Ok...."

"But then Lacing interjected, saying Macmaham was misrepresenting Drump's views and that he was only doing so out of jealousy, because his own bid for the Republican nomination had been nothing but a total failure."

"Oh that's right," Veldman snapped his fingers, "he was a Republican candidate too. I even remember seeing him in one of the debates for the second tier candidates. He was pretty funny actually, reminiscing about his parents' liquor store and how he learned to be diplomatic helping out in the bar and the pool room as a young boy."

"Well, he was in no mood for jokes yesterday," Richter said. "He called Drump's remarks about most Mexican immigrants being criminals and wanting to ban Muslims altogether 'very un-American', to which Governor Lacing replied the Senator should come out of the closet already, or man up and grow a pair."

"She said that? And how did he react?"

"Macmaham said he wasn't even going to dignify it with a reaction. Then Caitlin Shelly said something about there being no need for name-calling and quickly moved on."

"Clara Lacing…" Veldman scoffed. "Just imagine what would have happened if McCain had won the presidency back in '08 and then died in office."

Richter nodded. "Then it would have been President Lacing. Now there's a recipe for disaster."

"He is worse, though," Veldman said.

"Who? Macmaham?"

"No, Drump of course. Banning all Muslims from entering the United States, monitoring mosques, registering U.S. citizens as Muslims, deporting millions of Mexicans. What kind of country do you think *that* would be?" Veldman said with growing indignation.

Richter shrugged indifferently, but his eyes, alert and inquisitive, betrayed his real state of mind. The Dutchman's answer to his own question could reveal a lot about the depth of his resentment towards the Republican candidate.

"I'll tell you what kind of country that will be—a fascist police state, just like Nazi Germany, only this time the Muslims and Mexicans will fill the camps instead of the Jews." Veldman's pupils dilated as his anger rose. "I mean, there must be millions of illegal Mexicans in the country, and what, another couple of million Muslims? You can't deport millions of people without mounting an elaborate enforcement, detention and deportation-processing infrastructure. Racial profiling by the police would become the official policy, there would be raids and concentration camps, families would be dragged from their homes and jobs, kids taken from their schools and put on transport to camps in California, Arizona, New Mexico and Texas, before being deported to Mexico. And what are these people going to do in Mexico? Many of them have lived here all their lives."

He took the notebook out of his side pocket and held it up. "It's nothing new, we've been there before. I just can't believe that the same country that was so instrumental in ending the evil empires of Germany and Japan is now considering electing a President who could turn out to be a 21st century version of Adolf Hitler."

He placed the book on the bar and felt for the pen inside his jacket. "Registering Muslims just because they are Muslim, really? How much different is that from forcing a Jew to wear a yellow star? And what's next, Muslims being banned from holding public office, from working for the government, from voting, from teaching, from marrying non-Muslims? You think I'm exaggerating? Because I don't think it's that far removed from someone who has said that 'radical Islam is taking our children and turning them against us.' To Ronald Drump, every Muslim is basically just one step away from radicalizing and becoming a terrorist."

He held up the white gold fountain pen and looked at it. "For the last few weeks, I have been thinking about this pen. I got it from my dad, who said it had belonged to my grandfather. Here, have a look." He held it out for Richter, who reached over to take it.

"It's a Cartier," Veldman continued. "A few days ago, I took it to an antique dealer. He said it was from the 1920s and was worth over $10,000. But my grandfather was just a teenager in the 1920s and didn't have a pot to piss in for much of the 1930s, so how did he come by this pen?"

Richter passed it back. "You think he took it from some rich Jew or something?"

Veldman looked at the pen. "I honestly don't know. But how can I continue writing with it?"

Neither spoke for a while. Richter gestured the bartender for another round—he made sure Veldman never had to pay for anything—and considered several responses that could nudge the Dutchman another crucial step closer towards the inescapable conclusion.

He swirled the fresh cubicles in his glass and took a generous swig. "You know, even if Drump is elected, he will be gone in four, eight years tops. This is still a democracy."

Veldman shot him a derisive look. "That's exactly what the Germans said in 1933."

"That was different though," Richter responded, knowing it was not. "The Nazis came to power by force."

"You're wrong," Veldman said, taking the bait. "Hitler won the election of '33, then quickly introduced an emergency law in the *Reichstag* that would give him absolute power, while at the same time arresting all the Communist *Reichstag* members before the vote and intimidating the Centrist Party into voting for the law."

"Hmmm, okay, I didn't know that," Richter lied.

"You think a man like Ronald Drump will let himself be curtailed by something as weak and inconsequential as Congress? All it would take is one terrorist attack. One big attack, like 9/11, real or staged, before he could cajole Congress into passing a far-reaching emergency law giving him sweeping powers. Meanwhile, he would unleash war in the Middle East, using it as a pretext to pre-emptively arrest Muslim citizens and put them into internment camps. I mean if Roosevelt could do it, why not Drump?"

"So what are you saying? That he could be another Hitler?"

"I'm saying that just because he's blond and chubby and speaks English instead of German, doesn't mean he won't be."

14

Friday, September 9, 2016, 4:55 p.m.,
Kasernenstrasse 29, Zurich, Switzerland

More often than we think, the course of human history hinges on the actions of a single individual. And those actions, in turn, more often than not hinge on a single moment of inspiration, an instinctive decision, a tiny mistake, the boldness of attack—or restraint.

Consider the chauffeur of Archduke Franz Ferdinand, who takes a wrong turn in the center of Sarajevo on June 28, 1914. And nineteen-year-old Bosnian Gavrillo Princip, who accidentally finds himself at the perfect spot for a clear shot at the Archduke and his wife. Was World War I inevitable? Would it have broken out no matter the actions of this one Bosnian secessionist?

To answer yes, is to say that none of our actions matter—even if Gavrillo Princip had missed on June 28, 1914, war would have still broken out one month later. To answer no, acknowledges the possibility that one action, however small, might alter the lives of millions, perhaps for generations to come.

Of course, most of the time, the weight of individual actions is only added afterward. Trying to retrace the steps to a particular outcome, we go back in time and try to determine how much a particular action contributed to it. Where was victory secured? Where defeat imminent?

In the case of detective Hans Kreuzer of the Kanton Zurich *Kriminalpolizei*, the casual decision to put off getting a search warrant until after the weekend would prove to be the most weighted action of his professional career.

"Kreuzer."

—

"Yes, good afternoon. Inspector Kent, you said?"

—

"Of Scotland Yard. Right."

—

"Of course. How can I be of assistance?"

—

"Hold on, I'll write it down. Dieter… Zimmerman."

—

"The name vaguely rings a bell. Hold on, I'll check it right away."

—

"Yes. We have him on file here as a ballistics expert. I recognize him from his photo. I even worked with him once or twice actually."

—

"Yeah, he is most definitely a ballistics expert."

—

"Are you sure your man isn't pulling your leg or something Inspector? I mean, to be honest, Mr. Zimmerman doesn't exactly strike me as the type."

—

"Fair enough. So, a custom-made gun."

—

"Right."

—

"And what was so special about it?"

—

"Plastic, you say? Even the barrel?

—

"Custom-made bullets too. Hmmm. Well, as I said, he certainly knows a lot about bullets. Okay, we'll check him out. I'll get back to you within the next couple of days, alright?"

—

"And a nice weekend to you too Inspector. Good evening."

Kreuzer looked at the photograph of the bespectacled man with the friendly smile. He shrugged. A plastic gun? The only criminals that bought custom-made firearms like that were professional killers and it would highly surprise him if a man like Dieter Zimmerman consorted with the likes of those. Sounded more like this perp just wanted to have a little fun with the boys over at Scotland Yard. He looked at his watch. Exactly 5:00 p.m. He'd get the warrant Monday morning. It wasn't like Herr Zimmerman was going anywhere.

15

Tourists were basking in the afternoon sun on the grand marble staircase of the New York Public Library building on Fifth Avenue and 42nd Street, as Richter made his way up to the equally impressive entrance, where he joined a line of people in T-shirts, shorts and slippers, waiting to get in. He felt severely overdressed in his suit and tie, but for the past few weeks this is what he had been wearing whenever he met with Veldman. A grey or dark-blue suit with tie.

He knew the Dutchman was working today but not whether he had any plans after. Of course he could have called him, but he wanted to keep digital communication with Veldman to the absolute minimum, meaning zero. It always left a trace, there was no way around it. A phone call, a text message, there would be a record of it at the phone company long after Veldman's demise. If he used a burner they would not be able trace it to him, but they would still find the record of the message, maybe even the message itself. And that would mean a trail. For the same reason e-mail was out, Skype was out, Whatsapp was out, anything that could leave a digital slipstream.

But it was time to move to the next phase of Veldman's recruitment and for that he needed to meet him somewhere else. The bar on Amsterdam Avenue was where Veldman could confide in *him*, but now he needed a location where he could confide in Veldman,

93

to forge a bond of mutual trust.

The line moved slowly, and once inside he saw why. Every bag was checked by security personnel. As he shuffled along, the memory of an enormous, brightly decorated Christmas tree, erected in the middle of this majestic, white marble lobby, flashed up in his mind. It must have been in the late 1970s, early 80s, when they had visited the library during a school outing, the only time he had ever been here before. Funny, he thought, as fragmented images kept jolting his memory, he grew up in New York City and yet he had been here only once, at this iconic building that drew hundreds of thousands of tourists every year. He suddenly felt like a tourist himself.

After he was waved through (he didn't have any bag), he asked another security guard to direct him to the library's Map Division. Leaning against a wall, arms crossed, she slightly lifted her right index without moving anything else. "Past the gift shop, end of the hall, on the right."

Waiting in line just now, he had felt overdressed in his suit and tie, especially with the rest of the visitors dressed so casual, not to say sloppy. But walking through the impressive hallway, with its richly decorated, 40 feet high ceiling, his black leather shoes click-clacking on the marble floor, he felt almost sorry top hats and stylish walking canes had gone out of fashion.

He entered the Lionel Pincus and Princess Firyal Map Division behind two giggling teenage girls wearing jeans cut off so far at the top they failed to cover the lowest part of their behind. One of them was shapely enough to make it look sexy and tempting, with just the right amount of sleaze, but the other girl's bottom was too big and flabby to pull off anything other than slutty and easy. As they walked past the desk on the right, he saw Veldman looking at them.

"Hi Peter."

"Hey Don. What are you doing here?" Veldman smiled.

"I was in the neighborhood and remembered you saying something about always working at the library on Saturdays." He looked around for a moment, before continuing, "And I... eh, also wanted to talk to you."

"Well, you know, I was planning to go to Café Lambik tonight anyway."

"Yeah, no, I would prefer to talk somewhere else about this," Richter said softly.

"Oh, okay. Yeah, sure," Veldman responded, not wanting to embarrass his new friend. "Look, I'm almost done." He looked at his screen. "How about we meet at Bryant Park in about fifteen minutes?"

"Yeah sure, that sounds good."

"Great. I'll come to the fountain at the other end of the lawn."

Was Veldman ready for the Big Lie? It was impossible to say. He had dressed the part, let him know between the lines that he worked for the government and had combat experience, but nothing else. Then again, why wouldn't he believe it? And even if he didn't, it wasn't like he couldn't continue without Veldman.

It was something that had bothered him since the beginning, almost since Chris Mathers had brought it up, telling him he needed a 'Sirhan Sirhan' to make it look like the assassination was carried out by a leftist fanatic, a lone wolf.

In the early planning stages, he had chewed on the idea of using two identical guns. The biggest problem was always going to be getting away, and having a decoy—some fanatic with a gun right in front of the candidate—would give him much more breathing room. To maintain the illusion of a lone wolf assassination, he would ask Zimmerman to identically rebore two Smith & Wesson Model 629 .357 revolvers to a .44 caliber, so that the striations on the bullets from the spiraling grooves and the lands (the flat parts between the grooves) would be identical, making it seem like the bullets were fired from the same gun. He would then have his own S&W Model 629 outfitted with a standard 2X scope, maybe a 2-7 Burris or 2.5-8 Leupold. That, together with the 629's 8.375" barrel, should give him more than enough accuracy at a range of 50 to 100 yards. If his decoy could get off a couple of shots, great. He only needed one himself.

Later, crime scene investigators would discover that one of the bullets had been fired from a downward trajectory. They would also start matching the number of bullet holes with the number of shots fired and realize there might have been an extra bullet, and therefore a second shooter. But without any further evidence, law enforcement authorities would, in due time, be pressured to declare the case solved and closed, and move on. They had their shooter, after all. The theory of the second shooter would soon be relegated to the conspiracy theorists, as had been the case with the murders of JFK and RFK. Of course, he would be long gone by then, sitting on some tropical island drinking Mai Tais.

But then he had remembered the poisonous dart gun he had used for the hit on General Santos, realizing his chances of both success and escape would be even better using a sniper rifle version of that gun. Why had he still kept the decoy in the picture in that scenario? Because he remembered how Santos had painfully grabbed his ankle when he was hit. And with Drump it couldn't be his ankle, it would probably have to be a chest shot. How would it look if Drump rubbed his chest in pain in front of the cameras, maybe making some remark about a mosquito sting, then develop pulmonary edema the next day and die of heart failure one or two days after that? Suspicious is what it would look.

A thorough autopsy by the forensic pathologist would almost certainly reveal the tiny red dot on the chest, leading to suspicion of poisoning and a search for traces of slow-working poisons like ricin. The pathologist would determine the cause of death to be poisoning, investigators would launch a prolonged and intensive investigation into the identity of the mysterious poison dart assassin and the Mai Tais wouldn't taste half as good.

But, if Drump was also shot by a lone gunman, the narrative would be very different. In that case, the moment the candidate had rubbed his chest from a supposed bug sting would likely be lost in the pandemonium following the shooting. And even if the gunshot wounds he received weren't fatal, if he developed pulmonary edema and die of a heart attack a few days later, it would probably still be linked to diminished health and/or increased stress as a result of the shooting.

Then Dieter Zimmerman had told him firing a poisonous frozen dart from a range greater than twenty yards was impossible and the plot had evolved into a poisonous drone that could attack much more subtly. Did he still really need Peter Veldman in this scenario? Maybe not as much. With the drone he could go for an ankle hit, making any instinctive reaction—Drump grabbing his ankle in pain—look more natural and less suspicious. Then again, his death a few days later would still raise all kinds of questions, questions that merited a thorough autopsy and perhaps a close examination of the available video footage—especially the frames where Drump had grabbed his ankle—which might reveal the drone, hovering mere inches away from the candidate.

No. After all was said and done, he still felt that the benefit of having a lone wolf shooter greatly outweighed the relative low risk of trying to recruit one. And Veldman was almost there. In his mind, there was already very little difference between Adolf Hitler in 1933 and Ronald Drump in 2016, and you don't become involved in the Anti-Fascist League because you don't care about stopping fascism. In a way, Peter Veldman had been waiting for a man like Ronald Drump to rise up the way a professional soldier waits for a war to break out. The soldier might not wish for war, but deep down he knows his existence is tied to it, that without it, he can never truly fulfill his destiny. It was—

"Don, there you are." Veldman was walking towards him. "You want to get a table or something?"

"Nah, let's just walk around a bit."

"Sure. Why don't we walk around the lawn, that's what I always do on my lunch break—well, in spring and summer anyway," he grinned, leading the way down the stairs and onto the gravel path.

For a while, neither of them said anything. They just walked, passing young lovers smooching on the grass, two girls chatting and sunbathing, a couple of kids running around, an old homeless man sleeping next to his few possessions, a guy in a suit loudly conducting a business deal on the phone, pacing up and down the lawn as if it was his office.

"Look, I need to tell you something," Richter began, the grey gravel crunching under their feet. "I mean, you might find out sooner or later anyway, watching TV or something, and I'd rather have you hear it from me."

"What, are you a celebrity or something?" Veldman sniggered.

"No, not exactly, but I have been working for one."

Veldman turned towards Richter. "You know, I don't even know what you do. I think you said something about working for the government, in the military or something?"

"I have indeed worked for the government in a military capacity, but that was a long time ago. Truth is, for the past fifteen years

98

I have worked for the Secret Service."

"Get out of here," Veldman laughed.

"No, I'm serious."

"Come on, you're messing with me, right?"

"Look at me."

Still grinning, the Dutchman looked Richter in the eye, but this time there was no mocking twinkle in the deep sky-blue irises. "Okay, so you're not joking," he said, not sure what to make of it and feeling slightly uncomfortable.

"There is more," Richter continued, as they turned left, passing the bronze statue of William Bryant. "A little over a month ago, I was assigned to the security detail of the Republican presidential candidate."

"Wait wait wait," Veldman stopped Richter in front of Bryant, the latter stoically continuing to survey his namesake park like an umpire a tennis court. "Drump? You're saying that for the past few weeks you have been working as a bodyguard for Ronald Drump?"

Richter nodded, his hands in his pockets.

"Why didn't you say something before? I mean, we've talked about him quite a bit I'd say."

"I know. Look, to be honest, I was embarrassed about it. You know I don't like the guy—in fact I hate everything he stands for—but I still might have to take a bullet for him one day. Can you imagine that? Having to take a bullet for that fascist?" He scoffed. "I'd rather put one between his eyes."

They passed a juggler who was entertaining a three-year-old by keeping four brightly colored balls in the air. The little blond boy was marveled in a way we experience only rarely in later life, gazing with big, bright eyes and wide open mouth.

Richter sighed. "I know, super unprofessional of me, right?"

"What, that you would rather kill that fascist than protect him?"

Veldman shook his head. "That doesn't make you unprofessional, it makes you human. As a matter of fact, you probably should put a bullet between his eyes, before it's too late."

Richter stared across the lawn. "No, I could never do that. I mean, I could never betray my duty like that."

He glanced at Veldman. "I can see you disagree," he smiled. "I don't expect you to understand."

Veldman shrugged. "It's not my place to say anything about it, but I know that duty—the sense of duty—can drive someone far beyond what can reasonably be expected of them."

They walked past *Le carrousel,* playing Edith Piaff's *Non Je Ne Regrette Rien* as the kids went round and round on the richly decorated, colorful wooden horses.

"Actually, I imagine my grandfather felt that same sense of duty," he continued. "And sometimes I honestly wonder who were worse: the half-hearted collaborators who only joined to enrich themselves and fled at the first sign of trouble, or the true fanatics like my grandfather, who fought themselves to death for an ideal that was as close to evil as we have ever come."

"Hmm, maybe you do understand," Richter said approvingly. "Listen, to make it up to you, I can probably get you into the third and final presidential debate, on October 19. It's in Vegas. Very exclusive, they don't sell tickets for it, but we always get a couple. All I need is a copy of your passport. Unless you're not interested of course."

Veldman's face lit up. "Are you kidding? I would absolutely love to go! If you come to Lambik tonight, I'll make sure to bring a copy of my passport."

"That would be great. And I'll be on duty next week, so that'll give me a chance to get you on the audience list."

"Awesome!" Veldman beamed. "Vegas here I come!"

16

It was 6:00 in the morning, an hour before sunrise. The narrow, cobble stone streets were still silent. A cold, ash-grey fog was quickly rising up from the Limmat River, painting the heart of Zurich's sleeping *altstadt* with a mystic, sinister brush. The sparse light emanating from the classic street lanterns barely made a dent in the dense, grey soup. On a park bench on the eastern bank of the Limmat, next to the Münsterbrücke, Conrad Richter cursed in silence. His view of the house on the corner of the Kämbelgasse and the Wühre—on the western bank—had been perfect, but in the space of less than a quarter of an hour it had turned to absolute shit.

Other than an old woman walking her dog and a young couple giggling and stumbling their way home, there had been no activity for the past hour in front of Dieter Zimmerman's house, but in a thick fog like this the entire Zurich police force could set up shop in the gunsmith's home without anyone noticing. He put the small binoculars in his side pocket and considered his options for a moment. The chance that Dieter Zimmerman was somehow compromised was slim to none of course, he knew that very well. He had done business with the Swiss gunsmith for over twenty years. The man had always delivered, kept to himself and lived a modest, even boring lifestyle—at least as far as he could tell. Nothing was impossible, but usually those were not the kind of people popping up on anyone's radar. But even if chances were small, he didn't like diverting from his security procedures. They were an integral part of a playbook developed from years of training, experience and costly mistakes—both by himself and others. He would not have survived this long without it.

Meetings with (potential) clients and suppliers were always a risk, and follow-up meetings even more so. True, ninety-nine out of a hundred times you were waiting for nothing, in the soaking rain, freezing cold, blazing sun or middle of the night, but that one time it saved your life. He got up, crossed the bridge and strolled along the Münsterhof, taking a right onto the Storchengasse and another right into the Kämbelgasse, approaching Zimmerman's house from the other side. Passing the gunsmith's house, he slowed and looked around for an instant, before quickly patching a device no bigger than a quarter at the bottom of the side wall next to the heavy oak door. Not ideal, but it would have to do, he thought by himself as he strolled on.

10:00 a.m.

"Ah, Herr Kruger. Please come in," Zimmerman smiled, as he turned around and began climbing the stairs. "I think you'll be very pleased with what I have for you," he said, looking back over his shoulder and half-stumbling over one of the staircases.

Richter followed Zimmerman upstairs, feeling more alert and less comfortable than last time. He couldn't put his finger on it, there had been nothing unusual on the listening device—Zimmerman hadn't received any visitors during the past hours—but somehow, something felt off.

Zimmerman entered his office. "Would you like an espresso, *ja*?" the gunsmith asked, already walking in the direction of his beloved La Pavoni espresso machine.

"Eh, no Dieter, thanks. I'm actually quite curious as to what you have come up with."

"Of course, I understand," Zimmerman said, making a half-turn and going behind his desk. He reached into his right-hand pocket, took out a small bronze key and unlocked the upper left desk drawer.

"First, the gun," he said, taking out a small, white cardboard box and placing it on the desk. "It has the 2.5" barrel, as you request-ed." He opened the box, took the double-stacked barrel out and handed it to Richter.

"To reinforce the structural integrity of the barrel, I used ma-chined zirconia, over-wrapped with resin-coated carbon fibers. It should prove quite durable," the gunsmith said confidently, a hint of pride in his voice. He took out the grip and trigger part. "The barrel and grip are joined the same way as on the original Bond Arms guns, only I used a plastic screw. I've also manufactured a plastic 4" Allen wrench," he said, plucking the small tool and the screw from the box and holding them in the palm of his hand. "If you'd like to try."

Placing the barrel on the desk, Richter moved its screw open-ing—sitting on top—between the ones on top of the grip, placed the screw on top of the aligned opening, carefully fixed the Allen wrench on the screw's head and started turning it.

"You will find it fits perfectly," Zimmerman said. "I have not test-fired the gun myself, but from my measurements I concluded that everything is perfectly aligned."

After tightly fixing the screw, Richter pushed the barrel in the groove running atop the trigger part; a plastic-sounding click confirmed the barrel was locked-in. He tried to wiggle it, but found it was solidly fixed. Pushing down the lever next to the trigger released the barrel from the groove. Satisfied with the gun's structural integrity, he clicked the barrel back in the groove again and cocked the hammer.

"Cocking the hammer changes which barrel will fire," Zimmerman said. "The firing selector is a hammer head, right there, in the hammer," he leaned over to point it out. "When it drops—like it did just now when you cocked the hammer—it means the lower barrel will fire. It's exactly the same as with the original Bond Arms guns."

Richter cocked the hammer and pulled the trigger a few times, to observe the principle. "Excellent piece of work Dieter," he finally said. "Truly excellent."

"Thank you, Herr Kruger," Zimmerman replied, sounding both proud and noticeably relieved.

Richter put the gun on the desk. "And the drone?"

"Ah yes." The gunsmith walked around the desk and reached inside the upper left drawer again, this time taking out a small, tiffany-blue jewelry box.

"Here it is," he beamed, placing the little box on the desk and turning it a few degrees so it aligned perfectly with the angle of the table.

"I've also prepared this." He put a slim, oblong metal container on the desk and clicked it open. "Three vials of ricin and a USB stick with the latest version of the navigational control app. You could also download the app from the company website, but that would leave a trail to your phone, which I thought you'd probably want to avoid.

"You thought right," Richter nodded, still feeling rushed and uncomfortable for some reason. But he was here now, so it was best to get it over with.

"So, here we are," Zimmerman said, opening the box and carefully taking out a tiny creature with six grey-black legs and two dragonfly-shaped wings. "The body is made of carbon fiber. It is very light, weighing only 5.5 grams, and that is including the camera and wireless communication." He picked up the drone and put it on his left index finger. "The wingspan is just three centimeters, a little over one inch."

Richter was impressed. Looking at the tiny drone on Zimmerman's finger he wondered whether it would one day make the sniper rifle obsolete. After all, why would you try to hit a target from a mile away—which was extremely hard—if you could simply fly an artificial insect to it, land undetected on a piece of clothing and pierce the skin with a poisonous needle? Nobody would even know the hit had been executed until the target keeled over his coffee table a few days later. And even if the hit was noticed, how would they ever catch the killer? He could be miles away, in a house, a car, a movie theater.

"How does it fly?" he asked. "Does it actually flap its wings?"

"Oh yes. It uses high-performance piezoelectric actuators that flap the wings at 120 times per second." He pointed to the small pyramid on top of its head. "And this is what enables the drone to keep its balance: a sophisticated light sensor that, according to the manual, works much the same way flying insects use sunlight to stabilize their flight and keep a sense of direction. It's really quite ingenious."

He carefully picked up the drone and placed it on its side on the palm of his hand. "And here, hanging on a toothpick-sized rail under the body, is the syringe. The needle is only half an inch, but that is quite sufficient. Now, inside the syringe's cylinder sits a plunger, fitted with a rubber piston. I have removed the gripper that was originally located here and modified its operating mechanism, so that activating it first pushes the syringe forward along the rail and then pushes the plunger down, which in turn forces the liquefied ricin through the needle. Tapping the operative button a second time will move the syringe back to its original position—thereby retracting the needle—and push the plunger up. That is also the easiest way to fill the syringe by the way, though it is also possible to uncouple the syringe from the rail and operate the plunger manually."

"I'm impressed," Richter said. "And how about the controls? I mean, is it difficult to operate?"

"Why don't you try it?" Zimmerman smiled, gingerly placing the drone on the desk and taking his iPhone out of his inside jacket pocket. "I have the same app version as the one on the USB stick." He tapped the drone control app's icon, turned the phone to landscape and showed it to Richter.

"So, let's switch it on first," he said. "You do that by tapping this green square here… now the screen comes on… yes… and we're seeing what the drone is seeing. By the way, the wings are covered with photovoltaic cells. The electricity this generates is not enough to power flight, but it *can* be used to switch on the main power source, so it won't be drained from being in stand-by mode for long periods."

"Hmmm, a very useful feature." Richter said.

"Yes it really is quite a nifty trick. Okay, then we have the transparent circle on the right here, which allows you to move the drone up, down, left and right. Accelerating and slowing down is controlled at the center of the circle, with the two little arrows at the upper part for accelerating and the two arrows at the lower part for slowing down."

Zimmerman pointed to the smaller transparent circle at the left side of the screen. "This is also an important button. It activates stationary hover mode, which is really the easiest way to tell the drone to keep its current position." He briefly looked at Richter to make sure he wasn't moving too fast, but the American's eyes were intently focused on the screen.

"Ah, and these two are also very convenient," he continued, pointing at two rectangular buttons at the bottom of the screen, one green-striped, one red-striped. "The green button will take the drone a few inches into the air, the red one will automatically land it."

"And this button here, the semicircle with the curved clockwise arrow?" Richter asked.

"That, as far as the drone's flight capabilities are concerned, is the *pièce de résistance*," Zimmerman answered, emphasizing the French words while pointing his right finger in the air. "You see, normally, the drone flies horizontally, like this." He held out his right hand palm down. "But then how do you land on a wall? You can't. But the developers wanted to mimic the movement of a fly as closely as possible, so they included an option for the drone to come to a vertical position and land up against a wall. Look," he lifted the artificial insect and turned it upside down, "it even has tiny suction cups for feet," he chuckled, looking up at Richter. But when the American didn't show any reaction, the gunsmith quickly reverted back to serious mode.

"Yes, well, I've tried it a few times and it really works. Swiping the button clockwise will land the drone in vertical position, swiping it counter-clockwise will unlatch it again and put it in horizontal hover mode."

"And this, I take it, will activate the syringe?" Richter said, ignoring the awkward moment and pointing to the red square on the left bottom.

"Eh, yes, correct. And remember, the second tap will push the syringe back to its original position."

Zimmerman looked at the screen for a few seconds, trying to think of something he might have forgotten, but all the important functions had been discussed. "Well, that's about it. Would you like to take it for a spin now?" he smiled, offering the iPhone to Richter.

But the American, looking at his watch, demurred. "I'm actually in somewhat of a rush Dieter, if you don't mind. I'm sure it will perform great."

"Oh… eh, yes, okay. As you wish of course," Zimmerman said, sounding a little disappointed. He slipped the phone back into his inside jacket pocket, carefully picked up the drone and gently placed it back into its little tiffany-blue box.

"Now, as to your fee…" Richter said.

"Yes, of course." The gunsmith walked around his desk. "I have prepared a financial statement as usual. The drone itself was €12,000, including the app. The… eh, mark-up from the credit card buyer was 50 percent—so, that is €6,000. Then there are my own hours, for manufacturing the plastic gun, modifying the drone, testing everything and producing the ricin. A total of 54 hours. Per the usual €400 an hour, that comes to €21,600, making for a grand total of 39,600 Euro."

"I take it that's including taxes?" Richter joked.

The gunsmith produced a modest laugh. "Ah, yes."

The American reached into his jacket and took out four tight banknote packages, vacuum-sealed in plastic. "I know you don't like denominations of €500, so here are four packages of 50 €200 bills. Count it if you want."

"That won't be necessary Herr Kruger. I'll just open one to get you your change."

"No need. Consider it a tip for a job well done." He pocketed the white cardboard box, the jewelry box, the metal container with the three vials of ricin and the USB stick and walked to the door. Then, as if realizing he forgot something, he turned around and brought his hand to his head in a casual salute. "Until the next time."

"It will be my pleasure Herr Kruger," the gunsmith smiled. "As always."

It was 10:42 a.m.

17

Monday, September 12, 2016, 12:30,

Zurich, Switzerland

"Yes?"

"Mr. Zimmerman?"

"Yes…"

"I am detective Hans Kreuzer of the Kanton Zurich *Kriminalpolizei*, this is detective Georg Wassermann."

"Good afternoon gentlemen. You look very familiar Herr…. Kreuzer is it? Have we worked together before?"

Kreuzer nodded somewhat uncomfortably.

"Is this about a new case? Because you didn't have to come here to pick me up for that," he smiled friendly. "If it's in the Zurich area I only require an address, then I'll get to the crime scene on my own."

"No, uhm, I'm afraid it's something else, Herr Zimmerman. We have a search warrant for your house."

"A search warrant?" Zimmerman looked more confused than alarmed. "For my house? I'm sure there must be some kind of mistake."

"I'm afraid not Herr Zimmerman. Please take a look for yourself," Wassermann said, presenting the stunned little gunsmith with the document.

When Zimmerman saw his own name, his stomach shrank to the size of a golfball and the blood withdrew from his face like an army on the run. Oh God.

"I, eh, am still finishing my lunch," he stumbled, "could you perhaps return an hour from now, or towards the end of the afternoon?"

Kreuzer shook his head. "I'm afraid it doesn't work like that Herr Zimmerman. Please," he gestured the neatly dressed ballistics expert to step aside.

In the movies, search warrants rarely yield results, perhaps because there is nothing spectacular about a policeman finding a suitcase full of money under the bed or a pound of cocaine in the sock drawer. In the case of Dieter Zimmerman, however, it took detectives Kreuzer and Wassermann less than two minutes to come across the kind of evidence that made it clear there was more to the mild-mannered ballistics expert than met the eye.

Whenever Zimmerman collected a payment from another satisfied customer—always in cash—he would bring the money to the bank at the end of the day, depositing it in a safety deposit box. Many years ago, he had started with a modest 3" x 5" x 24" box. When it was full, he had rented another one, and when that was full, he had switched to a medium sized box, before moving up a final notch, to a box the size of a wine crate, which at present held a little over $2 million in medium denominations of Deutsche Marks, Swiss Francs, French Francs, U.S. dollars, Euros and a variety of other denominations. He had never spent any of it, never invested any of it, never even exchanged his Deutsche Marks and French francs for Euros, afraid he was going to get caught. Any ten-year-old could tell you it's no use keeping cash money in a safety deposit box for thirty years, but for Dieter Zimmerman, it was never about the money.

The four packages of 50 €200 bills still lay on the antique mahogany desk, vacuum-sealed in plastic and impossible to miss. Within the next half hour, Kreuzer and Wassermann found undeniable evidence of sophisticated gunsmithing in the large workshop in the cellar, along with blueprints of dozens of custom-made guns and what at first glance seemed to be a design for a remote controlled syringe, fixed to a kind of rail.

But the real treasure trove was the five feet high, steel filing cabinet in the office upstairs, which held files on all of Zimmerman's clandestine custom jobs over a period of three decades. Like many of his generation, Zimmerman had never been able to completely divorce himself from the deeply felt belief that to own something was to be able to take it in your hands whenever you wanted, to have it parked in your driveway or stowed in your home. He certainly was no stranger to technology—in fact, he had become quite the programming hobbyist these past few years—but there was something fundamentally beautiful and personal about a handwritten document that could never be matched by any digital version, kept in a digital folder, instead of a five feet high steel filing cabinet. He knew it would save time to create and store his files on a computer, but he had never been a man to rush himself. He loved running his fingers over the folders in the filing cabinet, leafing through the calendar on his desk and writing down a new appointment with his Sheaffer fountain pen. And detective Hans Kreuzer loved him for loving it.

The dossiers didn't mention any real names, they were all filed by nickname—'Tommy', 'Zossen', 'Afrikaner', 'The American'—but Kreuzer quickly pushed away the stinging disappointment he initially felt, realizing that asking for real names would have been pushing his luck.

"Herr Zimmerman, what are you doing there?" Kreuzer asked the gunsmith, who was standing next to his desk.

"Nothing," he responded weakly, sounding like a schoolboy caught cheating by the headmaster.

"Yes you are, you just put something in your right side pocket. Take it out please."

There was no sense in denying. He took the small book out and put it back on the desk. Kreuzer walked over and picked it up while Zimmerman retreated, as if he was afraid the detective would smack him over the head with it.

"Well well, what have we here?" Kreuzer said softly.

He leafed through the pages until he found what he was looking for. He put his index finger on the upper left corner of the page. Monday, September 12. Today. "Who is the American?" he asked.

To his credit, the little gunsmith never said a word. He was interrogated for hours and threatened with a long prison sentence if he didn't cooperate, but Dieter Zimmerman kept his mouth shut. Not because he was afraid for reprisals from his unforgiving clientele, but because he loathed betrayal. He took pride in his work and in the reputation he had acquired among the select group of mercenaries he had worked with for the past decades, as a man of precision, a man who could make any gun and always delivered on time. He was not about to tarnish that reputation.

Then again, he didn't really have to say anything, the elaborate project files he had kept from the beginning spoke for themselves. They held blueprints for every gun he ever made, notes he had taken during meetings with customers, receipts for materials he had bought—some from companies that had been out of business since the late 1990s—invoices detailing hours, material costs and acquired services from third parties (such as the credit card buyer he sometimes used to purchase certain items anonymously), handwritten summary documents listing each project's opening and closing date, cost and profit. The only thing missing were the customer's real names.

Kreuzer contacted Inspector Kent from Scotland Yard to thank him and tell him his perp had spoken the truth about Dieter Zimmerman. Within a few days it would be established the man the Yard had in custody was the one nicknamed 'Tommy' in the files—if only Tommy had known how meticulous his Swiss gunsmith had recorded every weapon he had ever commissioned, he might have thought twice about mentioning him—but without real names, it would be difficult to apprehend any suspects based on Zimmerman's files alone.

There was one nickname in particular that bothered Kreuzer. The American. At first only because he had apparently just missed him by two hours and any criminal buying custom-made guns would be an interesting by-catch, but after he pulled Zimmerman's file on the American, his slight annoyance was replaced by a growing sense of alarm.

First, there were the weapons he had commissioned, or to be more precise, the two latest weapons he had commissioned. A small plastic gun with a detachable double barrel and what looked to be a tiny drone armed with a syringe—which also explained the detailed design of the remote controlled, rail-fixed syringe they had found in the cellar earlier.

Then there was the invoice for the American's latest purchase, which among other things listed 'three vials of ricin' (over the next couple of days, a crime scene investigator of the *Bundeskriminalpolizei*, the Swiss Federal Criminal Police, would discover that Herr Zimmerman had indeed manufactured ricin in his workshop).

And the grand total on the invoice. Who would pay €40,000 for two highly specialized weapons that could fool metal detectors and—in the case of the drone—kill undetected? A contract killer, and not just any contract killer but one who was obviously extremely well-paid. Who had that kind of money and was willing to pay what could be hundreds of thousands of dollars for a single assassination? It was certainly far beyond the kind of money paid by criminal gangs or syndicates to get rid of the average unwanted element.

And why the need to kill with ricin? To stay undetected? So it wouldn't look like an assassination? It made him think of something the CIA or the FSB would do, but they wouldn't need to hire someone like Dieter Zimmerman, they had their own gunsmiths, lab technicians and expert assassins. No, this was something else, something big, and it was likely going to happen in the next few months, maybe weeks, or even days. And whoever this American was, he had to be very good, because according to Zimmerman's files he had been a customer since the mid-1990s.

Suddenly it occurred to Kreuzer the American might still be in the country and would possibly fly out of Zurich in the coming hours. How many Americans would depart from Kloten Airport today? Hundreds probably, if not thousands. He looked at his watch. 2:45 p.m. He pulled his phone out and called the *Bundeskriminalpolizei*.

"Karl. It's Hans. Listen, I need your help with something."

—

"Yeah it is. Listen, how long would it take you to get access to today's passenger data for Kloten?"

—

"I'm not sure it's terrorism."

"Yeah I know that's the magic word nowadays to get a quick green light, but I don't think that's the case here. We are at the house of an illegal gunsmith and it seems a professional assassin has just taken delivery of an all-plastic gun and some sort of drone, armed with a poisonous syringe."

—

"No, a drone."

—

"Yes. No it's very small apparently. The size of a housefly."

—

"Yeah, no I didn't know that either. Anyway, the guy was just here a couple of hours ago, so he might still be in the country, possibly flying out today."

—

"We don't know for sure. The gunsmith calls him 'the American', but that doesn't mean he is from there of course."

—

"He's not talking, we got it from documents found in his house."

—

"Yeah, that's what we thought. But there is more. This guy, the assassin, he has apparently been in business since the mid-1990s, and the first weapon he commissioned from the gunsmith was an M40A1 rifle."

—

"I just looked it up, it's a bolt-action sniper rifle exclusively used by the United States Marine Corps."

—

"Yeah that's what I thought."

—

"Look, I think we need to move as fast as possible here. Our best bet is that he is an American citizen, possibly a former United States Marine, between the ages of 40 and 70. I don't think there are many of those flying out of Kloten today. We should get the passenger data and then you guys can contact the FBI and have them check our list against military records."

—

"Don't worry about me, I just want the guy stopped before it's too late. I'll send over the necessary info within the hour."

—

"Yeah you too. Keep me posted."

When Kreuzer came off the phone, Conrad Richter had just cleared the French border and was driving on the A35, a few miles from Mulhouse, just before the exit to the A36, direction Paris.

After leaving Dieter Zimmerman's office, he had found himself unable to shake the slightly nauseating feeling that something was wrong. He couldn't say what it was, maybe this particular job just made him a little bit more paranoid than usual. But his grandfather always used to say it was the paranoid who survived. That the experienced Marines at Peleliu and Iwo Jima—those who had survived earlier engagements—had developed an uncanny sense of hidden danger, lurking up ahead in the jungle or on the other side of a creek, even though there were no discernible signs of enemy presence. Over the years, Richter, too, had learned not to ignore his emotions and treat them as an asset instead of a liability.

So, instead of buying a ticket to Charles de Gaulle on the first available flight out of Zurich, he had decided to drive to Paris, renting a BMW 320i Automatic at a local car rental company under the name of Don Jensen. He would never know how right he was. Unfortunately, he was equally unaware he was no longer just a hunter. He was now also being hunted.

18

Monday, September 12, 2016, 4:30 p.m. (CEST),

Zurich, Switzerland /

Washington D.C., United States

Four hours after *Kanton Zurich Kriminalpolizei* detectives Hans Kreuzer and Georg Wassermann had knocked on the door of Dieter Zimmerman—and less than six after Conrad Richter had left through that same door—*Bundeskriminalpolizei* Inspector Karl Deiss was on the phone with the FBI Legal Attaché Office at the American Embassy in Bern.

The Legal Attaché himself, special agent Mike Burkhalter, was gone for the day, as was the Assistant Legal Attaché, but the office assistant picked up the phone within five seconds. Deiss briefly explained the situation and sent over the report he had just received from Kreuzer—which included photos of Zimmerman's file on 'the American'—together with the passenger list of U.S. nationals departing from Zurich International Airport on September 12.

No, it wasn't much to go on, Deiss agreed, but given the current intel he thought their best bet was that the individual was indeed a U.S. citizen. Yes, of course he would sent the file to INTERPOL as well, including today's complete passenger list for departures from Kloten Airport.

After they had hung up, the office assistant immediately contacted the International Operations Division (IOD) at FBI Headquarters, in Washington, D.C., who subsequently passed it on to the Criminal Investigative Division (CID), until it finally landed in the inbox of special agent Jake "Goldilocks" Underhill, of the CID's Violent Crimes Section, Specialty Weapons Department, around noon, local time. Doing right by his nickname, earned for always trying to ditch both the easiest and the hardest cases, in favor of the not too difficult promising ones—in addition to having a full head of wavy blond hair—it took Underhill about thirty seconds before he started complaining about being sent on another wild goose chase for some guy who bought some illegal guns in Europe. "Jesus, who cares if they bought a couple of guns from some gunsmith? Honestly, I don't see what the big deal is."

"What is it this time Goldilocks?" Senior special agent Steve Berenson sighed, without looking up from his paperwork.

"The lottery just assigned me this case about some moron who apparently bought some guns from some illegal gunsmith in Switzerland."

"And this is our concern because….?"

"Pfff, who knows. It was dumped on us by IOD. I guess the Swiss called the local Legat Office. Europeans are always so touchy about guns."

"Hmmm," Berenson agreed.

Underhill continued to make a variety of complaining noises, ranging from 'bleh' to 'hurgh!'

"What kind of guns?" Berenson asked, jotting down a few notes in an old-fashioned Moleskine notebook.

"Hmmm?"

"What kind of guns did he buy? From the gunsmith?"

"I don't know, who cares? Maybe a Swiss Army Knife with a tiny Glock 22 hidden inside it? Look, if you're so interested, why don't you take it?"

Contrary to Underhill, Berenson really believed in what he was doing. Many little boys want to be a policeman when they grow up, Steve Berenson had still wanted to be one by the time he had. For most of his leftist-activist college friends, law enforcement had been an easy target, for Berenson, it had been a calling. And although, at 45 years old, his hairline had started to recede, his physical condition had started to deteriorate and his waistline had started to expand, his desire to man the wall was as strong as ever.

"Okay, hand it over," he gestured with a sigh.

"Really?"

"Yes, really. Come on, before I change my mind."

"Sure thing buddy, hold on." Lunging forward, Underhill, suddenly as focused as an Olympic athlete, made a few rapid-fire clicks with his mouse, before gleefully announcing to Berenson: "You've got mail. I've signed the case over to you."

For the next two minutes, Goldilocks silently congratulated himself a couple of times for handily forking over a worthless piece of shit case to "Boy Scout" Berenson, who could always be counted on to do the right thing.

"Hmmm, that's interesting," Berenson said softly, almost to himself.

"What is?"

"Well, apparently this guy has been a customer of that gunsmith for over two decades."

"If you say so," Underhill said, sounding about as interested as a French civil servant during work hours.

"And you know what the first gun was that he had made?"

"Ehmm, a rocket launcher with one of those Swiss cow bells attached to it, so he could hear whenever someone was trying to steal it? I don't know, I give up."

"An M40A1 rifle."

Underhill looked up, a flicker of interest visible in the v-shaped wrinkle above his nose. "Isn't that an early version of the standard issue sniper rifle of the Marines?"

Berenson nodded.

"Huh…"

"And the last weapons he commissioned are even more unusual."

"Okay, you got me," Underhill grinned, throwing his hands up in the air and pushing back his chair. "What were they?"

"Nah, don't you worry about it. I'll take it from here," Berenson said, picking up the phone and punching in the number for INTERPOL Washington (the United States National Central Bureau, USNCB), to notify them he would be the FBI liaison for the case.

While Steve Berenson was running a military background check on all 783 male U.S. citizens who were both on the departing passenger list of Zurich International Airport on September 12 and born before 1980, Conrad Richter checked in at Hotel Splendide at Rue Jean Moulin, in the 14th *Arrondissement*. It was 8:00 p.m. The assassin had 24 hours to kill.

19

There were three former U.S. Marines on the passenger list for departing flights out of Zurich on September 12 (there was also one active Marine, but he was born in 1991). The first was a 91-year-old veteran who, according to his record, had been part of the 1st Marine Division that had fought at Peleliu and Okinawa—so he was probably out. The second was a banker at JP Morgan Chase. Berenson had called the bank, which confirmed what he had already suspected, that extremely well-paid workaholics putting in 60 hours or more a week managing assets for the extremely wealthy do not have the time, nor the inclination, to travel the world as contract killers.

The third was more interesting. Pete Riggins from Houston, Texas. Born in 1971, joined the Marines in '89, mustered out in '94. Mr. Riggins had boarded a Swissair flight to Chicago yesterday, at 12:55 p.m. Zurich time, arriving at O'Hare at 3:45 p.m. local time. At 5:30 p.m. he had subsequently boarded a United flight to Houston, Texas, which had landed at IAH at 8:17 p.m. Flight data from the last three years revealed Riggins had re-entered the United States from a variety of European as well as more exotic locations, including Dubai, Tel Aviv, Amman, Hong Kong, Moscow and Abuja.

Berenson briefly considered contacting the HPD and asking them to pay Mr. Riggins a visit at his home and check him out, but if this really was the guy they were looking for it could easily end with two dead Houston police officers.

"Agent Underhill, are you busy?" Berenson looked across his desk.

"Not really. I'm filing my expense reports."

"Well then maybe you can add a plane ticket to Houston, Texas, because we're going on a little trip. That is, if you're interested in getting back on the case of the illegal weapon's purchase in Switzerland."

Underhill peeked around his screen. "The M40A1 guy?"

"That's the one. Turns out one of the American passengers out of Zurich was a Marine until '94. A Texan, lives in Houston. He landed at George Bush International yesterday evening, so chances are he's home right now."

"So why not just notify the Houston Police Department? Let them have a chat with him," Underhill suggested.

"No. I'm not going to send the boys in blue to have a chat with someone who may or may not be an armed and lethally dangerous international contract killer. That's our job. But hey, if you don't want to come, you're welcome to continue filing your expense reports of course," Berenson said sarcastically.

By the time Berenson and Underhill boarded United 1594 from Dulles to Houston International, at 12:20 p.m., it was 6:20 p.m. in Paris and Conrad Richter had already observed café *Le Bouquet d'Alésia* for several hours.

At *Le Zeyer*, across from *Le Bouquet d'Alésia*, he had first enjoyed a lunch of steak tartare topped with raw egg yolk, which he had washed away with a single glass of 2009 *Féraud-Brunel Côtes du Rhône Villages*. Forgoing dessert as usual, he had ordered an espresso and continued observing the bustling traffic on *Place*

Victor-et-Hélène-Basch like a regular tourist. It was one of those wonderfully chaotic Paris roundabouts whose logic could only be understood by a true Frenchman, and even they would never be able to explain how to apply just enough fender-bender defying machismo to vanquish Place V-H-B unscathed. Counting a total of nine different directions, danger was lurking everywhere and no quarter was given by anyone. City buses crawled along inexorable, honking their horns whenever some lower life-form obstructed their path, taxis mercilessly elbowed their way from one end to the next, taking advantage of every car that showed even the slightest hesitation, scooters zigzagged suicidally through every cavity, no matter how tiny or temporary. This was no roundabout for old men.

It was close to 4:00 p.m. when Richter settled his bill, strolled up the Avenue du Général Leclerc and, after buying the day's edition of *Le Monde* at a nearby kiosk, sat himself down on a public bench in front of the *Saint-Pierre de Montrouge* church, situated directly across from the construction site of the new movie theater. A few yards to his right, next to the exit of Metro station *Alésia*, a serious-looking little Indian was selling oranges, peaches and pineapples from a makeshift fruit stall.

An hour and half later, Richter folded his paper and went for a coffee at the Burger King next to the church, whose second floor offered a good vantage point from where to monitor the café. It was from this position that he saw Jackie arrive, at 7:15 p.m., just beating an Asian family of four to the last free table on the terrace. He saw her open her laptop—a different one than last time, no sticker with the black logo of the *Parti pirate*—and almost immediately start hammering away at her keyboard. Nothing appeared out of the ordinary, the slender French-American girl seemed relaxed and composed. After ordering something from the waiter, she put her headphones back on and returned to her screen. Nobody appeared to make contact, no sign of the French police, or—what would be much worse—the *Direction générale de la sécurité intérieure* (DGSI), the French equivalent of the FBI. At a few minutes to 8:00 p.m., he walked down and crossed the street.

"Yes?"

"Good afternoon sir, I am special agent Berenson, this is special agent Goldilocks—I mean Underhill, " he showed his badge and looked at Underhill with slight embarrassment. "Oh yes of course," Underhill mumbled, and got his badge out too.

Pete Riggins studied the badges for a moment. He offered a short "Okay," then looked expectantly at the two agents.

While Riggins was studying their badges, Berenson was studying Riggins. His furrowed, bronzed face showed no signs of alarm at all. If anything, his expression was calm and confident. He was looking at a man who feared little, if anything. A true Marine. About average in height, wearing khaki pants and a grey T-shirt stretched tightly around a muscular frame. Berenson instantly knew that, even together, he and Underhill would have no chance in hell if it came to fighting the man currently studying Underhill's badge.

"May we come in?" he asked.

"May I know what this is about?"

That was always the problem with these 'feeler interrogations', not having enough to justify a warrant and come in with a complete team, while at the same time knowing that the wrong question—or rather the right one—could turn things very ugly very fast. He didn't want to alarm Riggins, but he couldn't say nothing either.

"We're interviewing all passengers from Swissair flight 484, and according to the passenger manifest you were on that particular flight."

"That is correct. Did anything happen?"

"We'd rather discuss this inside if you don't mind," Berenson tried again.

"Yeah sure. Come in."

The two FBI agents followed Riggins into his spacious but sparsely decorated living room.

"Can I get you anything?" the ex-Marine asked.

"No thanks," Berenson said. "The reas—"

"I'll have some lemonade if you have it," Underhill interjected. "It's so hot outside, I feel I could drink a whole pitcher in one big gulp."

"Eh, yeah, sure man, I think I have some in the fridge. Just a sec." Riggins walked out of the room.

As soon as he was gone, Berenson slapped his partner against the shoulder. "Are you out of your mind?" he whispered angrily. "We're in the house of someone who may or may not be a professional hit man and you give him an excuse to disappear out of sight?"

"I was thirsty," Underhill shrugged.

"You were thirsty," Berenson mumbled under his breath. "Moron. If he comes back with a cocked MP5 I'll ask him to shoot you first." He silently unlocked the strap over the holster holding his Glock 23.

When they heard Riggins return a few moments later, Berenson's hand instinctively moved to the grip of his gun, but when he entered the room carrying a tray with three glasses and a pitcher of lemonade, Berenson quickly lowered his arm again.

"I know you said you didn't want any," Riggins smiled, "but your partner is right, it's pretty hot out there today and I thought you might change your mind." He put the tray on the table and poured three glasses.

"I believe you were about to tell me the reason for your visit, agent… Berenson?"

"Ah yes. You see, according to our Swiss colleagues, some weapons might have been smuggled out of the country on Swissair flight 484, and they asked us to look into it."

The Texan didn't buy it for a second. "Someone smuggling weapons *to* the U.S.? Sounds a bit far-fetched if you ask me," he grinned knowingly. "Look, I'm not sure what you are really looking for, but I'm pretty sure it's not an illegal arms shipment from Zurich to Chicago, and on a commercial flight at that."

He opened his hands disarmingly, "But, in case you're thinking I have something to do with anything, I was only in Zurich for a two-hour layover, waiting for my flight back to the States. I never even left the airport."

Berenson and Underhill exchanged a brief look. "Where were you coming from?" Berenson asked.

"Dubai."

"Could we see the ticket?"

"Sure." The ex-Marine opened his phone, scrolled through his e-mail until he found the reservation and showed it to Berenson.

"I go there a couple of times a year actually," Riggins explained to Underhill while Berenson was checking the ticket. "I have two clients there."

"May I, ehh, ask what you do for a living? This lemonade is excellent by the way," Underhill smiled, taking another swig.

"I am a private combat instructor. I give weapons training, teach martial arts skills, that sort of thing. I'm also frequently hired to drill some sense into lazy, spoiled rich teenagers, which is what I was doing in Dubai."

Berenson handed the phone back. He had seen and heard enough, this was not the man they were looking for.

"I think we're done here," Berenson said to Underhill. "Thank you for the lemonade and your time Mr. Riggins. We'll show ourselves out."

As they walked out, Underhill suddenly stopped and turned around. "One last question Mr. Riggins. During your time as a Marine, did you have any experience with the M40A1 rifle?"

Riggins grinned and shook his head. "I'm afraid I wasn't enough of a marksman to merit training with the M40A1."

Underhill smiled. "A friend of mine was actually in the Corps as well and he still can't shut up about that rifle."

"That sounds familiar enough," Riggins chuckled. "A buddy of mine was a scout sniper and I can tell you, he treated that gun like it was his mistress and wife rolled into one and in that order. Even slept with it, I kid you not."

He reflected for a moment. "Haven't seen that guy since the '90s," he mumbled with a smile, more to himself than Underhill. "Funny, he mustered out around the same time I did. Maybe I should contact him, see where he hangs out these days."

"You think he took the rifle with him when he left the Marines?" Underhill asked.

"Oh you can't. They are custom-built by Marine Corps armorers at MCB Quantico. You can't even own one legally, it's all property of the Corps. But I'm sure there are gunsmiths who can build you a replica, though, and that quite a few former Marine scout snipers have one such custom-made version at home. After all, it's hard to part with something you've been taught to love so unconditionally," he smiled.

A short minute later the two agents walked back to their car, each lost in his own thoughts. When they got in, Berenson looked at Underhill and smiled approvingly. "Well done Jake."

"Good evening Jackie."

No reaction. The hacker remained immersed in her work.

Kids these days, Richter thought. How can you ever be alert, or even simply aware of your surroundings, when you are always drilling music into your ears? He liked music as much as the next man, but it seemed this generation couldn't put one foot in front of the other without looking at their phone or blasting their ears with whatever crap went for music these days. Shit, he was getting old. He sat down.

Jackie took her headphones off and gave a cute smile. "Sorry, noise-canceling headphones. They're really great, though, nothing gets through."

"That much I understood," Richter said with a wry smile. For the first time he saw that for all the boyish, chaotic, hyperactive behavior, Jackie was an attractive young woman. Not a classic beauty. Even if she would have possessed the physical features of one—and she did not—her style and natural demeanor, rough-shod and direct, conflicted too much with the for such a classification required composure. But the strains of short black hair dancing on her forehead, the full but elegant eyebrows, the puckish grin and slim neck, the perky breasts constrained by nothing but a tight, light-grey T-shirt. Yes, she was definitely pretty.

"So what do you have for me?" he asked, to rid himself of things that would only weaken his mind. "Did you succeed?"

"I should think so," she smiled confidently. "Remember that zero-day I told you about?"

"Vaguely." Computers weren't really his thing, never had been.

"My Jedi Knight powers tell me that you prefer to forgo all the exciting details of my cat burglar-like, NSA-style hack…" she paused for a short moment, perhaps hoping he would come to his senses and beg her for all the juicy details, "so… to make a long, interesting story short and boring: it turned out I indeed had to break into both systems, but the zero-day—the backdoor—also worked on both systems, so we got two for the price of one. Yay."

"And did you find the invitation list for the October 19 event?" Richter asked.

"I did. There are about 6,000 names on it, which is relatively modest considering the Center normally seats over 18,000. Anyway, when I got in, the list was already complete, so I had to hack into the Thomas & Mack Center system as well, to see if they had their own copy of the list."

"*Monsieur, wot ken I get fore u?*" The neatly uniformed waiter stood straight like an arrow, tray in hand, white napkin draped over his arm.

How in hell did the waiter know he wasn't French, Richter thought. He even had a fumbled copy of *Le Monde* lying in front of him. Did he not look French? As if the man could read his mind, he said: "*I remember u fromm sze laast time. A Heineken, wasz iet not?*"

A lousy accent but a fabulous memory, that much was clear. "Yes, thanks. Oh, and don't forget the cups with the olives and the salty peanuts."

The waiter smiled the way only French men can. "*I nevur doo sir.*"

When he was gone, Jackie leaned across the table. "It's amazing how bad the accents are, huh?" she whispered. "It's like it's in their genes or something. I mean, my parents sent me to a bilingual, French-English school in New York and there were all these French expat kids, and after a couple of years their English accents were still horrible."

Richter also leaned forward. "Why are you whispering," he whispered, "and if what you're saying is true, then how come your American accent is so flawless?"

She sat up straight. "Because I'm not French," she smiled, "I'm Dutch."

"Really?"

"100 percent. Well, that is to say, I've never actually lived in Holland. I was born right here in Paris and we moved to New York when I was six, but both my parents are Dutch, so, you know..."

"You don't say." He couldn't help thinking of Peter Veldman, another Dutchman. These people got around.

"Yep."

The waiter returned. "*Szaire ve are monsieur. Le Heineken and les olives and sze nuts u like so muds.*"

"Thanks."

"*Avec plaisir monsieur.*" He made a quick, proud bow and disappeared.

Richter popped an olive in his mouth. "So, did they?"

"I'm sorry?" Jackie looked confused.

"Did they have their own copy of the guest list over at the Thomas & Mack Center?" Richter asked, before taking a swig from his beer.

"Ah, yes, yes they did—they do. So I'll have to add your personal data to both lists. The University of Las Vegas is ultimately responsible for the list, it seems—at least their document has an older date stamp—but we can't bank on them sending an updated version to the Thomas & Mack Center at a later stage, so you'll need to be added to the Thomas & Mack version of the list as well."

Richter nodded.

"Right, so if you give me your passport data I'll get it done right away," Jackie said.

"What, right now?"

"Yeah why not? No time like the present." She saw the guarded look on his face. "Don't worry dude, I checked the backdoor just before you arrived, it's still good, and from past experience I can tell you it'll probably remain good for months, if not longer. And even if they'd find out they were hacked—and they won't—I've made sure the data leads back to some government building in Beijing."

Richter considered this for a moment. She really seemed to know what she was doing, but if for some reason she was already being monitored by the DGSI, being physically present at the moment of the hack would put him in a compromising position. Then again, he'd have a much bigger problem than being complicit to hacking a University computer system if the DGSI was really onto her.

"Did you buy a computer specifically for this job, like I asked?"

"You're looking at it," Jackie said.

"Good." He reached into his pocket, pulled out the folded passport photocopies in the name of Peter Veldman and Daniel Greenwald—a fake identity he would only use for this one, specific event—and handed them over. "I'm going to need those back," he added.

"This a Dutch passport," she said as soon as she saw Peter Veldman's passport photocopy.

Richter shrugged. "So it is."

"I mean, it's no problem or anything, it's just weird to be looking at a Dutch passport. I have one myself you know."

Richter said nothing.

"Anyway…." Jackie said, slightly embarrassed by his sudden silence, "let me just get in there…."

For the next couple of minutes Richter simply enjoyed his beer and peanuts, watching the sun slowly set over the red rooftop of the *Saint-Pierre-de-Montrouge* church. He had a vague feeling he was forgetting something. It wasn't something bad, he just couldn't see it clearly enough. Instinctively he squinted, as if trying to zoom in on his own brain. But however distinct the feeling, he couldn't articulate it into something useful. He looked at Jackie, a little concentration wrinkle showing right between her eyebrows, the eyes focused, the fingers flying over the keyboard. She was even cuter this way. But no. He was old enough to be her father for Christ' sake. Well, not that that had ever stopped him before. But no. Besides, he knew better than to mix business with pleasure.

Suddenly he remembered.

"The seating," he blurted out.

"Hmmm…" Jackie responded, without looking up from her screen.

"Veldman, he should be in the front, as close to the stage as possible."

She grinned. "Going for the best seats in the house, huh? Okay, no problem, I'll get you guys in there."

"No, not me—not Greenwald. He should have a seat on the upper layer, all the way to the back."

Jackie looked confused. "Wait a minute. Okay, so you want Veldman all the way to the front and Greenwald all the way up top and to the back?"

"Exactly."

20

"You know, these documents are all in German," Underhill said, as he rummaged through papers spread out over his small airplane table and the empty seat between them.

"Ah, so you noticed," Berenson snickered.

"There's no need to be nasty. I'm just trying to familiarize myself with the case. I mean, I get the highlights, I only wish I could get the details as well."

"I know, I already asked Muller to translate them."

"Muller speaks German?"

"Yeah, his family is from Germany," Berenson shrugged.

"Hmmm, I did not know that." Underhill took a moment to digest this eye-opening piece of information. "So how'd he end up at the Bureau then?"

"I might ask you the same thing," Berenson mumbled.

"What?"

"Nothing. Ehmm, I guess he wanted to be an FBI agent, maybe thought it was cool or something? Jesus, what do I know?"

"No, I mean because you said he was from Germany."

"His family," Berenson gesticulated. "His family is originally from Germany. Muller is from Newark. Anyway," he sat up straight and leaned over to Underhill's side, "he told me this morning he was still working on the translation but that he had already found something interesting." He pointed to the papers. "You know the one-sheet with the summary, the '*Zusammenfassung*'?"

"*Jawohl mein Führer*," Underhill quipped.

Berenson raised his right eyebrow and gave a disapproving look. "Anyway… Muller told me that the gunsmith wrote in the summary that the American had initially requested a different weapon than the drone. Apparently, he had wanted a sniper rifle version of a gun that could fire a poisonous frozen dart."

"Come again?"

"Yeah, that's what I thought. So I did a little research and it turns out the CIA actually developed such a gun in the 1960s," Berenson said.

"A gun that can fire a poisonous frozen dart? Jesus, that is some real James Bond shit," Underhill whistled. "So why didn't the gunsmith manufacture that rifle?"

"Do you have the document?" Berenson asked, gesturing Underhill to get it.

"Eh yeah, wait…" he searched among the stack of papers for a moment, fished out the one with *Zusammenfassung* written at the top and handed it to Berenson, who quickly glanced over it. "Here," he said, pointing to the word he was looking for, "the one that is underlined. *Unmöglich*. Impossible. Apparently the gunsmith believed it couldn't be done."

"So where does that leave us?" Underhill asked.

"Not much further I'm afraid," Berenson sighed, "though it does prove that our assassin prefers a sniper rifle, and given the fact that the first weapon he ever commissioned from the gunsmith was a custom-built M40A1, a sniper rifle Marine scout snipers apparently have a serious love affair with and that is normally custom-built by Marine Corps armorers at Quantico, I'd say there is a pretty solid chance that our man was indeed a marksman in the US Marine Corps and mustered out somewhere in the early 1990s."

"Now, assuming he's not much over 60," Berenson continued, "which would seem a bit too old to still be traveling the globe as a professional killer, and given the fact that he had to be at least around 20 when he got out of the Marines, our killer is likely a male U.S. citizen between 40 and 65 years old."

"Well, there is a small chance he is actually a she," Underhill said.

Berenson looked confused. "Are you saying our Marine slash contract killer slash sniper rifle fetishist might be a transgender?"

"No, a woman, a natural born woman."

"No," Berenson shook his head. "*Unmöglich.*"

"Why?"

"Because women weren't allowed into the Marine Corps infantry in the early 1990s."

21

Wednesday, September 14, 2016,

Charles de Gaulle Airport, Paris, France /

Washington D.C., United States

The drone, without the syringe, was hidden underneath the silver cushion of the tiffany-blue jewelry box, stowed in his backpack. In the groove on top of the cushion, he had inserted a simple golden ring. Closer inspection was highly unlikely, but in any case there was nothing illegal about bringing a 5.5 gram drone with a wingspan of 1 inch onto a 800,000 pound plane with a wingspan of 200 feet. The small syringe he had tucked away in the hollowed out heel of his right boot, together with the barrel of the plastic gun. The grip and trigger part of the gun, together with the plastic screw and 4" Allen wrench, he had hidden in the other heel. The ricin powder he had put in three small packets of Splenda, stowed in the front compartment of his backpack, together with a tea egg and specialty tea he had picked up that morning at *Mariage Frères*, the gourmet tea store at Rue du Bourg-Tibourg, in *Le Marais*.

From experience, Richter knew customs officials always looked at three things: the document, the individual and the story. Being clean-shaven, Gucci sunglasses stylishly on top of his head, a tight-fitting, grey T-shirt hanging from his broad shoulders—'*Don't Be a Hater*' imprinted on it in ruby-purple—wearing light-blue shorts revealing muscular calves and Vans lace-up sneakers on bare feet, Richter looked every bit the hipster who would travel with his personal tea equipment.

In short, he did not expect any trouble going through customs at Charles de Gaulle before boarding his American Airlines flight back to New York, which was set to depart at 1:20 p.m. Paris time and expected to arrive at JFK around 4:00 p.m. EST.

"You know, this guy is not your average garden variety contract killer." Hunched over the translated Zimmerman files, his head cupped in his left hand, Underhill looked over at Berenson.

"Oh yeah?" Berenson didn't look away from his screen. He was looking at an anonymous tip about a guy in Huntsville, Alabama, who was supposedly selling homemade grenade launchers from his barn.

"He has ordered nineteen custom-made weapons from this Zimmerman guy over the past twenty years. Nineteen. It's almost like he has a weapon made special for each job."

"One job a year. Sounds like a cushy life," Berenson said from behind his screen.

"Couple of years ago, he paid ten grand for a gun that looked just like a cell phone. Chambered for .22 LR... operated through the key pad. Could hold three bullets. Actually... the phone part still worked as well." Underhill looked up. "I mean, you don't spend that kind of money just to clip a local drug lord."

"'Clip?' Have you been watching *Goodfellas* again?"

"And that gunsmith," Underhill continued, "he must be loaded. $10,000 for one gun, Jesus. And he had been operating that little shop of his for more than 20 years without any problem. Who knows how many customers he had."

"Are you thinking about a career change?"

"Being a gunsmith?" Underhill scoffed. "I can't even drill a proper hole in the wall to hang up a painting, let alone rebore the barrel of a Remington 700."

Berenson chuckled.

"Look, seriously though," Underhill went on, "I think this guy is almost certainly a high-value target contract killer, and he must be very good at is his job, since he has been doing it for over two decades. Are you listening?"

"Uhuh."

"It feels like you're not really listening, though."

"I'm listening," came from behind the screen.

"Okay. So, what we have here is a professional killer who shells out 40 grand for an all-plastic derringer and a drone the size of a housefly that we didn't even know was on the market, armed with a remote controlled, poisonous syringe. What does that tell you?"

Berenson popped his head around the screen. "What does it tell *you*?"

"You want me to come out and say it? Fine, I'll say it," Underhill said, leaning back and throwing his hands in the air. "I think he was hired to kill Valery Clayton."

"étaler vos bras s'il vous plaît."

"Excuse me?"

The Frenchman had a difficult time hiding his annoyance with yet another American who didn't speak one word of French. "*Your arms, spread szem pleesz.*"

He routinely padded the American down before quickly waving him on. His next customer, an Arab with a thick beard wearing a chestnut-brown dishdasha, got a much more thorough working-over, though.

Richter collected his things at the end of the conveyor belt and waited for his backpack. When it came out, another customs official indicated he had to have it checked at a station a few feet away.

A man with a proudly waxed handlebar mustache asked him to open his bag as if he had asked that same question a hundred times already today—which he probably had. He sifted through the clothes and opened the toiletry bag. "*Szisz isz too bieck,*" he sighed, holding up the tube of tooth paste. "*I am zorry, yoe cannot take szies on sze plain.*" He looked at Richter, perhaps waiting for him to complain, but when the American simply shrugged, he stashed it somewhere below the counter. He went back into the bag, and after some rummaging fished out the jewelry box. "*Ah, marriage, hein?*" he chuckled, forgetting for a moment he hated his wife almost as much as this job.

Richter smiled back benevolently.

The customs official looked at it for another moment, then put it back. Finding nothing else interesting, he moved to the front. Meanwhile, the Arab in the chestnut-brown dishdasha was waiting with his suitcase behind Richter. Evidently, he had been picked out as well. The official shot him a quick look and sped up the pace. He took out the bag of Darjeeling from *Mariage Frères* and smiled. "*Ah, my wife, elle vraiment adore le Mariage Frères.*"

"Oh my boyfriend too, absolutely adores it," Richter said.

The Frenchman raised an eyebrow. Boyfriend? "*Alors, u can go,*" he said curtly, putting the tea back and zipping up the bag.

As Richter walked on, the Arab put his suitcase on the counter. The ring was for the boyfriend? What was the world coming to? Queers and Muslims, everywhere you looked. He shook his head and looked up at the Arab. "*Ouvrez,*" he sighed, gesturing at the suitcase.

Berenson forgot about the guy who sold homemade grenade launchers from his barn for a moment. "Valery Clayton?" he said, as he leaned back in his chair, his voice dripping with skepticism.

"Okay… and of course you have a logical explanation for this… theory."

Underhill stood up.

"Yes, by all means, stand up, make your case," Berenson gestured like a conductor indicating the choir to rise.

"Fact," Underhill began, raising his index finger, "we are talking about an elite contract killer who has been operating for more than twenty years."

"Fact," he continued, raising a second finger, "the killer is able and willing to pay 40,000 dollars—I mean Euros, which is even more—for a plastic derringer and a tiny drone armed with a remote controlled, poisonous syringe." Underhill looked at Berenson, but he stayed silent, at least for the moment.

"Fact," another finger went in the air, "he only made this last purchase very recently, meaning he will most likely use it somewhere in the coming weeks."

Berenson showed no reaction but he had to admit that was a good point, it *was* likely the killer needed the weapon for a job in the coming weeks.

"Fact, he is using a drone for the hit either because he needs time to get away or because he doesn't want it to look like a hit."

"Or both," Berenson added.

"Very well, or both," Underhill acknowledged, encouraged that Berenson was apparently at least listening intently. "Now, if it is because he needs time to get away, that means by definition we are talking about a very well protected target, and I'm not talking about a bunch of thugs hanging around some organized crime boss' kitschy lair, but someone who is guarded by the kind of people who have the authority to check for weapons and target open windows with counter-sniper teams when their man—"

"Or woman…"

"Or woman," Underhill repeated, pointing at Berenson, "is, you know, speaking at a public event or something."

"You're talking about someone acting in an official capacity," Berenson suggested.

"Yes, exactly," Underhill pointed at Berenson again.

"Okay, let's assume you're right so far. A professional super killer has accepted a contract on someone so high-profile he can only get to him—"

"Or her…"

"Or her," Berenson nodded with a smile, "using a stealthy drone no bigger than a housefly. Granted, there aren't very many targets that come to mind, but to finger Clayton just because this country is readying itself for one of the most contentious, hard-fought, bitter elections in modern politics is more than just one bridge too far."

"You're forgetting that using poison will also disguise it from looking like a political assassination."

Berenson shook his head. "We don't know that's the reason. As said, it might just be to give the killer a better chance to get away." He sighed. "Look, ask yourself this: why can't the target be Vladimir Putin, Benjamin Netanyahu, Recep Tayyip Erdogan or Abdel Fattah el-Sisi. All four are highly controversial political figures, have powerful enemies and are extremely well-guarded."

Underhill considered this for some time, pacing the room in silence. Meanwhile, Berenson drifted back to his screen and the grenade launcher entrepreneur. Homemade grenade launchers sold out of a barn. Jesus. Who bought these things? Probably mostly local gun fanatics. Seemed this was something the Huntsville Police Department best take care of. He looked up the number.

"No," Underhill suddenly said, staring at the carpet. "No. Our guy is an elite sniper, he would always prefer using a sniper rifle over anything else, and he could get to Putin, Erdogan and the others that way if he wanted to, just as he could get to Senator Clayton that way."

"So it's not about creating a getaway window?" Berenson asked.

"Maybe that's a bonus, but I think the main reason is to make it look like a natural death, or at least not like a political execution. And you see, I don't think this would factor in with assassination plots for people like Putin or Netanyahu, because they are already in power and have so many enemies, nobody would think twice if everything pointed to a political assassination."

"Clayton has enemies," Berenson said.

"She does, but she's not in power yet. And if she would be shot on the eve of the election, it could actually help the Democrats win the White House, albeit it with another candidate. Then the conspirators would have taken all that risk for nothing. But if she were to suffer a heart attack a few weeks before the election, making it look like a natural death, the vice-presidential candidate—who would probably move to the top spot on the ticket—would have only a very short period to campaign. Meanwhile, the people, though sympathetic, won't have anyone to blame and come November 8 might very well elect the better known candidate on the right. But even if they don't, at the very least Clayton will be out of the way, and you know how deep the hate for Valery Clayton runs in some places."

Berenson looked intently at Underhill for a few seconds, before abruptly giving his verdict. "You know what?"

"What?"

"You should have been a writer."

22

Thursday, September 15, 2016,

Upper West Side, Manhattan, New York City

When Conrad Richter was ten years old, all he had ever wanted for Christmas (that year at least) was a little remote controlled BMW that had two speeds and actual working headlights, so you could even drive it in the dark. Finding that little beige car in a box on Christmas morning, gift-wrapped and tied with a golden bow, feeling the eager adrenaline rush as he ripped away the wrapping paper, opened the box and put the batteries in the compartment underneath the car and at the back of the remote control, is what he thought of when, on the morning of September 15, 2016, he carefully unplugged the minuscule drone from its charger and put it on the bar counter at the edge of his living room kitchen.

He had always had a weakness for gadgets and this was without a doubt the coolest gadget he had ever owned (at 400 times the price of the remote controlled BMW, it was also by far the most expensive gadget he had ever owned). He picked up his iPhone and tapped the drone app icon, bringing up the control screen. Tapping the green square brought the drone's camera view online, showing the left side of the shiny metallic faucet above the sink. Hmmm, not the most impressive view. He carefully turned the little drone in the direction of the window on the far end of the living room. Now the camera showed his table, the two chairs, the bookcase and the window, even the fire escapes hanging from the neighboring building.

So far so good. The transparent circle on the right, with the little arrows for up, down, left and right—and the ones for accelerating and slowing down—the green-striped rectangular button for automatic take off and the red-striped one for automatic landing, it all looked tantalizingly simple. He tapped the green-striped button. Almost immediately the drone's tiny, dragonfly-shaped wings began to vibrate, lifting the artificial insect about three inches above the counter without making a sound. Richter leaned in closer, until he could almost feel the streaming air from the fanatically flapping wings brush up against his eyebrows. It was a surreal sight, this little fly hovering mere inches away. It looked almost alive, or was that just because it moved in such a controlled manner? Shooting a quick glance at his phone, he saw his eyes looking at something on the right.

After moving to the side, the camera showed the table again. He tapped the forward arrow and the little insect set itself in motion, whizzing past him. Observing that the drone was slightly off course for the middle of the table, he briefly touched the leftward arrow, causing it to veer a couple of degrees to the left, until he tapped the forward arrow again. A few seconds later, when it had nearly reached its destination, he tapped the transparent circle on the left side of the screen, to activate stationary hover mode. To his relief, the drone slowed down immediately and came to a full stop above the center of the table. For the last part of his first drone flight, he tapped the red-striped rectangular button. Without making a sound, the fly started descending with the speed of a falling feather, gently touching down on the wooden surface a few moments later.

Richter moved one of the chairs back, sat down and tapped the green square on/off button, putting the drone in stand-by mode. Looking at the little insect standing there on its six legs as if nothing had happened, he got the paradoxical feeling that although this first flight had gone more smoothly than he had expected, it was going to require a lot of practice to make him capable enough to navigate the drone along the ceiling of a packed Thomas & Mack Center, maneuver it behind the presidential candidates, descend it unseen to just a few inches from the ground and then slowly, stealthily, pilot it towards the calves of Ronald Drump. A lot of practice.

After a modest lunch of two grapefruits, a small omelet and a kale-based salad, Richter went to the PetSmart in East Harlem, on East 117th Street, where he bought two rats with accompanying rat starter kits the pet store help said were top of the line. Aside from a food dish and drip resistant water bottle with spring hanger, the starter kits included a flying saucer exerciser, two solid surface shelves, easy to climb treaded ramps and a comfortable hammock. It also came with food and bedding.

The store help, a 22-year-old blonde vegan with dreadlocks, a nose piercing and a perennially sad look on her face, had recently been questioning the ethical validity of selling animals, reasoning that if humans shouldn't eat animals, keep them for dairy products and use their skin for clothing—which, being a vegan, she firmly believed—what then gave them the right to keep animals in bondage for their pleasure? But the tall, good-looking blond man buying the two rats and deluxe starter kits rekindled some of her lost faith in the animal that was man and almost made her rethink her position on animal slavery. He was so kindhearted and forthcoming, petting the rats, instantly bonding with them. She could always tell when an animal liked its new owner and in this case there was no doubt whatsoever. The rats and the nice blond man were perfect for each other. And although she knew he was way too old for her—he must have been somewhere in his forties—she had still flirted with him, even given him her number, under the always helpful pretense of being available for any kind of advice on how to treat the animals. "Day or night," she had said with a seductive smile. How much clearer could she have made it? She hoped he would call.

Back home, Richter put the bedding in the cages, filled the water bottles and put some food on the dishes. Then he got the rats out of their cardboard box, satisfied himself they hadn't bitten each other senseless and put each rat in its own cage. The one in the left cage immediately went for the food dish and started packing it in as if his life depended on it. The other one didn't even look at the food but climbed up the ramp and quickly made his way to the hammock. Once there, he dove right in—almost certainly not the first time he had done that—and started swinging from left to right like a vacationer under a palm tree on a Hawaiian beach. Amused, Richter took the scene in for a few minutes. After checking the time on his phone, he said jokingly: "Okay Biggy and Lazy Pete, be good now, daddy has to go out for a while."

Like most New Yorkers, Richter thoroughly hated rats and cockroaches, but thinking about his new pets as he walked around in the drugstore on West 72nd Street—where he picked up a box of surgical gloves and a couple of surgical masks—he had to admit that seeing them munch their food and swing in that cute little hammock almost made them adorable.

An hour later he was back. Putting the surgical masks and the box of gloves on the counter, he went over to the cages to take a look at how his new friends were adjusting. Biggy had fallen asleep on the lower of the two solid surfaces—the food bowl licked

147

clean—but Lazy Pete was still swinging in the hammock, curled up like a fetus in its mother's womb.

Richter went back to the kitchen and took the jewelry box out of the top drawer next to the stove. He picked up the drone and carefully placed it on the counter. Lifting the jewelry box's silver padding, he took out the small syringe barrel, the Luer connector (the syringe hub) and the hypodermic needle. Holding the needle between his thumb and index finger, he embedded it in the connector, which he then screwed onto the syringe barrel.

Next, he strapped on one of the surgical masks, pulled two gloves out of the box and put them on, before taking the metal container with the Splenda packets out of the drawer and placing it on the counter. This is where it got tricky. He took a 25 cc bottle of water from the fridge and emptied it above the sink until only a small sip remained, then cut off a small corner of one of the Splenda packets and carefully shook a quarter of its powdery contents in the bottle. Satisfied nothing was spilled, he folded the corner of the packet and put it back in the metal container, screwed the bottle cap back on and swirled the bottle for a few seconds. After concluding the powder had blended with the water, he unscrewed the cap again and placed it on its bottom on the counter, then slowly poured the spoonful of liquefied ricin in it.

Now he took the small syringe. Holding the tip of the needle in the spoonful of liquefied ricin and the tiny syringe barrel between his left thumb and index finger, he slowly pulled on the plunger, sucking up the fluid. Zimmerman was right, he thought, doing this manually was a forbiddingly punctilious little job. Still, he preferred to be in complete control for this most vital part. When the syringe was filled, he placed his thumbs on the plunger and index fingers on the barrel, then pushed the plunger down a bit, to press the air out of the barrel and force the first drops of fluid through the needle. Satisfied the syringe was now ready for use, he fastened it on the rail underneath the drone.

He closed the metal container with the Splenda packets and put it back in the drawer, threw the bottle cap, the bottle, the surgical mask and the gloves in the trash can and walked over to the two deluxe rat cages. "Okay, here we go," he said, pointing at Biggy's cage. "Eeny, meeny, miny, moe—catch a tiger by the toe. If he hollers, let him go. Eeny… meeny….miny… moe."

23

At two in the morning Berenson surrendered for the third night in a row. He switched on the light on the bed stand and stared at the ceiling for a while, following the hairline cracks and studying the ragged edges around the spots where the plaster had chipped off. There was something very sad about staring at a cracked ceiling at two in the morning. But what else could he do? Watch a movie? Pace the room? Take a walk around the block? Actually he could do all of those things, but it wouldn't make a difference, and none of those things were more attractive than staring at the ceiling—at least not at two in the morning.

He couldn't stop thinking about what Underhill had said a few days ago, about the American being a contract killer who was planning to assassinate Senator Clayton. He had made fun of it at the time and Underhill had been insulted—or at least acted insulted—for two days, but for the last couple of nights he had been unable to shake the feeling that Underhill was somehow right.

But right or wrong, there was simply not enough information to go on. Almost everything they had was based on conjecture. Actually, when it came right down to it, the only real fact they had was that someone had recently bought a very expensive housefly-sized drone, armed with a remote controlled poisonous syringe, together with a custom-made plastic gun. The gunsmith who had manufactured / modified these weapons called his buyer

'The American', but that didn't prove he was indeed an American, nor did the fact that the buyer had two decades ago commissioned an exact copy of an M40A1 sniper rifle from the same gunsmith prove he had been a Marine scout sniper at some point.

He had read the Zimmerman files a dozen times now, even meticulously read the German version, alongside Muller's translation, to see if Muller might have somehow missed something. It didn't seem to be the case. Yesterday, he had called Hans Kreuzer of the Zurich *Kriminalpolizei*, to find out if they had made some progress with Dieter Zimmerman. He knew it was a long shot— Kreuzer would almost certainly have informed the Legal Attaché office in Bern if they had—but any shot was better than to keep going around in circles. Kreuzer had been nice enough, but he said Zimmerman hadn't talked at all, not one word, and that it seemed unlikely that was going to change.

He had also notified the Secret Service National Threat Assessment Center (NTAC), but while the guy he spoke to had told him the Secret Service always took every threat against the President or a presidential candidate seriously, he had also quickly concluded that the evidence they had at this point was simply too thin to mount any sort of investigation, adding reassuringly that in reality most of the actual threats investigated by NTAC came from mentally unstable people anyway.

Of course that guy had been right. Without at least some solid indication this would-be assassin was indeed planning to strike against Senator Clayton, and without any sort of identification information about him, without knowing when he planned to strike, or where, they really had nothing, except the how.

He knew all that. He knew it. Why then, was he still staring at the ceiling at two in the morning?

24

"Never."

"Never?"

"Never. You know, guns are not allowed in the Netherlands," Veldman said.

Richter scratched the back of his head. "Well yeah, but I mean, not even on a hunting trip, or at a shooting range or something, just for kicks?

"Nope. The closest I ever came was holding a Glock 17 at a gun store in San Marino, a tiny city state in Italy I visited once on holiday to buy one of those imitation gas guns."

Richter looked stunned.

"The gun laws in San Marino are much more relaxed," Veldman clarified.

"Well, at least you *held* an actual gun once, I guess that's something," Richter snickered.

They both stared across the lawn at Bryant Park for a while, sipping their espresso from the Pain Quotidien stand next to the fountain. Suddenly Richter slammed his empty paper cup on the table. "Come on," he said, standing up.

"Where to?"

"We're going to take a little drive, you'll see. You're not working today, right?"

"Never on Mondays," Veldman confirmed.

"So, let's go," Richter repeated, sounding fired up.

"Okay, sure, why not," Veldman surrendered, standing up. "Lead the way."

Two and a half hours later, Richter flicked up the turn signal lever of his black Chevy Tahoe and took exit 7A from I-95 S, toward Trenton, New Jersey.

"Trenton. Hey, I read about Trenton," Veldman said. "Wasn't there an important American Revolutionary War battle fought there? Early in the war, an American victory I think."

Richter nodded approvingly. "You know your history. It's where Washington defeated the Hessian mercenaries after crossing the Delaware, in December 1776. The victory gave a much needed morale boost to the Continental Army, after they had been chased out of New York and New Jersey the previous months."

"It's funny," Richter continued after a short pause, "looking back, it always seems like things couldn't have gone any other way, right? I think it's because we prefer it that way. We prefer destiny over randomness."

Veldman nodded. It was a theme that had fascinated him for years. "Destiny adds weight," he said.

"Exactly," Richter turned his head towards Veldman for an instant. "Destiny adds weight. If something that is, had to be, it adds significance. We prefer to believe the United States was destined to be born, but in reality there were many moments in the years leading up to the revolution when King George III could have placated the colonists with slightly more independence, more representation and repealing some of the harshest taxes."

"Sounds like you really know your history too," Veldman said, clearly impressed.

Richter smiled. "Well, I'm a bit of a history buff, especially of American history. The point is, history is littered with examples of seemingly small acts that fundamentally changed the course of history. If Washington hadn't crossed the Delaware in December 1776 and provided his troops with a morale boost by defeating those Hessians, another six months of desertions and defeats might have forced the young country to its knees. If Lee Harvey Oswald hadn't killed Kennedy—well, if indeed it was him—the United States might have never been involved so deeply in Vietnam. If Martin Luther King hadn't been assassinated, he might have been the first black president of the United States, decades before Barack Obama."

He paused for a moment, then looked at Veldman. "I guess what I'm trying to say is, one man can change the course of history with just one act."

He took exit 49 from I-95 s and merged onto PA-332 w, toward Newton. A few miles later they passed Tyler State Park.

"Swamp Road," Veldman chuckled, "I just saw a sign that said 'Swamp Road.'"

"Means we're almost there," Richter said.

"Where?"

"You'll see," Richter said with a wry smile.

Ed Cahill, Jr., was leafing through an old issue of Guns & Ammo, pausing at the review of the Sig Sauer P220 Match Elite 10mm, while waiting for the update of Sniper 3D Assassin: Shoot to Kill to finish downloading on his iPhone.

It had been a slow day so far.

The reviewer extolled the virtues of the 10mm version of the Sig Sauer P220, which, he asserted, could stop a polar bear dead in its tracks. "Hmmm, ain't never done that," Cahill mumbled under his breath. He had, however, killed two whitetails with the Sig Sauer P220 10mm in Owen County, Kentucky, just a few months ago, and he remembered those deer had indeed dropped to the ground as if they had been switched off.

Hmmm, it said here the Danish Navy had even issued 10mm Sig Sauer P220s for defense against polar bears in Greenland. Damn, he would love to bag himself a polar bear. But where in the hell was Greenland? He googled it on the desktop computer. Northeast of Canada. Fuck. Must be ice-cold. When he checked Wikipedia, he found out the population of Greenland was only about 55,000, that it was part of Denmark—sort of—and that its capital city was Nuuk. Nuuk? What the hell kind of a name for a city was that? Oh, but at least they had an airport. He didn't notice the update for *Sniper 3D Assassin: Shoot to Kill* had finished.

Of course he would never go to Greenland to shoot a polar bear, he had never even left the states, why would he? But a man had a right to his dreams, didn't he? And just as he'd love to shoot himself a lion in Africa someday, he'd love to shoot himself a polar bear in Greenland. And of course kill an Islamic terrorist and be the hero of Bucks County. He was just about to check for flights from Philadelphia to Nuuk, when Richter and Veldman walked in.

Richter slowed the Chevy down and made a right onto the gravel drive leading to a red farmhouse about 500 yards further down, marked by a 25 feet flagpole proudly flying Old Glory.

"Now, I know you think you know America, because you've lived in New York for a few years— "

"Seven," Veldman interjected.

"Alright, seven years, but trust me when I tell you that New York is *not* the United States."

"I know that."

"I know you think you know, but I doubt you've met many Americans who are part of the 'other half', as in the half that thinks the liberals are basically destroying their country."

Veldman shrugged, but said nothing.

"Now," Richter continued, "the guy who is running this shooting range belongs to the far right of that half, so it's probably best if you talk as little as possible."

"This is a shooting range?" Veldman asked, his voice rising in excitement.

"It's about time you became a man Peter," Richter smiled.

He parked the car next to the flag pole. They got out and Richter opened the back. "A few ground rules," he said softly, taking a black gym bag out. "Don't call him Junior, don't let him lure you into a debate about what the best pistol is in a firefight—you'll be trapped for hours—and no sudden moves."

Veldman chuckled. "You're joking, right?"

A smug smile appeared in the corner of Richter's mouth. "Yeah."

"But don't, though," he cautioned, as they walked towards the farm's porch.

"Afternoon Ed. How've you been?"

Junior looked up from his screen. "Hey Don! Been a while! Shoot, I think the last time you were here was, what, January?"

"Yup, think so too."

"Who's your friend there?"

"This is Peter Veldman," Richter said.

"Pleasure to meet you Peter, my name is Ed Jr., but everybody calls me Ed."

"Unless they're looking for a fight," Richter joked.

"Right," Ed grinned. "So, what can I do you for today? You're here to do some long-range target practice as usual? The 1,000 yard range is free, hell everything's free at the moment. It's been a bit slow today."

"Actually, Peter here has never fired a gun."

Ed looked confused. "What do you mean? Like a rifle? Or a pistol?"

"Neither," Richter nodded with a knowing smile.

If it were possible to represent the brain's operative process through a wall of tiny lights switching on and off, with a screen in the middle displaying the outcome of that process, Ed's thinking at that moment would be a furious flickering of thousands of lights for a full ten seconds, before displaying the inevitable outcome: *Cannot compute.*

"I don't understand."

"Peter has never fired any firearm," Richter said, before adding: "he is from Europe."

That made more sense. "Oh." He shook his head. "Bunch of pussies over there. No offense Peter."

"None taken," Veldman smiled.

"I mean, that's why the Ruskies are eyeing your countries over there, you know, because you've forgotten how to defend yourselves."

Veldman opened his mouth to respond, but Richter quickly gave him a small kick to the shin.

"So, I think we'll just be using the beginner's range today."

"Sure," Ed chuckled, turning to the computer screen to type out their order. "So that'll be one adult and, eh, well, two adults I guess."

"Cut it out Ed," Richter laughed, "we all started out as virgins once."

Junior's surprisingly agile fingers ran back and forth over the ancient, sticky keyboard. "Speak for yourself Don, my dad taught me how to shoot when I was five."

"Yeah, how is Ed Sr. these days?"

"He's still there, but the cancer has advanced to stage four," Junior said, without looking up from the screen. "He looks terrible, a shadow of his former self. You remember the way my dad looked before, oak of a man. Arms like this," he showed with his hands. "But you should see them now, thinner than a deer's leg." He hit the enter button. Behind him a matrix printer from the Reagan era began screeching out a document.

"That'll be $40."

Richter got out his wallet and handed over two twenty dollar bills.

"So, what gun will be plucking his cherry?" Ed grinned.

"I was thinking a Glock 26," Richter replied, putting his wallet in his back pocket.

"The baby Glock?" Junior scratched his goatee. "Sure, you could go with that. Not very exciting, though. Or manly, for that matter. Why not the cz 75b? Also a 9 mil and its steel frame reduces recoil, although the dual recoil spring on the GEN4—I take it we're talking about a GEN4 Glock?—"

Richter nodded .

"—Well that does a good job of reducing recoil too." He put the bills in the till. "Still, the baby Glock… you see, what I don't like about it—I mean it's very reliable and all, and great for concealed carry—but the grip is too short to leave room for your pinky finger, which doesn't make it a very stable platform for shooting. Of course you can use the 15-round magazine, which is longer, but then that leaves a little ridge between the grip and the lower end of the mag, which moves a bit when you fire it; very uncomfortable."

He reflected for a moment, casually trying to draw Richter into an argument, but the former Marine had learned the hard way this was one of those moments he better keep his mouth shut, lest he'd be stuck at this counter for the next hour and a half.

"Or you could go with the Glock 17 GEN4. Also 9 mil but a little bit more masculine. Or maybe the Springfield XD-9, because of its grip safety, loaded chamber indicator and cocking indicator. Not sure I'd take a gun with a safety grip into a firefight—actually pretty sure I won't—but for training purposes it's great."

"I hear you," Richter responded. "Unfortunately, I only brought the Glock 26 today," he smiled. "So, eh, what range would you recommend for us? Because I'm sure our European friend here is eager to have his cherry popped," he gave Veldman a look, who immediately nodded enthusiastically.

Ed looked outside for a moment. "Ah, take the three, 25 yards and I just restocked the target sheets."

"Alright then, off we go," Richter said, rapping the counter. "See you in a bit Ed."

"You guys have fun and be safe," Ed said, seeing that his *Sniper 3D Assassin: Shoot to Kill* upgrade had finished and tapping the icon to start the game. Baby Glock... pfff, ain't nothing like the Beretta M9 daddy had taught him to shoot with. Damn, he had forgotten to mention that one.

"Okay, I'm going to give you a crash course in handgun shooting, so that by the end of the day you'll be able to hit a target from at least 10 yards away." Richter opened the black gym bag and got out the small Glock.

"Alright, what we have here is a Glock 26 GEN4, says so right here on the side, see?" He showed the gun to Veldman, who was standing back a little, his hands locked together behind his back. Aside from that one time in San Marino, he had only seen real guns when they were holstered on the hips of police officers. Seeing one out in the open like this, unholstered, naked, no uniforms around, almost seemed illegal.

"It has a large mag release button… here… safe action trigger—no safety switch—texture on the grip, adjustable backstrap, front sight, rear sight. Standard magazine capacity is ten rounds, but any Glock 9mm magazine will fit." Richter moved the slide to check the chamber, then presented it to Veldman. "Here, take it, it's not loaded."

Veldman hesitated, keeping his hands at his side after unlocking them.

"Come on, it won't bite, I promise," Richter chuckled.

Still hesitant, Veldman stretched out his hand and carefully took the weapon with two hands, as if it was a newborn kitten.

"It's not made of glass either. Trust me, this is one of the most durable handguns in the world. People have driven over them with trucks, shot at them, thrown them out of airplanes and still the damn things worked. So I'm pretty sure it can survive the deadly grip of Peter Veldman."

Veldman smiled and folded his right hand around the grip, his index finger automatically moving towards the trigger.

"See? Your hand instinctively knows what to do. Now, wrap your right hand—is that your strong hand?—"

"Yes."

"Okay, so wrap your right hand as high around the grip as possible, without hindering the slide. You want as much skin on the grip as possible, because a strong grip will increase stability and help absorb the recoil. Move the slide back and forth a couple of times with your other hand to make sure it can move freely.…yes, that's it. Okay, keep your right index finger aligned with the slide, your right thumb forward, and wrap the remaining three fingers

160

around the grip….yeah, like that. Now wrap your weaker hand around your firing hand, and put the knuckles of your strong hand in the weaker hand where the fingers join the palm… make sure the weak thumb isn't making any contact with the slide…. yes, that's good. Hold that."

With the help of Richter's instructions, the Glock now looked fused with Veldman's hands. "Now, put the pad of your right index finger, your trigger finger, on the trigger. Don't touch the trigger guard….keep the rest of your finger square with the gun….like that. Yes. Remember that the lighter the pull, the better the shooting. So don't squeeze the trigger like you're trying to open a soda can. Easy does it. Try it… a good, steady squeeze, from the front to the rear…"

Click.

"There you go," Richter said approvingly. "Alright, come over here." He guided the Dutchman to the beginning of the range. "Now, one of the most important elements of good shooting is your stance, which, ideally, should both maximize your stability and enable you to move quickly."

He took another gun from the bag, a Sig Sauer P229 chambered in .357 SIG, and took position next to Veldman. "Okay, so this is called the Fighting Stance. As you can see, I'm square to the target and my feet are positioned at slightly wider than shoulder width, but my firing side foot—in this case my right foot—is slightly behind my support side foot. Look at my right foot, it's at the instep of my support foot. My knees are flexed, my body is slightly leaning forward and my arms are extended straight out."

Maintaining the stance, he looked at Veldman, to make sure he got it. "Okay, now you try it."

After Veldman had assumed the proper position—his hands still wrapped around the gun, the barrel pointing at the target board—he looked like a rookie parachutist who is both eager and afraid to get on with it and jump through the open door.

"Okay, the last two things I want to mention before you're going to pop of your first few rounds are sight alignment and trigger control. Most beginners look at the target and then jerk the trigger, but if you shoot like that you can easily miss a 300 pound offensive guard from three yards away—or worse, shoot him in the foot so that he can still kill you. The right way is to only look at the front sight when you squeeze the trigger."

"Bring up your gun a bit… yeah, like that."

"Okay, now first line up your front sight with your rear sight, so that there is an equal amount of light on both sides of the front sight." He looked on as Veldman adjusted his gun somewhat.

"Got it?"

Veldman hummed to confirm.

"Now, the trigger pull itself is the hardest to master, but it's also the most important," Richter continued. "All the other things—grip, stance, sight fixture—are enablers, to help you arrive where you are right now: target in sight. If firing a bullet would not produce any recoil and the only thing you had to do was think about it, you would hit the bull's eye every time. But unfortunately there *will* be recoil and your brain knows that. It wants to prepare you for it, which is why it's so hard not to flinch when pulling the trigger. In the end, the only thing that will teach your mind not to prepare for recoil is practice. Practice, practice, practice, to keep looking at your front sight when you pull the trigger nice and easy, to keep your focus on your front sight… front sight… front sight… and bang, the bullet is off to destroy the target."

Richter looked at Veldman, trying to gauge the level of intake of this first part of the crash course. Was it too much? Of course it was, but they had to start somewhere and if the Dutchman was going to have any chance of success a month from now—that is, if he was even going to do it in the first place, still very much an unanswered question—he would have to learn how to hit a torso-sized target from at least 5 to 10 yards away.

"Okay, yeah, I think I've got it," Veldman said, still focused on the target, looking through the front sight, his hands wrapped around the grip. "Let's try it."

"Alright then," Richter smiled. He walked to the target board and carried it to the 10 yard mark. "I know this is a little far away for a first try," he said over his shoulder, "but at this point it doesn't really matter. Just hitting the target board at all on your first try would be an achievement."

He went back to his bag and took out a 15-round magazine. "Gun," he said, holding out his hand. Veldman relaxed his grip and handed over the weapon. Richter slid the slide back while pushing the slide lock up, clicked the magazine in place and pulled the slide back again to release it and move it back into its starting position, putting a round in the chamber. "Now listen carefully. Whenever you're handling a weapon, always check if it's loaded first—that means not just checking the magazine but also the chamber—always keep it pointed downrange, in a safe direction, and keep your finger off the trigger until you are ready to fire."

He handed the Glock back to Veldman. "Right, wrap your right hand around the grip as high as possible again... index finger aligned with the slide... thumb forward, three remaining fingers around the grip... your left hand around them... try not to squeeze your right hand too tight around the gun but form a tighter grip with your left hand instead... yes, that looks good. Now, take the proper stance. Feet apart... right foot slightly behind the left foot... arms fully extended. Okay, line up your front sight with your rear sight... make sure there is an equal amount of light on both sides of the front sight… you have it?"

Veldman hummed.

"Okay, now, with the target in sight, focus on the front sight and squeeze the trigger smoothly….focus on the front sight….focus on the front sight…"

Bang!

Richter and Veldman both looked at the target board. The bullet had gone right through the middle of the bull's eye.

"Wow!" Veldman said.

Richter was impressed, but he damn sure wasn't going to show it. "Right. Now do that 100 times in a row and you're all set for today."

25

Around the same time Peter Veldman fired a gun for the first time in his life, Jake Underhill hit upon an idea Steve Berenson couldn't believe he hadn't thought of himself in three sleepless nights.

To be sure, Underhill never had any sleepless nights himself. As far as he was concerned, there were very few things worthy enough to lose sleep over—and none of them were work related. Not that he had many cares in the first place. He had married into money and his wife was gorgeous and adored him. They had no kids yet—they wanted them eventually, but she was only 27 and he 33, so there was still plenty of time for that—and their careers were chugging along nicely. There was the townhouse in Washington, the villa in Tuscany and the condo in Chesapeake Beach, which offered a great view of the bay.

Recently, he had also developed a budding interest in yachting, something that hadn't escaped Elizabeth DeWitt-Underhill's attention, if only because he had been watching YouTube videos of expensive, sea-worthy yachts in bed every night. She knew it was only a matter of time before he would start campaigning for them to buy one, conjuring up images of silently gliding on a calm ocean, making love like sea otters in a blue lagoon, or on deck, at night, a million stars looking down on them like voyeurs from afar. He had a way with words she just found irresistible. Of course she would mention the tiny little fact that he didn't even know how to sail yet, but at the end of the day she loved his childlike enthusiasm much more than the boring details of reality and they would buy the boat. They always did. Besides, she also knew he would jump in head first and learn everything there was to learn about sailing, and that next summer he would sail them out of the harbor on their new boat as if he'd been doing it his whole life.

To Jake, working at the FBI was not unlike owning a yacht. He had wanted to work there because he had seen too many movies. His idea of what it meant to be a special agent was glamorous, exciting, a chance to be a hero, to foil the plots of ruthless terrorists. But even if he was about 85 percent wrong about what it meant to be an FBI agent, Jake Underhill had an uncanny knack of recasting reality after the image of his fiction.

With a PhD in Forensic Psychology from Dartmouth he had also been too qualified to ignore, and after his assessment revealed he had one of those rare minds both highly analytical and masterly creative, capable of thinking far out of the box while almost simultaneously breaking down those newly constructed concepts to their usable essence, he was quickly accepted into the training program.

He could go far, but he wasn't interested in making a lifelong career out of working at the FBI. He was more of an observer than a participant, who wanted to watch his own story of being an FBI agent unfold—preferably with a hero's ending—before moving on to a next chapter in his life.

That is why he tried to chuck both the routine cases and the most challenging ones. But a highly qualified professional killer acquiring state-of-the-art weaponry for a hit on what must be an extremely high-profile target? Now *that* was interesting! Of course, his mind was already skewed toward uncovering the edge-of-your-seat kind of plots that made people buy books and watch movies—nobody would read a book about the dull life of special agent Steve Berenson—which increased the risk of delusional theories that would lead nowhere beyond the thrill of the hunt. It had happened before. Then again, every dog has its day.

"You know, I keep thinking about that frozen dart gun," Underhill said, shooting a black dart with orange tip at a target circle the size of a coconut, taped to his desk lamp.

"Don't you have anything better to do?" Berenson said. Not having had a good night's sleep for days he was not in the best of moods, and Underhill killing time shooting those stupid darts, while he was going through a pile of routine cases himself, didn't make it any better.

"I am doing it. I'm thinking."

"Still thinking about that stupid case?" Berenson grumbled.

"It's not stupid, we're just not looking hard enough," Underhill said, sticking another dart into the barrel of his plastic gun.

Berenson scoffed derisively. "We have looked at it from every angle, there is nothing more to do until we receive new information—if we ever do."

Underhill carefully aimed his dart gun. "Or… uncover… our… own," he mumbled, focusing on the front sight before smoothly squeezing the trigger. "Bull's eye!"

Berenson looked up from his laptop. "Okay, out with it," he sighed. "I know you won't give it a rest until you've told me anyway."

Underhill pulled the three darts from the target board. "I just told you, the frozen dart gun, I keep thinking about it."

"Oh wow, sound the alarm, call the director on the red phone right away, there has been a break in the case! Special agent Jake Underhill here has been thinking about the frozen dart gun."

"Tell me, had you heard about that gun before?" Underhill asked, ignoring the sarcasm.

"The frozen dart gun? No. You?"

"No. I asked Muller and Sandowski too, they hadn't heard of it either. And we're the Specialty Weapons Department."

"Maybe we're not as informed as we think," Berenson suggested.

"Yeah, you see I don't think that's it. I think knowledge about that weapon just remained very limited even after that Congressional Commission—"

"The Church Commission."

"Right, even after the CIA admitted to the Church Commission they had developed and used such a weapon and the Commission published its report in the late 1970s. I mean, who would have picked up on that information? Who ever cares about anything Congress does, let alone a Congressional Commission? And this was way before the internet too, when information was not nearly as easily accessible as it is today."

"Your point being? Berenson gesticulated impatiently.

"I think that aside from a few 1970s journos and political junkies and of course the Church Commission members themselves, the only people knowing about this gun were people inside the CIA."

"So, what, you think our guy knew—or knows—someone in the CIA?

"No, I think he was in the CIA himself."

Berenson looked confused. "I thought we established that he was most likely a scout sniper in the Marines?"

"I still think he was." Underhill leaned forward. "Look, it's really not that crazy when you think about it. Let's say our guy joins the Marines somewhere in the 1980s, where he develops into this excellent marksman and falls in love with his custom-built M40A1 sniper rifle. Then he's recruited by the CIA. I'm sure they had a use for accomplished snipers fighting their secret wars, you know, against those communist regimes in Latin America, Africa and Asia. And where better to find loyal, well-trained, highly skilled snipers than in our own special forces?"

"Hmmm, I don't know Jake," Berenson said, after having considered it for a moment. "I mean, I see what you mean, but it seems a bit of a stretch."

"Not really. In times of stress or difficulty people almost always revert to what is familiar. Assuming our killer is faced with the challenge of taking out a high-profile political target without it looking like an assassination, it is actually extremely likely he would revert to something he knows will work. He simply can't afford the risk not to, because he knows he'll only get one chance. Come to think of it, I think he has probably even used that gun himself before."

"Well, you're the psychologist," Berenson said, though still sounding unconvinced.

Underhill suddenly realized something else. "Wait, when was the first time he commissioned a weapon from Zimmerman? That M40A1? Wasn't it '94?" Pointing his left index finger in the air, as if instructing Berenson to hold on for a moment, he checked the Zimmerman file timeline he had made a couple of days ago.

"Yep, 1994," he said triumphantly. "Right around the time the Clayton administration was making those massive cutbacks in the budgets of the intelligence services because of the end of the Cold War. You think it's a coincidence that our guy went into business for himself right around that same time?"

Berenson tilted his head. "Hmm, well, it definitely could be, but I'm beginning to see a flicker of merit in your theory." He took a pen and a pad and started a bullet point list. "So, we are looking for a male U.S. citizen, who joined the Marines in the 1980s or early 1990s and trained as a scout sniper, mustered out somewhere in the same period to join the CIA—most likely in a position where his skill as a marksman could be put to good use, meaning the clandestine service—and then left the agency no later than 1994."

Berenson looked at what he had just written down and searched his gut feeling. What was the chance that the person Mr. Zimmerman had code-named 'The American' was indeed hiding somewhere between the lines?

He sighed. They were all still conjectures, ranging from possibly to probably—even almost certainly—but none of them hard facts. He liked facts. Facts led to asking the right questions, finding real answers, other facts. Conjectures only led to other conjectures. But as much as he liked facts, he had to admit his intuition agreed with Underhill.

And there was something else. If they did nothing and a day, a week, a month from now Senator Clayton died of a heart attack, they would know it had not been an ordinary heart attack, they would know she'd been poisoned. They would have to come forward with that information and they would be crucified, not just by the conspiracy theorists, but by the media, the politicians, the Bureau... everybody would fall on them like football players on a bouncing pigskin.

"We'll have to get clearance for this," Berenson finally said. "We can't get into CIA personnel records without special clearance." He looked at his watch. "Alright, why don't you prepare a brief and I'll ask for a meeting with Longstreet for tomorrow morning first thing. Send it to me tonight, so I can have a chance to look it over before the meeting. And you better make it good, because if we don't get clearance, we're done with this case."

26

"No beer tonight, only whiskey will do. You're a man now!" Richter said, slapping Veldman on the shoulder as they walked into Café Lambik. "Martin, two Johnnie Walker Blues, neat."

The bartender looked back over his shoulder. "Johnnie Blue you said Don? You know that's $55 a pop, right?"

"I don't care. We're celebrating. Peter here fired his first gun today!"

Martin put three beers and two glasses with something brown on the waitress' tray, then pulled the bottle of Johnnie Walker Blue Label from the back bar. He took two glasses, placed them in front of Richter and Veldman and poured the liquor. "So how'd you do? Did you hit anything?"

"I'll say!" Richter said, before Veldman could open his mouth. "He's a natural, this guy. Never shot a gun in his life and the first time he pulls the trigger he hits the bull's eye."

"Yeah? Good for you. How far was the target?"

"10 yards. And at the end of the day he even hit the bull at 20."

"Yeah, but that was more luck," Veldman smiled shyly, a little embarrassed by his mentor's lavish praise.

Richter shook his head. "No, no, don't be so modest. You have a gift, trust me, I would know. You should have been a marksman."

"What, and miss out on all the excitement of working at the library?" Veldman said self-deprecatingly.

"No ice for you Don?" Martin asked.

"No thanks. At $55 a shot, the only thing I want touching my lips is the liquid brown gold itself."

The bartender nodded and leaned against the back bar. "Never fired a gun myself either, you know. How was it?"

"Awesome," Peter said without hesitation. "Powerful. Liberating. I mean, for a few seconds everything else disappeared, nothing mattered except the gun and the target… the absolute focus on the target and the immediate, gratifying result after squeezing the trigger. Really, it was one of the most honest, purest experiences in my life."

"That's pretty deep man," Martin smiled. "Maybe I should give it a try myself one of these days. Well, enjoy the Johnnie Blue guys, and let me know when you're up for another." He rapped the bar with his right fist and moved to the other end of the counter, where another waitress had just pushed her tray on the counter.

For Peter it was a day of firsts. He had never taken more than a sip of whiskey a few times, each time deciding hard liquor wasn't meant for him (or the other way around). But when someone who just taught you how to shoot a gun, buys you a $55 whiskey to celebrate, what can you do? And when Richter ordered another round, followed by another round and another round, Veldman emptied those too, not wanting to look like a boy who couldn't hold his liquor—though he was most certainly that. Halfway through his fourth glass, he loudly declared: "Next time let's shoot a deer or something!"

But he wouldn't remember any of it the next day.

27

Claire Longstreet was not in a good mood. This morning, she had found the passenger window of her Cadillac Escalade smashed, the interior looking as if a barbarian horde had just come through. After arriving fifteen minutes late at the office instead of the regular hour early—with her assistant already at her desk, which she absolutely hated—she had gotten a call from the office of FBI Director Leavy, telling her the 4:30 p.m. appointment was off and requesting to have her assistant reschedule a new one. On top of everything else her macchiato was cold, the air conditioning was broken and last night's date had been a bona fide disaster. In fact, she was beginning to wonder whether there were actually any normal, nice, good-looking, sufficiently manly men left in Washington. Men like her ex-husband Greg, only without the cheating.

The guy from last night had basically fucked it up in the first five minutes. Of course he had asked her if she was by any chance related to Confederate General James Longstreet, thinking he was original. They all did. Annoying, but this was Washington D.C., and most guys she dated were either lobbyists or working for the government and they all loved Civil War history. The fact that she actually *was* related to Robert E. Lee's most trusted general—he was her great, great and a couple of more greats grandfather—never actually mattered to any of these guys, though. All they cared about was showing off their knowledge about him. It was a guy thing, they always felt they had to prove their worth. And frankly, the ones that didn't were either extremely uninteresting or so soft and sensitive she felt like slapping some machismo into them.

The guy from last night was not one of those, but he instantly went to the top of the sleazeball list when he seemed to suggest he was sorry the Confederacy had lost the war. And he wasn't even a right-wing Republican from South Carolina or Texas—at least that would have made some sense—but some pacifist loser from Boston. After asking her if she had any artifacts or family heir-looms from General Longstreet, like his revolver or sword—she didn't—he went on to say the Northern States had been wrong in using military force to prevent the Southern States from seceding. Maybe he had said it to please her, somehow thinking that 150 years after the end of the Civil War the descendants of Confederate soldiers were still sorry slavery had been abolished, or maybe he really preferred slavery over war. Either way he was a spineless, gutless, eager-to-please, nasal-talking douchebag. Besides, if there was anything she hated it was pacifists. Yes, this was definitely the last time she'd agreed to let her sister set her up with someone.

She checked her schedule for the day. Oh, right, Berenson and Underhill from Specialty Weapons. She opened her inbox and glanced over the 37 new e-mails. Nothing from Berenson or Underhill. She pressed the intercom. "Susan, did anything come in from Steve Berenson or Jake Underhill this morning?"

"No, but actually both of them are walking in just now. Shall I send them through?"

Longstreet sighed. "Might as well."

"I'm sorry Claire, is that a yes?" the voice came back.

Grrrr. "Yes!" she answered, just a little louder than necessary.

Outside Longstreet's office, her assistant offered a word of advice to the two special agents standing in front of her desk. "Watch out guys, she's in a mood today."

"Special agents Berenson and Underhill, please take a seat," she gestured, before tucking a runaway strand of blond hair behind her left ear and folding her hands on the blotter.

"When I asked Susan to pencil you in for today, I was under the impression I would receive some sort of brief in advance, explaining me what this is about," she began, her tone moving up slightly at the end of the sentence.

Berenson had received Underhill's brief yesterday evening. It had been clear and concise, the way it should be, and he had shot Underhill a short reply saying exactly that. So why hadn't he sent it? He looked at Underhill. "Jake?"

Underhill coughed. "Yes, well… I, eh, thought it easier to just bring the brief with me, so you could read it right now."

Berenson didn't understand, but Longstreet got it right away. She hadn't become Director of the CID in just eight years without being a master in this kind of inter-office tactics herself. "You thought I wouldn't have agreed to a meeting if I'd read the brief beforehand," she smiled slyly, appreciating Underhill's cunningness. "You thought you would need to do some verbal convincing." She stuck out her right hand. "Alright, let's have it. But it better not be more than five pages, because I'm kicking you out in ten minutes."

"Actually it's only three, well, two and a half to be precise," Underhill said, as he handed her the brief.

She took the brown folder and placed it on her desk. "You guys want to get some coffee or anything? Because if you do, bring me back a macchiato."

Berenson and Underhill looked at each other. "No, we're good."

175

"Yeah, we'll just wait."

"Suit yourself," Longstreet said, already reading.

Some executives, habituated to ceaselessly projecting an image of being constantly busy, will immediately rush in with questions if handed a report, demanding clarification about something they read in the first line of the executive summary that is answered in the second line. Claire Longstreet was not one of those executives. She never went off half-cocked. She quietly and carefully read the brief, while Berenson and Underhill waited.

"So you want clearance," she said matter-of-factly after a few minutes.

Underhill looked at Berenson. "Eh, yes," he confirmed.

"Clearance to cross-reference CIA employment records with US Marine Corps employment records, to locate snipers who have worked for both and got out in….what was it, '94?

"Yes. We feel there is a good chance our man—"

"Yeah, yeah, save it agent Underhill," Longstreet interrupted, putting one hand up. "I know I implied you could make your case, but there is really no need to add insult to injury." She looked back at the three pages and shook her head. "Look, there are so many conjectures in here you could start a religion with it," she scoffed. "If this would be the standard of our investigations, we'd never get one criminal convicted. The Bureau would be turned into one big criminal warning apparatus—waving our arms like a couple of clowns at the first sign of mischief—that is until the government shuts us down, tired of paying for all the lawsuits from innocent citizens we needlessly harassed."

"So… that's a no then?" Underhill said, slowly getting up from his chair.

"No… it's a yes." She put the pages back into the folder, folded her hands on top of it and looked at the two men in front of her.

"I don't follow," Underhill said, looking at Berenson.

"Really? Because it's quite simple. What we have here is Operation Cover Our Asses," the CID Director said. "Whose brilliant idea was it that Valery Clayton might be the target of this mysterious assassin?" she asked.

Underhill hesitantly lifted his right hand.

Longstreet gave a cynical smile. "Now why am I not surprised? Yes that'll do agent Underhill, you can put your hand down now."

"Now that it has been suggested by agent Conspiracy Theory here," she gestured in Underhill's direction, "that Clayton might be the target of a professional hit man, we cannot afford *not* to investigate it as thoroughly as possible. Because if we don't and she is indeed assassinated—or even dies of seemingly natural causes—our careers will be just as dead."

She picked up the folder. "It doesn't even matter that any reasonable assessment, based on the string of circumstantial evidence you have collected here, would conclude that the chance this particular plot actually exists is slim to none. For Christ's sake, even NTAC concluded there was nothing to go on, and they go after everyone who so much as sneezes suspiciously in the general direction of the President."

Longstreet sighed. "But if she dies, we would be obligated to share our information about a possible contract killer who may or may not be a former U.S. Marine and who acquired some unusual, custom-made weapons from a Swiss gunsmith now in custody of the Swiss police. And if we don't, and it comes out anyway—and these things always have a habit of coming out—not only would our careers be over, we would go to jail for obstruction of justice, if not for aiding and abetting, in the unlikely event your man would actually turn out to be Clayton's assassin."

She threw the folder back on her desk. "So, I have no choice but to pursue this case, however unlikely it may be." She got up, indicating the meeting was nearing its end.

"You've got your clearance. Report back to me as soon as you have a list of people who fit the profile."

She waved to the door. "Now get out of my office, I have a macchiato to order."

28

Acquiring sensitive information from large organizations is almost never easy. Lower-level employees generally have—or think they have—better things to do than helping outsiders to company information and will certainly not risk their own hide for it, so they'll either bounce it back, or, if there is some sort of authorization they can't ignore, kick it up to their boss or another department—preferably both, to ensure maximum hide-covering security. The more sensitive the request, the higher it must go before finally reaching someone who has the authority to green-light it. Of course, requests like these are never a priority, and because nobody takes ownership, the person making the request is often sent back, forth and astray within the organization while it slowly makes its way up the ladder. And that is just for regular organizations.

The CIA is notoriously reluctant to release any employment information to anybody outside 'The Company'. This is hardly surprising, considering it has been in the business of stealing sensitive information itself since World War II, when its predecessor, the Office of Strategic Services (OSS), collected intelligence on Nazi troop deployments in Europe, recruited double agents and decrypted German, Japanese—even Soviet—cipher traffic.

Berenson and Underhill had their clearance, but even if information retrieval in the digital age theoretically needn't take more time than a mere split second, human intervention would in this case turn those split seconds into days.

The CIA liaison officer who received the request, complete

with scans of the proper forms with the proper signatures, simply passed it on to Personnel Resources, since it was a request for employment records of CIA personnel. Theoretically, that should have been the end of it, but when the administrator receiving the request looked into it and saw that it specifically asked for employment records of CIA operatives who had previously served in the Marine Corps as a scout sniper, she realized it most likely pertained to former operatives of the Special Activities Division (SAD), and when it came to information about personnel employed by the Directorate of Operations (formerly known as the Clandestine Service)—which ran SAD—The Company was even less inclined to cooperate. She therefore sent a short e-mail to the head of the Office of Security—responsible, among other things, for all personnel security—with a *cc* to her boss, the head of Personnel Resources. The latter subsequently also shot a quick note to the head of the Office of Security, stating she deferred to his decision in the matter.

The Director of the Office of Security happened to be at his daughter's wedding on Oahu, Hawaii, when he felt the phone buzz in his pants. He cast a quick glance, saw that it didn't involve terrorists overrunning Langley or CIA Director John O'Hannon asking him to prepare everything for an incognito visit to the Middle East, but that it was just about some FBI request, and decided it could wait until Monday.

Back at his desk on Monday morning after a fun-filled weekend, the Director of the Office of Security worked his way through the pile of unanswered e-mails, finally arriving at the FBI request just before lunch. He considered it for a moment, then decided, knowing how notoriously guarded—not to mention vindictive—George Piermont, the head of the Directorate of Operations was, to forward the request to Piermont himself.

George Piermont was one of those people who despised almost everyone, beginning with—but not limited to—everybody outside The Company. Among those he despised the most were, in no particular order, all 240,000 employees of the Department of Homeland Security, the Defense Intelligence Agency, his wife, his neighbors, liberals, and of course the Federal Bureau of Investigation, especially when they came sniffing around for information about his boys. He looked dismissively at his screen, hit the reply button, typed his two-word answer to the request and clicked the send button.

In the end, FBI Director Tom Leavy had to personally call CIA Director John O'Hannon, asking him for the personnel files and explaining it was of some importance to an ongoing investigation, of which he could unfortunately not divulge any details at the time. Like many of his lower-level employees, O'Hannon had better things to do than waste time on these kind of requests, and after hanging up he quickly shot a five-word message to Piermont. "Give FBI what they want."

It was September 26.

29

Monday, September 26, 2016, 9:00 p.m.,

Hofstra University, Hempstead, New York

Caitlin Shelly looked straight at him. If she disliked him personally, or his views, it didn't show. Her composure was perfect and she
was every inch the professional. She looked the part too. Potentially hipster strains of her short blonde hair were neatly tucked
behind her long ears. A little over a year ago her hair had still been
long and luscious, but at the height of a very public feud with the
same man now standing 10 yards from her, she had chopped it off.
An act, she later said, that had empowered her. Her complexion
was flawless, her expression stern but fair, with a dash of don't-try-
to-bullshit-me, the way a juvenile judge with twenty years under
her belt looks at a 15-year-old boy who is about to diss up a story
in her court.

She loved this moment, this exact moment, those few seconds
before asking the question, when the interviewee could do nothing but wait. Would it be a friendly question, or an axe to the legs?
With the applause behind her still going strong, she kept looking
at him. Was he looking at her too, or were his eyes fixated on the
audience behind her, drinking in the applause like the needy animal he was. She suddenly realized he was probably the only person she had ever interviewed who relished the axe, lived for the
axe even. The way he stood there, a pouting look on his face that
would look positively ridiculous on anybody else over the age of
five but somehow fit him like a glove. She couldn't help but think

that if a group of powerful aliens ever descended upon Earth, threatening to wipe out all of humanity if it did not immediately surrender, he would definitely be the guy best suited to negotiate on behalf of mankind. Because that smug and dismissive pouting look alone would be enough to convince even the most fearsome aliens of the universe that humans were simply too stupid to ever surrender. Of course it could also mean the end of mankind.

"Mr. Drump."

The audience kept clapping.

"Mr. Drump."

Audience minders gestured people to quiet down a bit.

"Mr. Drump."

"Caitlin," Drump said, not unfriendly.

"Mr. Drump, you have repeatedly vilified Senator Clayton for not disclosing transcripts of her paid speeches to Wall Street banks, yet you yourself are still refusing to disclose your tax returns from the past seven years. You have said that is because the IRS is still in the process of auditing your business—"

"It is," Drump said, his hands firmly on the glass lectern.

"Yet the IRS has said that citizens are always allowed to share their tax records, regardless of an audit. Will you promise to release your tax returns before the elections?"

"Look, there is nothing to learn from them," Drump said, raising his left hand from the lectern and pointing his index finger in the air, "you learn very little from a tax return really, it would just be an enormous waste of time. They are very complex, my tax returns, incredibly complex, because I have just so many businesses and assets all over the world. All that you would learn from them is that I'm really, really rich."

"For one thing, it would show if you have given as much to charities as you say you did. Wouldn't you agree that is something voters have a right to know?" Shelly rebutted.

"Voters don't care about tax returns, people like you do, politicians do, so they can fleece it for small things to nag about. I'm not a politician, I don't like fleecing, I'm not a monkey. The voters know me, they know I have given so much to charities, more than anybody. You could fund a small African country with the amount of money I give away. And in any case, the IRS won't let me," he stretched out both his arms in a helpless gesture.

"Actually," Shelly said, "the IRS, in an official statement, said in February of this year, and I quote: *Federal privacy rules prohibit the IRS from discussing individual tax matters. Nothing prevents individuals from sharing their own tax information.*"

"Yes, technically it is allowed, but every tax lawyer will tell you it's completely stupid to talk about your tax returns in public while you are being audited. Every tax lawyer can tell you that. It's stupid. But I will release them as soon as the audit is over. If that is before the election, I will release them before the election, it's as simple as that."

"Well, the election is in six weeks," Shelly said, without asking another question right away. It was a tiny slip-up, but enough for Ronald Drump to turn the tables.

"Look, I will release my tax returns, guaranteed 100 percent, just not as long as the IRS is auditing me—which is perfectly normal—but that's completely different from Senator Clayton's refusal to release the transcripts of speeches to Wall Street banks she was paid a quarter of a million dollars per speech for. Let's talk about *that*." He cocked his head in the direction of Valery Clayton, who had thus far just stood behind her lectern, listening. "Why won't you release them Valery? What, were you a little bit too nice to those big banks, promising to leave them alone if you'd get elected?"

Shelly broke in before Clayton could answer. "We'll get to that in a minute Mr. Drump. You said the voters don't care about your tax returns and that there's nothing to learn from them, but aside from information about your charitable giving, it would also show how much money you have parked overseas, would it not? And some would say that is not a very patriotic thing, especially not for someone running for president."

Drump threw his hands in the air. "Look, I'm greedy, alright? I love money. Guilty as charged, so sue me. But you know what, now I want to be greedy for America and stop the Mexicans and Chinese from getting rich off our country, stealing our jobs, exporting all that cheap, subpar stuff to us while good, American-made products are being pushed out. I'm filthy rich and I like being filthy rich, I've never made a secret of that. But Senator Clayton here is talking the liberal talk while secretly giving speeches to the biggest banks in New York, the biggest banks in the world, promising them God knows what. I mean, why would they pay her $250,000 for a speech that hoses them? I wouldn't, and I don't believe they would."

"We'll get to that in a minute Mr. Drump," Shelly said.

"What is this, ladies night? This is a legitimate question, let her answer it."

An electrifying rush went through the audience. In an instant, the auditorium was a sea of schmoozing.

Shelly was unfazed, or at least appeared to be. "Are you suggesting I am sparing Senator Clayton because she is a woman?"

"I'm not suggesting anything, I just want her to answer the question."

"You know what," Clayton said, as the audience grew louder. "You know what," she repeated, raising her voice a little, "I'll release the transcripts of my speeches the minute you release your tax returns!"

Clayton's supporters in the audience started clapping and cheering.

"And by the way, I have already released *my* tax returns…" she continued, raising her voice further and smiling broadly, the way a grandmother does when offering her four-year-old grandchild a cookie, "you can view them on valeryclayton.com!"

30

CHRIS ANDERSON: Yes, but 'ladies night?' I mean, how do you come back from that?

VAN SMITH, POLITICAL COMMENTATOR: I know, right? I mean, I know I wouldn't. Then again, he has survived so much already Chris. He has called Mexicans thieves and rapists, American prisoners of war losers, he has insulted countries, foreign heads of state…

JOHN PRINCE, DNN CHIEF NATIONAL CORRESPONDENT: Plus he is already considered a sexist.

SMITH: Right.

ANDERSON: So, what does that mean? That it doesn't matter anymore? That he basically gets a free pass to continue to insult everyone he has already insulted before? Because that's a long list.

GLORIA BURGER, DNN CHIEF POLITICAL ANALYST: Look, you have a candidate here who has been speaking his mind since the beginning, and he has alienated large groups of voters with it, but it has also endeared him to this large block of angry white voters.

SMITH, chuckling: Endeared?

BURGER, smiling: Well yes, I mean he's their champion isn't he? Their knight in shining armor who is going to make America amazing again. And their America *has* changed; the end of segregation, Mexican immigration threatening their jobs, manufacturing jobs going overseas…

PRINCE: Not all angry white voters are racists, though.

BURGER: No, but it is undeniable that life for the average white male was easier in 1960 than it is in 2016.

ANDERSON: Okay, so he has a core group of supporters who will vote for him no matter what. But that group is not big enough for him to win the election.

PRINCE: Looking at the electoral map it was always going to be difficult for any Republican to win, though, not just for Ronald Drump. For one, the Republicans need to do much better in the rustbelt states than they did in 2012, that means winning swing states like Ohio and Virginia, and doing well in states like Pennsylvania and Michigan.

AXEL DAVIDSON, DNN SENIOR POLITICAL COMMENTATOR: And this is even more true for Drump, because it is doubtful he can carry Florida.

PRINCE: Right, because he doesn't have the Latino vote and Hispanics make up about a quarter of the state's population.

ANDERSON: The latest poll numbers, from a poll held before tonight's debate, show Mr. Drump trailing Senator Clayton by seven points. After tonight's debate it seems likely that gap is going to grow. So what should he do to win in November?

BURGER, chuckling: Pray?

DAVIDSON: I think he is on the right path, even if it didn't pan out tonight. The best thing for him to do is to keep attacking her. Her paid speeches to Wall Street banks, her private e-mail server, her handling of the Benghazi attack, the preferential treatment given to donors of the Clayton Foundation while she was Secretary of State. Fundamentally, Clayton is a very unpopular career politician in a time both the left and the right are fed up with career politicians. And whatever you can say about Ronald Drump, he is certainly not a politician.

BURGER: No, but he is his own worst enemy.

DAVIDSON: I completely agree. But if he stops alienating female, black, Latino and moderate voters, he could still win this.

SMITH: That's just the thing Axel, I don't think he can do that anymore than Valery Clayton can become a likable, genuine politician like her husband. I mean let's face it, we have a presidential race here where both candidates are extremely unpopular, not just with the voters from the other party but also with a significant block of voters from their *own* party. If you ask me, I think this race will be decided by whoever succeeds the most in getting their lukewarm supporters to the polls in November.

ANDERSON: A hell of a way to win the presidency. We'll be right back.

31

Josh Cohen looked up from the latest poll numbers and smiled. These were the moments—the very rare moments—he lived for. When the numbers were so good there was really nothing left to wish for. 'Strong leader', 'Experienced', even in 'Trust' Clayton was beating Drump. The Latino vote, the black vote, the women's vote, they were all solidly in Clayton's camp.

"It's beginning to look a lot like Christmas," he hummed to himself, grinning like an ardent little schoolboy looking at his straight A report card.

He looked outside his glass office, at the flurry of desks, where the volunteers and junior staffers were furiously tapping away on their phones and keyboards, everything bustling with activity. Hell, they deserved to share in this moment. He stood up and went outside.

"Listen up my minions. Drop what you're doing for a moment unless you are about to wheel in a big donor for the home stretch."

About half of them looked up from their phones. The other half, realizing something was up, pulled out their earplugs. Most of them anyway.

"Hey, tell the Zen master over there to turn around for a moment and listen up," Josh said, pointing at a guy still happily typing away.

After someone tapped him on his back he turned around,

looked at Josh and quickly unplugged his earbuds. "Sorry chief, noise-canceling headphones."

"Yeah, that's Mr. Cohen to you, 'chief'. Supreme Leader would also be acceptable." He waited for some kind of acknowledgement, but the kid just sat there. These 20-somethings, he didn't understand them. They were constantly facebooking, tweeting and snapchatting, but when it came to common courtesy in the real world they acted like freaking *Rain Man*. God he was getting an old shit.

"Good news everybody. The numbers from last night just came in and they are excellent. We are up by 10 points now!"

Applause and a collective "wooow!" filled the room, bouncing off the mostly frugal, sterile interior.

"That's right boys and girls, we now have a double digit lead over Ronald Drump and his anti-Mexican, anti-Chinese, anti-Muslim, anti-women message. Clayton is winning on all fronts!"

After the applause and cheers had quieted down somewhat, he continued, "So what this means is that it's ours to lose. Now is not the time to let up, people, now is the time to redouble our efforts! We're in the homestretch, another six weeks and the Senator will be elected the next President of the United States!"

32

"Finally!" Underhill exclaimed when he checked his inbox.

"I take it our friends at the CIA have at last seen fit to release the personnel records we requested?" Berenson asked calmly.

"I'll say!"

"You sound excited. Tell me how many people are on the list and I might share your enthusiasm."

"Okay, hold on...."

"I barely can..." Berenson, typing a report on his laptop, said in the dry, subdued tone Underhill had come to almost miss hearing during the weekends.

"Twelve."

Berenson looked up. "What, that's it? Only twelve?"

"Yup. It says: "Names and partially redacted personnel files of CIA operatives falling in all three of the following categories: 1) CIA employment commenced between 1980-1994. 2) Served part of 1980-1994 as scout sniper in USMC. 3) CIA employment terminated between 1990-1994.""

"Hmmm, I would have thought the CIA hired more snipers during that period," Berenson mused.

"Well, they didn't all have to come from the Marines of course. I mean, you have the Navy SEALs, Delta Force, the Army Rangers,

I'm sure the CIA recruited marksmen from their ranks too," Underhill said, downloading the files to his desktop.

"You're right of course. Still, only twelve… we could probably pay each of them a personal visit then."

"I'm going to print these out," Underhill said, giddy as a schoolboy.

"Yeah, you do that. And get me a copy."

Fifteen minutes later Underhill's enthusiasm had somewhat cooled.

"Redacted… redacted… redacted, Jesus, these personnel files look like piano keys without the white ones. They could have just as easily sent us one page with twelve names, dates of birth, head shots and social security numbers, because everything else is redacted redacted redacted," he snarled.

"Come on Jake, what'd you expect? That they would hand over detailed information on all the 'wet work'—or whatever it is they call it—that these guys did? You know they'd never do that. Besides, we don't really need it either." He tapped his finger on a specific part of the page. "Although it is helpful we can at least see exactly where in the CIA they were employed. For instance, this guy… Martin Hernandez, says here he was employed by the Counterintelligence Center, while most of the others were active in 'DO-SAD-SOG'. Hmmm, what do you think 'DO-SAD-SOG' is?"

"Was just wondering that myself as a matter of fact," Underhill said, "looking it up as we speak. Okay, so…'DO' stands for Directorate of Operations."

"That's the Clandestine Service, right?"

"Right," Underhill said. "And 'SAD' stands for Special Activities Division, which is apparently divided into two subdivisions….the Political Action Group and the Special Operations Group."

"PAG and SOG," Berenson concluded.

"Right."

Berenson quickly leafed through the copied files. "3… 4… .7… 9… 10. Ten of the twelve worked worked for the, ehmm, SOG, the Special Operations Group. I bet that's the bad boy group."

"Yeah, you're right. I'm reading here that's the division responsible for the CIAs tactical paramilitary operations."

"Where snipers are always welcome," Berenson grinned.

After finishing his first reading of the personnel files, Berenson started dividing them into twelve different stacks. "We should start prioritizing the names, and then pay them a visit in that order."

"I agree," Underhill nodded, "but shouldn't we first check if any of them flew to Zurich in September? Because if one of them's a hit we're probably done right away."

"Good thinking. Okay, so let's divide the names and each check six. I'll take… Martin Hernandez… Mark Chandler… John Rizzo… Toby Conley… David Haldane… and Conrad Richter."

Unaware his name had just been mentioned by an FBI agent for the first time, Conrad Richter picked up his phone.

"Hi dad."

—

"Yeah, I've been back since the fourteenth."

—

"I know dad, I'm sorry, it's just that I've been pretty busy these past few weeks."

—

"You know, stuff."

—

"Yes, I know, you came home every night from your job. But you were a lawyer at Tripp, Stanwyck & Menken in Midtown

Manhattan, and 99 percent of your clients were Wall Street firms, whereas I work for a company that sends me to train and advise defense personnel all over the world."

—

"Yes, there too. What, they can't have an army? Look, I never criticized your job either."

—

"Ah, there is that word again. Respectable. Well, I assure you my clients employ a hell of a lot more lawyers than they do former Marines. We are all suckling on the same teat dad, your side is just fatter and wears more expensive suits."

—

"True. You have mom's cooking to thank for that."

—

—

—

"I know… I miss her too."——"How, eh… how are you holding up? Do Elizabeth and Mary visit regularly?"

—

"Well, her kids are much younger than Elizabeth's."

—

"Now don't start dad, we've been over this. You know I'm not the type for that kind of life. Besides, you have five grandkids already, so I really don't see the issue."

—

"Yeah, well, I'm sure there are still plenty of other Richters out there to continue the 'male line'. Look, I gotta go soon, I—"

—

"Tonight? Ehhh… yeah sure. What time?"

—

"Yeah I can make that."

"No, you don't have to send Sanchez with the car, but thanks anyway. See you tonight dad."

—

"Love you too."

Three of the twelve names on Berenson and Underhill's list showed up in U.S. flight records for September, but none of them had flown to Zurich. John Conley had flown from New York to Paris on the 5th and returned on the 15th. David Haldane had departed for São Paulo from Dallas on the 10th—with a return trip planned for October 5th. The third one was a domestic flight, a return trip from LAX to Bozeman Yellowstone Airport in Montana.

Of course John Conley could have taken a regional flight, or a train, from Paris to Zurich—or even have driven there—to meet with Zimmerman on the 12th, then made his way back to Paris and returned to New York on the 15th. It was possible, but not probable, especially since he had been accompanied by Mrs. Conley. More likely the trip to Paris had been a romantic getaway. A quick search into Conley's employment history revealed he was the owner / manager of three Wendy's fast food restaurants in Jersey City, hardly the kind of job that combines well with that of elite contract killer.

Around 11:00 a.m., Berenson contacted Hans Kreuzer and asked him to check if any of the twelve names showed up in Swiss flight record arrivals. Kreuzer subsequently called his contact at the *Bundeskriminalpolizei*, Karl Deiss, who was already on his way home but promised to try and get clearance for accessing the flight records within an hour or two.

Thinking about John Conley's trip to Paris, it occurred to Berenson that there was a chance that, even if their man was a U.S.

citizen, he had flown to Europe from another country and from this European destination had traveled by train or car to Zurich, especially since the European railroad network was better developed than the American and long-distance train travel was far more common there. So he contacted INTERPOL and requested it to assist in obtaining permission to check the flight records of all EU countries against the twelve names on the list.

As he went for coffee, Berenson contemplated the likelihood the American was traveling on an alternate passport. Based on the few facts and high probabilities they had on him, a picture of the American slowly began to emerge in Berenson's mind, of a meticulous, methodical man, trained by the best in a profession that demanded ruthless adherence to structure, organization and above all, patience. The kind of disciplined man, who, if he had an unforeseen chance to take out his mark with a 9mm handgun in a dark forest with nobody else around, would still do nothing more than mumble a greeting and walk on if he had planned to take him out a day later with a .300 Winchester Magnum from 800 yards away.

Planning, procedures, discipline, that's what had kept him alive and successful for more than 20 years. For each job he went through the steps, seeking out a location to strike, creating a timetable, commissioning a custom-made gun from his Swiss gunsmith. That M40A1 sniper rifle, the first weapon he had commissioned from the gunsmith—Berenson bet he almost never used it for actual hits. Perhaps he had thought he would in the beginning, before realizing that that was his old life. That there was a difference—if only a legal one—between killing in the service of the state and killing as a private contractor. Maybe he had done his first few hits with the M40A1, but before long he had seen it for what it was: a memento from another life, a relic.

Would a man like that travel under his own name, his own passport? Almost certainly not, at least not when it counted. Why spend $40,000 on a sophisticated drone but not $10,000 on a fake passport? He scoffed. Hell, for $40,000 you could hire a hacker to give you a whole new identity. Passport, driver's license, even a crispy clean social security number, complete with fake employment history. No, they wouldn't find the American by going over flight records. Still, they had to check. People make mistakes, even sophisticated criminals.

Meanwhile, Underhill had begun gathering information about the people on the list. For a first ranking, he looked at age, CIA employment history, post-CIA employment history and current employment, the latter two of which he obtained through a social security number trace.

In a few hours, he familiarized himself with the lives of their twelve persons of interest, uncovering their sometimes surprising—sometimes not so surprising—personal histories after leaving behind a life of violence and secrecy. What do you do when you're 30, 35 years old and all you've ever known is the soldier's life, first as a scout sniper in the Marines and then as Special Skills Officer in the CIA? Do you get a library card, open a retail store and pretend nothing ever happened? As it turned out, some of them did exactly that.

Dexter Lawrence for instance, who had grown up in Jackson, Mississippi, before joining the Marines in 1988, went back to Jackson after leaving the CIA in '94 and started a construction business. More than twenty years later, he still had it, and according to his tax records was making a decent living, although the recession of 2007-08 had hit him hard.

John Conley had gone to work in his father-in-law's Wendy's, taking it over after his death a decade later and opening two more Wendy's restaurants since.

Steven Dykman had also gone into the family business, taking over his father's 1,000 acre ranch in Paradise Valley, about 10 miles south of Livingston, Montana. A ranch. Allowing his mind to wander for a moment, Underhill wondered what the life of a rancher entailed. Grazing cattle? Mending fences? Hunting, fishing? Certainly a lot of solitude, with the nearest small town 10 miles away. Still, he could understand how somebody would choose a no-frills existence of peace and quiet in Montana after having done God knows what in the service of his country.

Then again, maybe Mr. Dykman had been splitting his time between cow herding and gun for hire these past twenty years, just to keep things interesting. Underhill took a quick look at flights from Washington D.C. to the airport nearest to Livingston, Bozeman Yellowstone International Airport. None of them were non-stop, though. They'd have to travel to Minneapolis first, then take a flight to Bozeman from there. It would take a little over six hours, including a layover of about an hour in Minneapolis. From Bozeman, it would be just a short drive to Livingston, but all in all it would take them the better part of a day to get there.

About half the people on the list had jobs that were related to their former employment in the military. One worked for private military contractor MilCorp., another was a security advisor for GenX Security. David Haldane owned a gun store in Wichita Falls, Texas, and Mark Chandler had worked as a salesman at Remington Arms almost since leaving the CIA in 1993. One had even re-enlisted as a Marine and was a scout sniper instructor at Marine Corps Base Camp Pendleton. If that checked out, it was almost certain he was not the man they were looking for.

Around 6:30 p.m. Underhill had completed his first, preliminary background check on all twelve persons of interest. He was just about to start ranking them when his wife called.

"Hi honey."

—

"Shit, I completely forgot the time. Why don't you start without me? I really want to finish this."

—

"The Larrabees?" That was tonight? I thought that was tomorrow."

—

"They're already there? Damn. Ehmmm, yes, I'll be right over."

—

"I don't know. How long does it usually take me? 30 minutes? Just tell them that I was working on something of national security. Hank Larrabee loves that kind of stuff."

—

"Yes honey, I'm leaving now."

—

"Yes I will. See you in a bit."

"Steve, I have to go," Underhill said.

"That much I understood," Berenson mumbled, as he was poring over the 2016 U.S. flight record data for Conrad Richter.

"Look, I finished the first background check on our guys and was just about to start prioritizing them, but I really have to go. Can you take a look, so we can set up an itinerary to visit all eleven of them in the most efficient way?"

"Eleven?"

"Yeah. William O'Keefe died in a car crash in 2004," Underhill said, as he quickly packed his stuff.

"Sure. Send it over."

With a few clicks, Underhill e-mailed him the document with all the information he had gathered so far. "Got it?"

"Yep. Now go to your dinner party," Berenson smiled. "I'll prepare a prioritized overview based on your information and send it to you later tonight, so you can go over it after your guests have left. Unless by then you have better things to do of course," he joked, moving his eyebrows up and down a few times.

"Thanks Steve, see you tomorrow," Underhill laughed as he hurried out.

Hearing Underhill say goodnight to agent Muller, who was apparently also still there, Berenson mumbled under his breath: "I guess I would hurry out the building too if I had a wife like that."

An hour later, Berenson e-mailed Underhill the following reworked and prioritized list:

1. **Conrad Richter**: 1967, New York City.
   DO-SAD-SOG at CIA.
   Employed by private military contractor MilCorp.

2. **Martin Hernandez**: 1969, Jupiter, Florida.
   Counterintelligence Center at CIA.
   Security advisor at GenX Security.

3. **Steven Dykman**: 1962, Livingston, Montana.
   DO-SAD-SOG at CIA.
   Owns a ranch.

4. **Joseph Moretti**: 1956, Toulouse, France.
   Instructor at Camp Peary, a.k.a. 'The Farm', at CIA.
   Yoga instructor.

5. **Toby Rizzo**: 1968, San Diego County.
   DO-SAD-SOG at CIA.
   Scout sniper instructor at Marine Corps Base Camp Pendleton.

6.   **Mark Chandler**: 1962, Huntsville, Alabama.
DO-SAD-SOG at CIA.
Salesman at Remington Arms.

7.   **David Haldane**: 1965, Wichita Falls, Texas.
DO-SAD-SOG at CIA.
Owns a gun store.

8.   **John Conley**: 1960, Jersey City.
DO-SAD-SOG at CIA.
Owns and operates three Wendy's fast food restaurants.

9.   **Winston Washington, Jr.**: 1963, Albany, Georgia.
DO-SAD-SOG at CIA.
Mayor of Albany.

10.   **Richard Lamotte**: 1959, New Orleans.
DO-SAD-SOG at CIA.
Owns a bar.

11.   **Dexter Lawrence**: 1966, Jackson, Mississippi.
DO-SAD-SOG at CIA.
Has a construction business.

12.   **William O'Keefe**: 1962, Boston.
DO-SAD-SOG at CIA.
Killed in car crash in Boston, MA, 2004.

33

Around the time Berenson e-mailed Underhill the prioritized persons of interest list from his office at FBI Headquarters in Washington D.C., the number one on that list walked into the 23-story residential building on 825 Fifth Avenue in Manhattan, New York, to have dinner with his father.

"Good evening Mr. Richter. Your father is expecting you," the doorman, dressed impeccably in black uniform with silver stitches and matching hat, nodded and smiled. He pressed a button and one of the elevator doors opened. "You can go right in Mr. Richter." Another smile.

Richter gave a polite smile himself as he walked past the reception, entered the elevator and pushed the button for the tenth floor. As it zoomed to its destination, he looked back over his shoulder. Yep, new couch again. Every year. He wondered what they did with the old couches. Well, old… most people would consider a one-year-old couch just shy of brand new. Maybe they gave them to the small army of doormen, handymen and manservants employed in the building? Maybe it was even presented as a perk to new employees: stay on for at least a year and you get a chance to win one of these kitschy, old ladies elevator couches.

Ping.

He got out, turned right towards apartment C—one of only three apartments on the tenth floor—and stopped before the black

203

oak door with the heavy bronze knocker. He sighed. Every time he faced this door, even now, at 50 years old, he felt himself shrink like Alice in Wonderland. Why? After the life he lived, the things he had seen, suffered and done, why did he still feel so small every time he came here? He was no longer a child, his father no longer had any hold over him, not since more than thirty years ago.

He heard a click and the door opened. "Good evening Conrad! Harry already called up to say you were coming." Wearing a khaki tie underneath a buttoned-down, grey-blue woolen vest with low side-pockets, his father greeted him warmly with bright blue eyes and a broad smile. Kissing him on the cheek, Richter felt his smooth face and smelled the all-too familiar aftershave—no doubt Sanchez had given his master an extra shave today, in preparation for the dinner. Flashbacks shot through his mind of his father telling him how to dress, eat, converse, sit up properly—the result of a strong belief that behaving like the upper class was the key to being accepted by the upper class.

"Well, what are you standing there like a mailman without a package? Come in."

As he followed his father through the hallway, toward the living room, the upbeat melody of the Allegro part of a Vivaldi concerto grew stronger. As a teenager, he had thoroughly hated classical music. Forbidden to listen to anything else, the sophisticated compositions of Mozart, Bach, Beethoven, Schubert and Chopin had felt like a corset, preventing him from developing his own musical taste. He did like the music his grandfather listened to—Frank Sinatra, Nat King Cole, Dean Martin—but he had almost completely missed out on the music of his own generation. It wasn't until many years after moving out of his parents' house that he had learned to appreciate, even love the music he had been force-fed during his childhood years.

"Sit, sit," his father gestured at one of the antique leather couches in front of the fireplace. "Sanchez is still working on the Boeuf Bourguignon, so best not to disturb him at the moment. Would you like a glass of this wonderful 2013 *Chateau de Beaucastel Chateauneuf-du-Pape* in the meantime? I already had a glass myself, it's really quite excellent."

"Sure," Richter said.

"We're having a bit of a French evening tonight," his father beamed. "Sanchez is even making crêpe Suzette for dessert."

"Sounds good." Richter looked past his father at the wooden easel and the large, still virgin canvas in front of it. On a table next to it lay dozens of tubes of paint, brushes, painting knives, white cloths and all kinds of bottles.

After he finished pouring, Joe Richter followed his son's eyes. "Ah yes, my new hobby. What do you think?"

"Of the painting? Yes, very modern," Richter joked.

"Well, I only bought the stuff today," his father laughed. "I thought painting could perhaps help me get my mind off things whenever I'm tired of reading."

Richter took his glass and leaned back in the couch. "You, tired of reading? I've never heard you say that before."

"Yes, well…" his father picked up his own glass and wrapped his fingers around it, "with your mother gone I sometimes have difficulty filling the days. I mean, Sanchez has been really great, but your mother always had a new project, you know, a new museum to visit, a movie to see, a concert to go to. I never realized just how much I depended on her for everything. To be honest, I think I would be completely lost if it wasn't for Sanchez." He looked around for a moment, then sat down in the tangerine bergère chair.

"But enough about me," he said in a forced upbeat tone. "What's going on with you?"

"Not much," Richter said, who never had been the talkative type when it came to his personal life, not even as a kid.

"Bought a rat."

"What do you mean?"

"You know, as a pet."

The old man looked confused. "A rat as a pet? What an odd concept. You mean you can actually buy them at a pet store? Or did you just go out and catch one in the basement or something?"

"Nope, bought it at the pet store, complete with a cage, food, water bottle, even got him a little hammock to lie in. And he does, all day long. I call him Lazy Pete," Richter grinned.

Sanchez inconspicuously entered the living room. Taking position at a respectable distance, he folded his hands in front of him, and waited.

Joe Richter still had a hard time understanding. "Who keeps a rat as a pet? Don't you know they carry diseases with them? They're vermin."

"Sanchez!" he suddenly said, a little louder and more familiar than Richter was used to from his father, "Conrad just tells me he bought a rat as a pet. Tell me, have you ever heard of such a thing?"

"Good evening master Richter," Sanchez nodded friendly to the younger Richter, before quickly adding: "a rat you say sir? As a pet? No, I can't say I've ever heard of that."

"Maybe I should get a pet," Joe Richter said abruptly. "Not a rat of course, there are enough vermin in the world as it is. A cat maybe?"

"Wonderful idea sir," Sanchez smiled broadly. "Ehh now, on a slightly different note, the Boeuf Bourguignon has taken a bit longer than expected, but I am ready to serve dinner now."

"Ah, excellent Sanchez, excellent. We'll be right there."

"Speaking of vermin," Joe Richter said a good twenty minutes later while slicing a piece of beef, "did you see the debate last night?"

Richter put down his glass. "I was wondering when you were going to bring that up," he said with a wry smile. "Yeah I saw it. Most if it anyway."

"Well, what did you think of it?"

"What's there to think about? It was a debate, they're politicians, trying to get elected. Actually it wasn't even a debate, it was a two-hour infomercial, a circus, only with talking heads instead of dancing monkeys. I don't think anybody is taking it seriously."

The old man swallowed, wiped his mouth with the white handkerchief resting in his lap and took a sip of his wine.

"Well they should," Richter Sr. said, as he carefully put down the Baccarat wine glass.

"Come on, you're not falling for the whole 'Drump is a danger to this country' crap, are you?"

"Language Conrad." His father shot him a stern look.

"I'm sorry, 'B.S.' then," Richter said with thinly veiled sarcasm, before continuing: "Look, the guy is just saying whatever he needs to say to get elected. They all do, only he is doing it louder and not as politically correct. You don't really believe he's going to ban Muslims and deport eleven million illegal immigrants do you? Come on."

"You know, we crossed swords once," Joe said, slicing off another piece of beef.

"What, your streams intersected in the bathroom of the Four Seasons or something?"

"Don't be so vulgar Conrad, you're always so vulgar. You know, sometimes it's like hearing your grandfather, the way you talk," the old man said, more reprimanding than annoyed.

"What's wrong with the way grandfather talked?"

"Nothing, nothing, you know I loved him very much. I just... I just wanted more for you," Richter Sr. said.

Two pair of the same shade of blue eyes interlocked. "Are we finally going to have this conversation?" Conrad asked.

"There's no need," his father smiled after a while. "We each have to carve out our own path."

They both fell silent. Not the kind of uneasy silence molded out of reproach and the failure to express regret, but a warm embrace of mutual understanding, perhaps the first they had ever shared.

A few minutes later, Sanchez discreetly entered the dining room. He filled their glasses, emptying the bottle of *Chateau de Beaucastel Chateauneuf-du-Pape*. "Would you like me to open another sir? I believe we have one more of the 2013 in the wine cabinet.

"Eh, yes please Sanchez."

"And would you like me to prepare dessert as well sir?"

Joe Richter looked at his son.

"Not for me dad. The Boeuf Bourguignon was excellent, though," he said to Sanchez.

"Thank you sir."

"I think we'll have that second bottle in the living room," Richter Sr. said.

"Very good sir."

"So, you met him once," Richter said, sitting in the same spot on the couch as earlier. "Drump."

Richter Sr. scoffed. "Ha! It was more than a meet and greet, if that's what you think. I was part of the legal team of a client threatening to sue him for reneging on a deal. His lawyers had proposed a meeting at our firm to discuss a settlement, but while we were in the middle of the meeting, Drump himself came by unannounced, bullied himself past reception and all but stormed into the conference room."

"You're kidding."

Joe Richter lifted his index finger. "That's not all. He ordered Ted Kinsen, their lead negotiator—*his* lead negotiator—who was sitting in the middle, to stand up, subsequently took the seat for himself and relegated poor Kinsen to one of the outer seats. Then he folded his hands on the desk and said smugly that he wasn't about to let himself be strong-armed out of $20 million and that there would be no deal. It was the most unprofessional thing I've ever seen."

"What, and that was that?"

"I'll spare you the legal details, but let's just say we weren't in that conference room for nothing. There was a preliminary contract and it was ironclad, ordering the party that reneged from the final deal to compensate the other party to the tune of ten percent of the value of the deal. Drump had been overeager in wanting to do the deal because he thought he was in competition with a rival real estate company. That turned out to be just a smoke screen, though, thrown up by our client. But by the time he found out, he had already agreed to pay a sum that significantly overvalued the asset."

He took a sip of wine. "The thing that baffled me at the time, was how a businessman of his stature could be so childish in accepting defeat. He must have agreed with his lawyers to settle beforehand, but apparently somewhere during the day he just snapped. Unbelievable."

"So did you go to court?" Richter asked.

"I would have liked that, but no. The next day he personally called Stanley Menken to say he was willing to pay the $20 million."

Richter snickered. "I'm sure he's not the only politician who is bad at losing, though, or plays dirty when he gets the chance. I mean, do you honestly believe Valery Clayton is any better?"

The old man wagged his finger. "That is not the issue Conrad. You saw him tonight. Half the time he doesn't know what he's talking about. And he has no moral compass, he'll do anything to win, not just the election, anything."

"Meaning what?"

"What, that isn't enough?" Joe Richter scoffed. "A narcissist without a moral compass, who doesn't know when to quit, running the most powerful country in the world in a time of increasing global tensions with the Russians and the Chinese? Would you want a man like that with his finger on the button? Do you have any idea how dangerous that would be?"

"I take it he doesn't have your vote then?" Richter grinned.

But Richter Sr. ignored the stab. "Look, I have been a Republican all my life, but unless Ronald Drump drops dead before election day, I'm voting Clayton."

34

"Okay, so yeah, I got your little list—thank you agent Berenson," Claire Longstreet gestured at Berenson, in an apparent effort to underline her gratitude, though the sighing tone of her voice revealed a fundamental annoyance with having to thank people for simply doing their job.

She looked at her screen. "I have to say I was a bit surprised by how short it is. Are you sure it's complete?"

Berenson and Underhill looked at each other. "Well," Underhill responded, sounding slightly insecure, "these are the ones that served as scout sniper in the Marines somewhere between 1980-1994 *and* were recruited by the CIA in the same period *and* left the agency again between 1990-1994."

"In other words," Berenson added, "it doesn't include members of other elite units, like the Army Rangers, SEALs, or Delta Force."

"Of course it's possible they were also part of the SEALs or Delta Force at one point, but the defining characteristic is that they were all scout snipers in the Marine Corps," Underhill tried to clarify.

"You lost me at 'well,'" Longstreet said. "I was looking for a simple yes or no."

"What was the question again?" Underhill asked.

"Is this list complete?" Longstreet shot back, pausing between each word and with the tone in her voice rising again, a clear sign of imminent overload.

"Well…" Underhill began.

"Yes," Berenson interjected, touching Underhill's arm for a moment.

"Thank you." Another sigh.

"So, what do you want from me now?—wait don't tell me," she put her hands theatrically on the side of her head and closed her eyes. "I see… wait, it's coming… plane tickets, hotel bills… am I close?—not a word, not a word—yes, I got it." Longstreet opened her eyes and continued in her normal, perpetually annoyed voice. "You want the Bureau to pay for a dozen flights all over the country, and one to the south of France no less—I could certainly use a vacation there myself too—so you can interview each and everyone on that list."

"Except William O'Keefe," Underhill said, "because he's dead."

"Yeah, but we should still pay a visit to O'Keefe's widow, to verify his death," Berenson remarked.

"And all on the taxpayer's dime, huh?" Longstreet mumbled cynically, looking at her screen again. "Look, these people are all over the place, you'll be on the road for so long the elections will be over and done with before you get back."

"Actually, by our calculation we'll be back on October 18 if we leave today," Underhill said, "a day before the last presidential debate in Las Vegas."

Longstreet reflected for a moment.

"You did say we should treat this as a potential assassination plot against a presidential candidate," Berenson said quietly.

"I know, I know," she looked away from her screen. "Alright. Visit these people, have a nice chat with them, be sure to type up a thorough report and then be done with it. And I want you back by October the 18th."

"We will be." Berenson and Underhill got up and and walked to the door.

"And keep me posted," Longstreet said. "Who are you going to talk to first?"

"The New Yorker," Berenson said, standing in the door opening, "Conrad Richter."

35

As Richter entered his apartment and walked into the living room, he was greeted by the soft squeaking sound of a tiny hammock being swayed back and forth by a black rat, dozing off in the day's fading twilight, coming in through the window.

"Hey Lazy Pete, did you have a good day?"

Ever so slowly, a pointed snout was lifted up and two beady little eyes opened.

"Wow, that good, huh?"

The next moment, the snout fell back into the hammock.

"Alright, let me just put my stuff away, and I'll get you some dinner."

He put down the gym bag, unzipped it and started unpacking, putting the Glock 23 and the two G17s in the safe and the three boxes of 9mm parabellum ammo and the six standard G17 magazines on the shelve above it.

It had been a good day, he mused, with Veldman hitting the bull's eye from 10 yards more than 90 percent of the time now. He had never really considered the possibility that his chosen one would not be able to hit a target from that distance—after all, anybody could be taught how to shoot fairly accurately, if given the time and determination—but he had to admit to have been very lucky with Peter Veldman; the Dutchman was a natural. Of course, the question remained whether he would also be able to perform in a stressful environment, when he *had* to hit his target and would get only one, or at the most two shots to do so.

He reflected for a moment on the feasibility of giving him a crash course in stress shooting as well, but what reason would he give? So far, Veldman thought he was just learning to shoot for fun. Richter had already determined that the best time to try and recruit the Dutchman would be one or two days before the event and to make it look like an unexpected opportunity that had just come up, a once-in-a-life time chance to make history. But giving him additional combat training before that time would make it look as if he had been preparing him for it. Besides, the most important part—aiming a gun at another human being and actually pulling the trigger—could not be trained for anyway.

He was just about to open the cupboard to get Lazy Pete's food, when he heard a knock on the door. Surprised, he went to the front door and looked through the peephole.

The sudden rush of adrenaline instantly activated his fight-or-flight stance, forcing him to back away for about half a second and assess the situation. Then he looked again. Two men, both dressed in a dark-blue suit, white shirt and tie. One a balding 40-something, the other younger, with a full head of wavy blond hair. Too sharply dressed for police detectives. FBI? Secret Service? Or perhaps some foreign service? Bodyguards? They had no guns at the ready.

Another knock. "Mr. Richter? We are from the FBI. We would like a moment of your time."

They knew his name. They knew he was home. Probably had been waiting for him. For how long? And what could it be about? Veldman? Had he been on their radar already, because he was the head of the Anti-Fascist League? Not very likely. Or had he done something, said something? Chris Mathers? No, impossible. Had something come up at MilCorp?

He had no choice. He opened the door.

"Yes?" He looked surprised and gave a polite smile.

"Conrad Richter?"

"Yes? And you are?"

"Special agent Steve Berenson, and this is my colleague, special agent Jake Underhill." They both showed their badges. Richter gave them a quick glance.

"May we come in?"

"Yeah, sure. I would just like to know what this is about." He stepped back and made an inviting gesture, then showed them into the living room.

"Would you like some coffee or something?"

"No that's alright, thank you, though." Berenson looked around. It was a modest apartment. Clean, white walls, no paintings, photographs, or posters. Hardly any furniture except for a table, two chairs and a half-empty bookcase. The bedroom was probably equally sparsely decorated. Clearly, Mr. Richter did not care for frivolous things. There was also clearly no Mrs. Richter.

"Oh look, what have we here?" Berenson squatted in front of Lazy Pete's cage. "Well hello there little fella. What are you doing there? Are you relaxing a bit?" He tapped the cage.

"That's all he does, I'm afraid," Richter smiled. "That's why I named him Lazy Pete."

"Lazy Pete, huh? Good name. Looks like you're enjoying the good life Lazy Pete, you even have two cages."

"Yeah, he, ehh… likes a change of scenery sometimes, so every now and then I put him in the other cage and move him to the other side of the room."

Berenson got up again. "Ah, the simple life. You're a lucky guy Lazy Pete, believe me."

"So officers, what can I do for you?" Richter said, feigning a bit of ignorance.

"It's special agent, actually," Underhill said.

"Oh, excuse me, special agent."

"There is nothing to be alarmed about, I assure you," Berenson said, "It's a matter of routine, really. Recently, there was a fatal shooting that involved the use of a high-powered sniper rifle, deployed from an extremely long range. Several witnesses reported seeing a man in his late forties, early fifties, leaving what was later determined to be the scene of the crime, with a rifle case. Considering the unusually long range of the shot, we are currently questioning elite snipers that have served in the special forces and are in their late forties, early fifties. Not that you don't still look very good for your age, of course." The little joke was meant to alleviate the tension, in an effort to lower Richter's guard. The lie about someone having been killed by a bullet from a high-powered sniper rifle served the same purpose. They needed Richter to be as much at ease as possible, so they could better measure his reaction when asking a question that should startle him—that is, if he was indeed the person they were looking for.

"What was the range, if you don't mind me asking? Professional curiosity, you understand," Richter smiled.

"Eh…" Berenson took out his phone and tapped it a few times. "1,940 yards."

Richter nodded. "That is impressive. And what kind of cartridge was used?"

Berenson couldn't tell if they were the ones being tested or if he was asking these questions out of genuine interest. If he was testing them, it meant he was doubting their story and was trying to find out what they were really here for. It could also mean he had something to hide. But because he was an elite sniper himself—and he knew they knew that—it was also perfectly normal for him to ask these kind of detailed questions, essentially giving him a free pass to interrogate his interrogators without arousing reasonable suspicion.

"Eh…, let me check that…" Berenson tapped his phone again, this time to quickly look up popular sniper rifle calibers.

"The .338 Lapua Magnum," Underhill came to the rescue.

Berenson couldn't prevent himself from giving Underhill a surprised glance. It did not escape Richter's notice.

"Ah yes, great cartridge," he said. "Shoots like a laser, farther and flatter than a .50 caliber. Its maximum effective range is just a little over 1,900 yards, but under the right conditions and with the right rifle and a high-quality scope, it's certainly possible to accurately hit a target at 1,940 yards."

"Mr. Richter, according to our data you joined the Marine Corps in 1986, is that correct?" Berenson asked, eager to move off the subject.

"Yes."

"And you were subsequently sent to scout sniper school at Marine Corps Base Quantico, where you graduated top of your class?"

"Correct."

"Then, in March 1988, you mustered out of the Marine Corps, and from September 1994 you were employed by private military contractor MilCorp."

Richter nodded.

"And were you employed by the Central Intelligence Agency's Special Activities Division between 1988 and 1994?"

A courteous smile appeared on Richter's face. "I'm sure you know that if I were, I could not publicly discuss it."

"Yeah, but we're not the public, we're the government," Underhill said.

Richter shrugged. "I'm sorry."

"Do you own a firearm?" Berenson abruptly changed the subject again.

"Yes. Several."

"And do you have a license to possess and carry firearms in New York City?"

"I do," Richter answered, taking out his wallet and showing the permit.

"This is an unrestricted concealed carry handgun license," Berenson said, inspecting the card. "I understand it's quite difficult to get one of these in the Big Apple. May I ask why you went through the trouble of acquiring it?"

Richter shrugged again. "I have been a soldier all my life. In my current job I use guns—handguns as well as rifles—on a daily basis. I regularly practice at shooting ranges to maintain my skill level. Frankly, it would be impossible for me to function professionally if I couldn't legally carry a firearm."

"I take it you have firearms in the house as well?" Berenson asked.

"Yeah, in the safe. I'll show you." Richter moved in the direction of the walk-in closet.

"No, that won't be necessary," Berenson gestured. "Okay, we're almost done here Mr. Richter. "You mentioned working at Mil-Corp. What is your job title there?"

"I'm a military consultant and trainer. Specifically, I give weapons and tactical training to special forces and law enforcement personnel in countries all over the world."

"I understand MilCorp also offers personal protection services. Do you ever function in that capacity as well?"

"On occasion."

"As a sniper?"

"I see where you're going with this, but no, never as a sniper," Richter said, adding after a short pause: "I could certainly make that shot though, if that's what you're interested in. And I'm sure that goes for most of the top guys at the special forces."

Berenson smiled. "Hmmm, yes, that's what we believe as well."

He shot Richter a sympathetic look." Mr. Richter, I have to ask: where were you on September 12, around 11:00 in the morning?"

"Pfff, that's more than two weeks ago, let me think on that for a moment." Richter looked down, pretending to be in deep thought. Of course he knew exactly where he had been on September 12, around 11:00 in the morning—or rather 5:00 in the afternoon CEST. In a rented BMW 320i Automatic, on a French highway, less than a 100 miles from Paris. That morning, he had had his final meeting with Dieter Zimmerman and taken delivery of the drone and plastic handgun. But of course he couldn't say that. He couldn't even say he'd been abroad, because U.S. flight records showed Conrad Richter entered the United States on August 3, and there was no record of him boarding another flight since then. He wondered why they wanted to know his whereabouts on precisely that day? Was it a coincidence? Something felt off.

"I think I was at home actually."

"Is there anyone who can verify that?" Berenson asked.

Meanwhile, Underhill stayed on Richter's right side, far away enough to be considered out of the conversation—so Richter would not feel the need to shift his eye contact from one to the other—but at the same time close enough to study the former Marine's body language and eyes.

"Ehm, I'm afraid not, I was alone."

"Maybe a neighbor saw you in the hallway? Or a delivery boy? Maybe a phone call was made to your home address, that you picked up?" Berenson tried.

"No, I don't think so, nobody but Lazy Pete here," Richter laughed.

The FBI agents laughed as well.

"We understand," Berenson said.

"I'm sorry I couldn't be more helpful," Richter said apologetically.

"Oh no, no, you've been very helpful, really," Berenson looked at Underhill. "Well, thank you for your time, we'll be on our way now. Is there anywhere we can reach you if we have some more questions?"

"Sure, let me give you my cell number."

A few moments later the special agents were on their way out. They had agreed beforehand that Berenson would ask the final question, the one that mattered, and that he would ask it after the interview was already over, to try and catch Richter off-guard. Underhill opened the door and stepped out into the hall. Berenson was a few steps behind him.

Putting aside the many assumptions and conjectures that had brought them here, there was one connection they knew to be real. A connection, moreover, whose discovery by Swiss law enforcement was almost certainly unknown to the person they were looking for. Of course, making the assassin aware of this might scare him off (an acceptable result in this case, even if they would never find out) but it would also likely startle him—a volatile, adrenaline-driven reaction that was hard to hide.

"One last question," Berenson turned around in the door opening, locking eyes with Richter, who was standing at the beginning of the narrow apartment hallway. "Do you know a Mr. Dieter Zimmerman?"

36

They had been in Richter's apartment for less than half an hour, but in those few minutes the ebbing twilight had completed its retreat into the dark of night. As they walked back to the subway station at 96 Street, Underhill was surprised to see how much brighter the ketchup-red neon letters of Big Daddy's Diner had become.

"So, first impression?" Berenson asked.

"Well, he certainly knew his rifles…" Underhill began.

"As do you apparently. How did you know about that long-range caliber?"

Underhill shrugged. "I've been studying up on snipers these past few days, to get a better handle on what we're dealing with. What kind of personalities they have, what makes them tick. They are very meticulous, methodical, dedicated. And competitive. I mean, you wouldn't believe how far they go just to add another 50 yards to a 1,900 yard range. I remembered reading something about the .338 Lapua Magnum cartridge in the autobiography of that famous Navy SEAL sniper they made a movie about, Chris Kyle. Apparently it was his favorite bullet."

"I'm impressed Jake." They crossed 95th Street and walked past the bank and a busy Starbucks. "So what did you think of Mr. Richter?"

"I don't know. I mean no doubt we are looking for someone *like* him. The mercenary type, highly knowledgeable about firearms, a loner, no family. But whether it really *is* him, I couldn't say."

They entered the subway station and passed the turnstiles. "He certainly doesn't seem to need the money," Berenson said, as they walked down the stairs to catch the downtown express train. "I mean, he had very little stuff as it is, and that job at MilCorp probably pays pretty well."

"*There is a Downtown 2 express train, approaching the station. Please allow the passengers off the train first,*" the computerized announcer said.

As they got on, Berenson looked at his watch. "You know, we've still got plenty of time to get to Jersey City and talk to Conley. Let's get off at Penn Station and grab a quick bite to eat first. I remember there's a good diner across the street from the station."

"Sure." Underhill never liked crowded trains like this. There was nowhere to move. He held on to the top handlebar running along the aisle between the seats, squashed between Berenson and a stylishly dressed Asian woman in her forties. In front of him, a 200-pound black woman, taking up three seats, was eating churros. "Maybe he's not in it for the money," he said to Berenson, "maybe he's in it for the action."

"What? I'm sorry, I didn't catch that."

"Maybe it's not about the money," Underhill repeated, considerably louder, just as the train was slowing down.

"Honey, it's *always* about the money." Underhill looked down and caught the black woman's cynical look. When he didn't immediately respond, she raised her eyebrows. Not quite knowing what to say, he remained silent. "Fine, be like that," she said, returning to her churros.

"I tend to agree with her," Berenson said, leaning towards Underhill.

But Underhill was not convinced. "I don't know. You think it's enough for a guy like that to train new recruits at the police academy of Abuja, after having been a Special Skills Officer in the CIA?"

"Look, I'm sure he is not going to—" Berenson began, before cutting himself short. "Let's wait until we are at Penn station."

As the Express 2 train carrying Berenson and Underhill pulled away from the station at 72nd Street, Conrad Richter hailed a cab on Broadway and 91st. He wasn't sure if he was being followed, but he would find out soon enough and if necessary take appropriate counter-measures.

He had prepared for this eventuality a long time ago, but never really expected it to happen. At times, the bug-out bag in the corner of his walk-in closet had almost seem silly, the indulgence of an overly cautious—some would say paranoid—mind. But, as his grandfather and the Marines had taught him, being prepared is half the battle, so silly or not, he had kept making sure he would be ready to go on a moment's notice. The bug-out bag held two sets of clothes, two sets of clean identity papers—passport, driver's license, credit card—$50,000 in $100 bills, €20,000 in €100 bills and £10,000 in £50 bills, a first-aid kit, a toiletries kit that also included a tube of temporary dark-brown hair dye, brown-colored contact lenses and clear lens horn-rimmed glasses, and a Glock 23 with four 13-round magazines. To this, he had added Zimmerman's custom-made plastic gun, the drone, the remaining two Splenda packets containing ricin powder and the Greenwald identity papers.

He told the cab driver to go to Times Square, where it would be easy enough to disappear in the crowds. From there, he would take one of the many cabs at Duffy Square, on 7th Avenue and West 47th Street, and get to a car rental agency on Federal Circle, at JFK. In a restroom, he would first change his appearance to that of Jack Dresden, one of the two clean identities, then rent a car under his new name—preferably something similarly inconspicuous as the black Chevy Tahoe he owned but which he had to abandon because it was registered in his own name—drive upstate and go off-road after 50 miles or so, to confirm he was indeed not being followed. Tomorrow, he would return to the city and get a room in some run-of-the-mill hotel—also in the name of Dresden—and wait.

He was close, too close now, not to go through with it. Strikingly, that had been one of the first things going through his mind as he had grabbed the bug-out bag. As much as he had been alarmed by the visit of the two FBI agents, he had also quickly realized they didn't have much on him, or else they wouldn't have taken such an oblique line of questioning. They were on a fishing expedition, and the question about Dieter Zimmerman revealed that the Swiss gunsmith was probably the source of the trail that had led them to him. But how? How had they gotten to him, after all these years? The man lived like a recluse, always alone, no kids. He had lived in that house for as long as he knew him, had a regular job, always wore those same boring charcoal-grey suits. Not exactly the kind of person that regularly showed up on the radar of police investigators.

But whatever the case, Zimmerman was not a hardened criminal and had probably sung like a canary, so he should assume that whatever the little gunsmith knew about him, the FBI now also knew. He couldn't immediately figure out exactly how Zimmerman's information could have led them to him—since Dieter didn't know his real name—but the fact that they knew the gunsmith's name and had asked him about his whereabouts on September 12—the day he had taken delivery of the drone—was simply too much of a coincidence to be a coincidence.

Berenson leaned across the table in Al's Diner, across the street from Penn station, and said softly: "I'm sure no one would murder a U.S. presidential candidate just for kicks. People killing or wanting to kill politicians are fanatics, crazies or hired guns, and the guy we're looking for is clearly the latter."

Underhill took a slurp from his coke. "I'm not saying he's not getting paid, or that he wouldn't want to get paid, all I'm saying is that we shouldn't discard Conrad Richter simply because he has a spartan apartment."

"So you think it could be him."

"Like I said, I think it's someone *like* him. But when we asked him about Zimmerman he didn't seem startled. As far as I could tell, it looked like he'd never heard of him."

"I agree."

"Tell you what, though," Berenson added, pointing his finger at Underhill, "if it really is him and he is as well-trained and experienced as we think he is, he has probably packed his bags already. In fact, he'll probably be out of New York before we are."

Underhill put his glass back down. "You think we should double-back, have a look?"

Berenson considered it for a moment, but then dismissed it. "Nah. If we do that with all of them it will add days to our schedule, and I don't think nurse Ratched will look too kindly on that."

"Longstreet? She doesn't look kindly on anything," Underhill scoffed. "Honestly, I feel sorry for the guy who has to live with her. Or the gal. Which is it, do you know?"

"Guy. But she's divorced. Rumor has it she's dating."

Underhill snickered. "Who would want to be dating her? Unless they're into sadomasochism of course."

Berenson smiled. "Come on now, that's not very nice. I'm sure she's not the same person at home as she is at the office."

"Yeah, well, I'm sure she is," Underhill shot back.

"Anyway, back to the matter at hand," Berenson said sternly but with a playful undertone, "I was thinking we could revisit the most promising candidates after we've talked to all of them. Because if it turned out someone indeed flew the coop, that would be a strong indication we have found our man."

37

Ronald Drump was nearing the end of his speech at the packed, 1,600-seat Mystère Theater, at the Treasure Island Hotel in Las Vegas. The crowd was boisterous as usual and had welcomed his stump speech points on the dangers of terrorism, immigration and jobs disappearing to China with roars of approval. But there was one person who hadn't come to hear Ronald Drump talk about the many things threatening the country and how to make America Amazing again. He had come to kill him.

In the finale, Drump always regurgitated the best bits, the ones that had received the most yelling and booing, to make sure he would leave his supporters even more fired up than he had found them.

"African-American youth has a very high percentage of unemployment, okay—it's huge. They want to work, they want to work, but they can't work, they can't work, because we're letting all these people pour into our country and they come from hostile countries, we have no idea who the hell they are, they have no papers, no documentation, they just pour in and these countries that they come from are tremendous in terms of terrorism.

Why are we letting these people in? And Venomous Valery

wants to let in even more, she wants to increase it by 500 percent. I'm telling you folks, we're going to have big problems if Valery Clayton becomes president. If you think Orlando was the end of it—with that pathetic, weak attitude of this president that we have—think again, because it wasn't folks, it wasn't. Unless we become tough and vigilant again, like we were before, because we have to say: 'you know, I'm sorry, but you're from a region in the world that has a lot of Muslims, and it's radical Islamic terrorism. It's a whole new thing.' We should be letting in more people from Europe, not from Africa and the Middle East and Turkey, because it's terrorism. It's a whole new thing."

Mark Bryson, a 20-year-old British national who had been living illegally in Hoboken, New Jersey, for almost two years, had followed Mr. Drump's prodigious rise and disparaging demeanor with growing frustration. Back home, he had lived in an assisted living apartment reserved for people with mental health issues—in his case Asperger syndrome—but in January 2015 he had impulsively decided to go to the United States, emptied his bank account and traveled to New York City under the Visa Waiver Program.

At first he had stayed at a budget hotel in Brooklyn, but after he ran out of money he had taken to living in his car, a 2006 Chrysler Town & Country he had bought for a song.

"And it's not guns. It's terrorism. And terrorism, you know, it's a terrible thing. I mean in the past, we had wars, you know, we would fight the British—like we did during the revolution, you know, when our amazing ancestors fought against the British Empire—we would fight the Japanese, and the Mexicans—yeah, you know this right, we fought wars with the Mexicans, we kicked their ass many times—but at least they were in uniforms, you could recognize them. But now, with these terrorists, we don't know who the hell they are. But we know they're Muslims, they're radical Islamists, they are from these countries like Syria, Afghanistan, Pakistan, and all those other 'stans', and all they want is to kill us. And it's gotta stop."

On September 26, 2016, after seeing the first presidential debate, Bryson abruptly decided he was going to do what he had already been dreaming of for over a year. That same night, he got tickets for Ronald Drump's next available rallies—one in the Treasure Island Hotel in Las Vegas, the other in Phoenix, Arizona, a few days later— and just like he had up and left his apartment in South London to fly to New York, he now put his clunky Chrysler in drive and left the street where he had parked for almost a year to embark on the 2,500 mile road trip to Las Vegas, Nevada.

"But I'm telling you, it's not going to stop with President Obama, and it's certainly not going to stop with Venomous Valery, right? Because nobody has the guts, nobody has the guts to do what has to be done—what I will do—to ban all Muslims from coming in until we have a way of tracking the bad ones, of stopping the bad ones. Because not all of them are bad, but a lot of them are."

Apart from reserving the tickets for the rallies, the only other preparation Bryson made was visiting a gun range outside of Denver, Colorado—a few miles from the I-76—to learn how to fire a gun. He had never fired a weapon before in his life, and although he had viewed a few instruction videos on YouTube, he thought he should test-fire at least a few rounds to get more comfortable with the recoil. At the gun range he answered yes to the question if he had any experience with handguns and subsequently picked out a Glock 17 GEN4, renting it for an hour. Contrary to his expectations, he found it relatively easy to fire the gun with reasonable accuracy from a range of about five to ten yards and after firing about 20 rounds he returned the weapon and got on his way again.

"Every time there is a terrorist attack, in San Bernardino, in Orlando, in Paris, in Nice—every time there is another radical Islamist going on a killing spree—a lot of the so-called moderate Muslims are dancing in the streets, you know, and in their living rooms. Dancing. And we have to track them, the Muslims, and stop them from coming in. They're shooting people and pledging themselves to ISIS as they are shooting. And we're letting in millions of people. This could be the great story of the Trojan horse. Because our President is weak and he doesn't protect us, all he does is talk. And he's letting in all these terrorists, and committing us to these bad trade deals with China and Mexico and it's costing us millions of jobs and trillions of dollars.

You know, I know about China, I know it very well, I've done many deals with China, with their biggest banks—they're buying condos like crazy—I know how to deal with China, and Mexico. I'm not knocking China, and I'm not knocking Mexico, and I'm not knocking Japan, I'm not knocking anybody. But they have to start respecting us again, because they don't respect us anymore, they think we're weak.

That's why I'm going to build the wall with Mexico—oh it's coming, believe me, we're going to have the wall, we're going to have the wall—and punish companies for shipping jobs to China and punish the Chinese for manipulating their currency."

The rally itself was an absolute torture for Bryson. Seated somewhere in the middle of the left section of the theater, he had to pretend to be an ardent Drump supporter from overseas, while the over-enthu-

siastic, extravagantly dressed real supporters around him made just
about every numbskull joke known to man about his British accent,
which they thought was 'soooo funny'. He had never been good with
people, had never really understood the need to socialize with them,
but in this case he had no choice. If he wanted to avoid arousing
suspicion, he had to play along. So he put on his best fake smile,
laughed at all the stupid jokes, delighted them with an extra heavy
Oxford English accent, cheered whenever they cheered and booed
whenever they booed.

"You know, the media, the mainstream media, they have these so-called experts that say that it can't be done, that you can't build a wall or punish the Chinese. But I have the smartest people, the most dedicated people, the best people, and they are all saying I'm right.

We are going to make this country great again. We're going to save the Second Amendment, because Valery Clayton wants to take your guns away. You know, in Paris, at that horrible, horrible shooting, only one side had guns—by the way France, toughest gun laws in the world, but that didn't stop the bad guys from having guns, it only stopped the good guys—but if just a few people, a man, a woman, had had a gun strapped to their waist, or their ankle, or inside their jacket, you know, they could have ended that terrible shooting by these Islamist isis fighters. Would have been a whole different story. You know, the hospitals in Paris are still loaded with people, it's terrible, terrible. And Venomous Valery wants to take your guns away, just like those poor people in Paris had no guns. How can we fight isis without our guns? How can anybody not understand that we need our guns to fight all these sick, perverted Muslim terrorists—not just the ones that are still coming in, but the ones already here. We need our guns, and I will make sure we get to keep them."

An upbeat country & western tune began playing over the speakers. Hearing his cue, Drump wrapped it up with his favorite finale. "I will make sure we will win again, that our military will win again, because I'm going to rebuild our military, and I will make sure other countries respect us again. We are going to win so much that you'll be sick of winning!"

As Drump was making his closing remarks, Bryson made his way down, together with other hard-core fans, towards the front of the left side of the stage, which was cordoned off by Las Vegas police officers.

Drump waved a few times, pointed at the crowd, smiled, and withdrew to the side of the stage, where his fans were clamoring for a handshake, an autograph, a personal remark, or just one of his signature broad smiles from up close and personal. No matter how big the crowds he drew, how loud the shouts of approval, this moment right after the speech, with his most ardent fans, was what Ronald Drump loved the most.

It was also the moment the Secret Service hated the most. Briefing a candidate on the exit procedure before an event was standard security procedure, but the special agents who were part of Drump's protection detail had quickly learned it was of little use in his case, because he would never forgo an opportunity to touch base with his fans.

He absolutely loved it when they pushed and shoved and elbowed each other to be as close to him as possible, even more when they were holding up his book, 'The Art of the Steal', for him to sign. He loved hearing them yell anxiously, almost desperately: "Mr. Drump! Mr. Drump!", followed by some request, ranging from 'would you sign your book' to 'do you have a job for me, I'll even work for free'. These were his people, his followers, his believers. How could he ignore them, how could he let them stand out in the cold, bereft of his presence, when they were so close? No, whatever the Secret Service guys said, he would always make time for the crowds nearest to the stage.

The LVPD officers sent to increase security and—more importantly—help with crowd control, had all been briefed by the Secret Service on the normal course of events during a Drump rally. That they should not be alarmed by angry shouting, heckling or aggressive chanting, and that at the end of the rally many supporters would try to make their way to the stage with Drump books, baseball caps, T-shirts and other paraphernalia, for an impromptu meet & greet with the candidate, who always took the time for his fans.

By the time Drump arrived at the left-side of the relatively small stage, there were so many people there that the police officers were being pushed against the stage by the crowd. Bryson struggled to get in front of a police officer standing less than ten yards away from Drump—who was shaking hands with some fans and signing a few books and baseball caps—and asked the officer to help him get Mr. Drump's autograph. In the split second Jamal Jenkins looked over his left shoulder to see where the candidate was—a reaction triggered more by instinct than a desire to help the young Brit—Bryson reached for the holstered but unlocked sidearm on officer Jenkins' right hip. He grabbed the gun and pulled it out of the holster, but before he had it completely out and ready to aim at Drump—who, unaware of the altercation taking place just a few yards to his right, was still shaking hands and smiling benevolent-

234

ly to the restive crowd below him—Jenkins' right hand prevented Bryson from completing the motion. With his other hand, he punched the would be-assassin in the throat, making him release the sidearm.

Twenty seconds later, officer Jenkins quietly led a cuffed and subdued Mark Bryson out of the Mystère Theater, while Ronald Drump was signing a T-shirt with the text 'Make America Amazing Again' printed on it in the colors of Old Glory.

38

When Conrad Richter read about Mark Bryson's amateurish assassination attempt he softly cursed. One idiot trying to grab a cop's sidearm and weeks of planning could be down the drain. After all, a small poacher could scare big game away. If Drump had any sense, he wouldn't get so close to his devoted supporters anymore after a rally or debate, making it much harder—if not impossible—for Veldman to get a clear shot from a reasonable distance.

He took the laptop off his lap, put it next to him and scooted down on the bed a bit, laying his head on the pillow. If this were any other target, he would have stepped away by now—actually he would've stepped away a week ago already, right after those FBI agents were out the door. But he knew he couldn't. This was the big one. Ten million dollars. A legendary hit. If he pulled it off, he could retire in luxury, maybe find a quiet farm in Tuscany and write his memoirs, or go somewhere cooler, like the Northern part of Norway, buy a tract of land there with a nice log cabin on it, hunt for moose and enjoy the silence. No, he couldn't step away now. It was worth the risk.

While Richter was laying low, dreaming about farms and log cabins and practicing flying the drone—which he soon mastered to perfection—Berenson and Underhill were crisscrossing the country to interview each of the twelve people on their list individually, with the exception of William O'Keefe, who had died in a car crash in his hometown of Boston, Massachusetts, in 2004, a fact confirmed by O'Keefe's mother and widow.

Two hours after talking to Conrad Richter, they had met with John Conley in his dingy office in the back of a Wendy's in Jersey City, one of three he owned. His blubbery, 300-pound figure belied his former existence as a paramilitary sniper for the CIA, but unlike Richter he was nice enough to confirm he had indeed worked for the clandestine branch of the Central Intelligence Agency in the early 1990s, though without going into specifics. They also interviewed a few employees about Mr. Conley's presence at their workplace, and they all confirmed he was always there, except for a couple of weeks during the summer and the last week of December. Those interviews were really a formality, though, because Mr. Conley could hardly lift a binder without gasping for air, let alone a fifteen-pound sniper rifle. It would be a miracle if he lasted the decade.

From Jersey City they traveled to Albany, Georgia, to talk to Winston Washington, Jr., Albany's mayor since 2012. Contrary to Conley, Washington still looked very much like a one-man war machine, albeit one with a disarming smile and a thousand dollar suit. He too confirmed he had at one time been employed by the CIA's Directorate of Operations, while his staff confirmed he was almost always the first one to arrive and the last one to leave, driving the interns crazy with his dedicated work ethic. In short, even if Washington still seemed physically very capable of living a mercenary's life, he simply lacked the time for it.

Martin Hernandez was a different story. He lived in Jupiter, Florida, not far from the headquarters of GenX Security, where he was employed as a security advisor. Contrary to most of the others on the list, Hernandez had not worked as a Special Skills Officer at the Directorate of Operations, but at the CIA's Counterintelligence Center. He was vague and uncooperative, but at the same time very observant. At first, his company was equally unhelpful, but after a short phone call from Longstreet, who happened to be friendly with one of GenX's senior executives, the company confirmed Martin Hernandez traveled extensively in his capacity as security advisor for some of GenX's biggest clients, which included multinationals and governments on all five continents.

According to U.S. flight records, Hernandez had traveled to Turkey on August 17, returning stateside on September 21. Seeking clarification on whether he had traveled anywhere else from Turkey in the meantime, Berenson reached out to INTERPOL Ankara for access to Turkish flight records. The response had been slow and unhelpful, though, perhaps in reaction to the United States' continued refusal to extradite the Turkish cleric and political figure Fethullah Gülen, for supposedly masterminding the failed coup of July 15 against his rival, Turkish President Recep Tayyip Erdogan.

Berenson would continue to press the Turks for the flight records, but all things considered they agreed Hernandez was probably not the man they were looking for. His reaction to their question about gunsmith Dieter Zimmerman had been one of seemingly genuine surprise and his general demeanor and employment history at the CIA pointed more to a career as a spook than a sniper.

Their next stop was Huntsville, Alabama. Like Conley, Mark Chandler had put on more than a few pounds since retiring from the CIA in perfect physical condition. His wife was partly to blame for it, though, as Berenson and Underhill experienced first hand when she regaled them with artisanal French cheeses, homemade chicken liver pâté, toast and white wine—not forgetting to join in herself—followed some twenty minutes later by homemade tiramisu with a splash of Amaretto Disaronno, "a veritable match made in heaven", as Mr. Chandler echoed Mrs. Chandler.

Another source of Mr. Chandler's morbid obesity seemed to be his job as a high-powered salesman at Remington Arms. Chandler regularly traveled the country to meet his clients—mostly large hunting and sporting goods stores and chains—but they also regularly visited the Remington plant in Ilion, New York, and the new plant in Huntsville, Alabama. Client visits always consisted of elaborate demonstrations of the newest rifle types, hunting trips and copious dinners.

Chandler's 2016 U.S. flight records revealed two dozen domestic flights so far this year, but nothing international. And since his busy calendar and traveling schedule in August and September really left no room for an unnoticed trip to Europe on a different passport, they scratched him off the list.

In Jackson, Mississippi they talked to Dexter Lawrence, who, like most of the others, had been a Special Skills Officer in the Clandestine Service, before leaving the Central Intelligence Agency in 1993. After working a few years in construction, he had started his own construction business and done quite well for himself. Soft-spoken and mild-mannered, Lawrence hardly came off as a former paramilitary scout sniper doing CIA wet jobs, though his still excellent physical condition would certainly not have prevented him from a continued career as a hired gun. But, as with Wendy's franchiser John Conley, Lawrence simply lacked the time for a secret life as an elite sniper, being completely devoted to his business, a fact corroborated by his employees.

The same held for Richard Lamotte, who for the last twenty years had owned a biker bar in New Orleans. Lamotte was 57, but with his dyed, half-long hair, tanned face and muscular build—emphasized by a tight-fitting white T-shirt—he looked at least ten years younger. The bar's customers didn't make the slightest attempt to mask their contempt for the two 'suits'—especially the blond and neatly coiffed Underhill—but from the derisive mumbling under their beards and horseshoe mustaches, the two special agents gathered that the bar was never closed and Lamotte had not missed a single day of work in the past twenty years, unlike "most of those pansy-ass, whining liberal hippies" American society nowadays produced according to the bar's clientele. They could of course be lying simply for the hell of it—a distinct possibility in this case—but Lamotte's first reaction to their question about Dieter Zimmerman was a high-pitched mocking "who!?", followed by repeating the gunsmith's name in a rather successful imitation of a German accent, to the laughter of his customers.

Then there was David Haldane, who owned a large gun store in Wichita Falls, Texas. He wasn't there when they visited, though, and employees confirmed Haldane was frequently absent. After some gentle persuasion, two female employees divulged he was having an affair with another employee—apparently not his first—whom he regularly took on extensive romantic trips under the guise of visiting gun shows. According to Haldane's U.S. flight records, he had traveled from Dallas to São Paulo on September 10 and should have returned yesterday, October 5th, but he wasn't at home—and neither was his wife, for that matter. The girlfriend's address was a room in a cheap hotel off Route 277, but there was nobody there either and the bored receptionist told them she hadn't seen the girl in almost a month.

Berenson had a gut feeling there was something fishy about Mr. Haldane, just not that he was the assassin they were looking for. For one, he would have had to have flown to Zurich the day after he arrived in São Paulo—to meet with the gunsmith on September 12—then fly back to São Paulo and on October 5 return to Dallas, Texas. It was possible, but not probable. And then there was the girlfriend, who would be a deliberate witness to this highly suspicious travel activity, an unlikely loose end for the kind of elite contract killer who has managed to stay in business for over 20 years. No, they would ask the two female employees to let them know when Haldane or his girlfriend showed up, but whatever he was involved in, he was most likely not their man.

From Wichita Falls Berenson and Underhill drove back to Dallas and boarded a plane for San Diego, which was about an hour's drive from Marine Corps Base Camp Pendleton, where Toby Rizzo was a scout sniper instructor.

On paper, Rizzo was an excellent candidate for a secret second job as a professional hit man. He had been at the top of his class as a young Marine at Camp Pendleton sniper school, had been employed as a Special Skills Officer at the CIA's Special Operations Group from 1989 to 1993 and returned to Camp Pendleton as a scout sniper instructor in 1996, where he had since served without interruption. With his short grey hair, heavy-set eyebrows, attack dog expression and puffed-up chest, Rizzo looked like the kind of guy who could have easily kept on killing for the CIA until well into his eighties, if only the agency hadn't ended his employment due to cutbacks in the early 1990s. But after a short talk with Rizzo, his immediate superior officer and a few of the other instructors, it quickly became clear sergeant major Rizzo was married to Camp Pendleton sniper school and had never left her for more than a few days in a row since re-enlisting in '96.

The trip to San Diego County was not entirely for nothing, though, because Rizzo did confirm Marine scout snipers have a special love for the M40A1 rifle. Extolling the many virtues of the "greatest sniper rifle ever to have seen the light of day", he even seemed to become a little moist-eyed. When Underhill subsequently gave Rizzo the exact specifications of the M40A1 rifle the 'American' had asked Zimmerman to built in 1994—including the Remington trigger tuned to 2.5 pounds, the USMC modified trigger guard, the McMillan M40A1-HTG stock and the Unertl 10x fixed-power scope—the sniper instructor confirmed that the person who ordered that rifle was very likely an ex-Marine who had started his scout sniper training between the late 1980s and 1990s, because it was exactly how M40A1s were built by the Quantico armorers during that period. He said he even knew a couple of ex-Marines himself from that era who owned an M40A1, custom-made by a quality gunsmith.

Interestingly enough, one of those ex-Marines turned out to be Steven Dykman, who owned a ranch near Livingston, Montana. Taking a Delta flight from San Diego to Salt Lake City on October 13, at 6:18 in the morning, Berenson and Underhill arrived at Salt Lake City International Airport at 9:14 a.m., where they boarded a Bombardier CRJ700 regional jet for the 9:45 flight to Bozeman Yellowstone International Airport, arriving there at 11:13 a.m. At Bozeman they rented a four-wheel Ford Explorer, to take them to the 1,000-acre Blueberry Creek Ranch, which was nestled against the Absaroka-Beartooth Wilderness. As they drove up to the log home, perched on a green hill and flanked by a small forest on the west side and a lake on the east side, Dykman was already standing on his porch, rifle in hand.

Upon exiting their car, Dykman asked them what they were doing on his land. Berenson showed him his FBI badge from about ten yards away, but Dykman just shrugged. "Doesn't take too much to fake one of those things," he grumbled. "In any case, I don't know what they look like, so why don't you just state your business."

His standoffish demeanor and imposing figure, not to mention the rifle barrel resting on his arm, made it clear Steven Dykman was a man not to be trifled with. After giving him the same explanation they had given the others—that they were questioning elite snipers in their late forties or fifties, in connection to a murder by a sniper from an extremely long range—Dykman rubbed his salt and pepper beard for a bit, looking from Berenson to Underhill before mockingly uttering: "uh-huh."

In the uncomfortable question-and-answer exchange that followed, the Marine-turned-rancher proved about as cooperative as a 100-year-old oak tree is with an Italian roadster smashing into it.

To the question where he was on September 12, he answered "here", and when they asked him whether he had at one time been employed by the CIA, he suggested they "drive that shiny Ford Explorer to Langley, Virginia, and ask 'em". When Underhill asked Dykman if he had a permit for the rifle he was holding—forgetting for a moment he was in Montana—the rancher grinned and said: "Second Amendment is my permit son. Issued on December 15, 1791, and it never expires." And to the question if he knew a Dieter Zimmerman, Dykman almost immediately answered: "Nope, don't know him", without his facial expression changing even in the slightest.

Seven minutes later Berenson and Underhill were back in their car, with the log cabin and its owner, still standing on the porch, in the rearview mirror. "Well, he definitely stays on the list," Underhill said. "Trained by the Marines, employed as a Special Skills Officer by the CIA, no wife, no children, no discernible stream of income and extremely guarded and uncooperative. I mean, the guy welcomed us with a rifle in his hand. Is that how he greets all his guests?"

"I don't think he gets many guests," Berenson said, as he drove back to Livingston over the sandy road.

"I'm telling you, that guy has 'professional hit man' written all over him," Underhill continued. "Let's go ask around in the town and see what we can find out about him." Berenson nodded, but he was less convinced about Dykman than his partner. The man was aloof, guarded, unpleasant, yes, but that was hardly exceptional. Maybe Steven Dykman was just a loner who wanted to interact as little as possible with the rest of the world.

Twenty-four hours later they were sitting on a zafu yoga cushion on a sunny rooftop terrace in downtown Toulouse. With the typical Toulouse-red rooftops of neighboring buildings to his back, yogi Shandor—formerly known as Joseph Moretti—smiled benevolently as he poured them both a cup of piping hot herbal tea.

"Quite a view you have here Mr. Moretti," Underhill said, gesturing with his hands to the city in front of him.

"Shandor, please," the former Marine scout sniper and instructor at CIA training facility Camp Peary requested with an even broader benevolent smile.

It was true, the feisty little Italian-American from Brooklyn, who had once held the record for longest sniper shot at Marine Corps Base Quantico scout sniper school, was long gone. Before them sat a slim yet muscular, relaxed, bald-headed sixty-year-old man who seemed at peace with the world.

"So, yoga huh?" Underhill said, feeling slightly nervous around the contently smiling man wearing nothing but loose-fitting white cotton pants.

"Ashtanga vinyasa yoga, to be precise, but it's so much more than just yoga, special agent Underhill. It is *asana*—posture—as well as *pranayama*—breathing—and *drishti*—looking," Shandor smiled, explaining each term with gestures. It is about purification of the body, the nervous system and the mind. Yoga is but a vessel, a vessel to meditation, which itself is but a vessel to enlightenment and true, inner happiness."

"Wow," Underhill grinned, "and here I thought it was just some Indian gymnastics for pretty young women in stretch pants."

"No, that is not at all what it's about," Shandor said, managing to keep his benevolent smile shining, albeit with a hint of restraint.

"Anyway, Mr. Moretti—I mean Shandor—" Berenson began, seeking to interrupt what could be the beginning of a pointless philosophical argument about the path to happiness, "we are questioning certain elite snipers who served in the U.S. special forces in the late 1980s, early 1990s and subsequently in the Central Intelligence Agency."

"Ah yes," Shandor responded, sliding back into his position of enlightened benevolence.

"Did you serve in the U.S. Marine Corps between 1984 and 1988 and were you after that employed as an instructor at Camp Peary by the CIA?" Berenson asked.

"Well, Joseph Moretti was…" the lightly dressed Ashtanga vinyasa yoga teacher offered, before adding, in response to Berenson's unwavering expression: "yes, he was—I mean I was. But you have to understand that was in a former life. That person does not exist anymore. The best explanation I could offer as to what happened to him—at least to an unenlightened layman such as yourself—is that he died and moved on to a higher plane of existence, where Shandor was born."

Berenson and Underhill looked at each other. "Right…" they responded in sync.

"So… do you still keep up your sniper skills? Because from what we understand you were a hell of a shot back in the day."

"No," Shandor said, as sweet and caring as saying no could ever sound.

"No firearms in the house then?"

"No. But you are of course welcome to look around special agent Underhill. As are you special agent Berenson."

"No thanks, we don't have any jurisdiction here," Berenson said.

"Oh but that's quite alright. I am gladly giving you my full permission to go through what little things I have."

The two special agents looked at each other again. "No, no, I don't think that is really necessary."

"Don't forget to drink your tea gentlemen, its herbs are best absorbed while the tea is still hot."

"Right, yes, of course." Underhill took a small sip of the terrible smelling tea. Yuck, tasted the same.

"Just to be thorough, can I ask you where you were on September the 12th?" Berenson asked, while Underhill kept looking as if he had just swallowed a dead mouse.

"Can I ask what day that was?"

Berenson looked at the notes on his phone. "Ehmm, a Monday."

"Mondays I always give my Chakra Wisdom Course," he smiled somewhat embarrassed. "It is also the one course I sometimes still have difficulty teaching in French. I can give you a list of my students if you'd like."

"That would be great," Berenson nodded.

"Oh darn it," Shandor slapped his knee, "I just remembered something. The Chakra Wisdom Course was canceled that day, because I was grieving for the victims of 9/11."

"On September 12?" There was a hint of confusion in Underhill's voice.

"Yes, this year the attacks happened exactly fifteen years ago, so I decided on a three-day mourning period."

"I understand," Underhill said. "Did you, ehh... have friends or relatives who lost their lives during the attack?"

"Yes, yes I did, sadly enough. My mother's cousin."

"So on September 12 you were... ?"

"Right here, meditating, from 7:00 in the morning to 7:00 in the evening."

"And can anyone verify that?" Berenson asked.

"Well, no... other than that my students can attest to the fact that the course was indeed canceled."

"Alright, I think we have enough information for the moment," Berenson said.

"Of course," Shandor said, getting up from his lotus position. "I'm sorry I could not be of more help to you," he gestured them towards the stairs.

"Oh, that's quite alright. As I indicated before, this was mainly a routine formality."

"One for which you nevertheless came all the way to the south of France."

"Well, we had to be in Europe anyway," Berenson explained. "Speaking of which, do you happen to know a Mr. Dieter Zimmerman?"

For a split second the benevolent smile disappeared and Moretti's pupils widened. But the next moment the smile was back again, though remaining limited to the immediate area around the mouth this time. "No, can't say that I do. Should I?"

A few minutes later they crossed the *Place du Capitole*, in the center of Toulouse. "Yoga teacher my ass," Underhill said. "That guy has something to hide."

Berenson nodded. "I agree, but we are on foreign soil and we really don't have anything solid on him. Our best chance still is that the Swiss *Kriminalpolizei* gets Zimmerman to cooperate, so he can help us ID our guy. In the meantime, we should get back, write our report and brief Longstreet, see if she wants us to look deeper into the ones on our short list: Conrad Richter, Martin Hernandez, Steven Dykman and Joseph Moretti," Berenson counted them off on his right hand.

"You mean Shandor."

"Oh, shut up."

39

Around the time Jake Underhill tasted the worst tea in his life, Conrad Richter steered his rented black Chevy Tahoe onto the gravel drive of Ed Cahill's shooting range, with Peter Veldman sitting next to him.

Over the past few weeks, the Dutchman had gone from a complete beginner to a surprisingly accurate shooter. Richter knew he should consider himself fortunate—not everybody could be taught to hit a bull's eye from 10 yards in such a short time—but today he had other things on his mind. Today was not about target practice, although Veldman didn't know that yet. Today was the culmination of two months of preparations. After roaming the internet to find a suitable person—someone who viewed Ronald Drump as a 21st century version of Adolf Hitler and who had the character, the conviction and the balls to put his words into action—after grooming that person, getting to know him, testing him, teaching him how to handle a handgun confidently and accurately, this was the day all that work could turn to shit in two minutes.

But that was putting it negatively. Richter had determined early on that a late-stage crash approach would have the highest probability of success. Had he tried to recruit Veldman earlier, the Dutchman would have had weeks to change his mind, an ocean of time, for second-guessing, getting cold feet or contacting law enforcement authorities out of remorse or God knows what else. This was a civilian after all, an amateur, and a troubled one at that. The more time he would get to fuck things up, the more likely he would do just that. So he had decided it was to be today, two days before the actual event.

In his backpack he had Zimmerman's plastic 9mm derringer, assembled and ready for use. He had also brought the Glock 17 and 26, to start off with.

"So I looked up some information about the deer hunting season in upstate New York, and guess what?" Veldman said, as they walked to Cahill's farmhouse in the early afternoon sun.

"What?" Richter said automatically, while going over the different scenarios of the coming session in his mind.

"The regular hunting season starts next week, October 24," Veldman said, his eyes lighting up. "We should totally go! What do you think?"

"Eh yeah, sure, that's a great idea."

"There's one thing, though," Veldman continued, as they climbed the wooden stairs up the porch, "I'd have to learn how to shoot a rifle. Do you know any good sniper rifles? You know, with a scope on it and everything?"

Richter halted on the porch for a moment. "Yeah, I think I can arrange something like that. But first I have to show you something else."

"Like what?"

"Patience, young *Padawan*, patience," Richter smiled, opening the ramshackle door to the shooting range's equally run-down reception.

When they came in, Ed Jr. was watching *The Godfather II* on his phone and had just started shoving a homemade two foot sub into his mouth, four layers of indistinct pink meat slices hanging over the side, a few drops of mustard and ketchup dropping on the counter.

" 'On, 'Eter!" Ed Jr. greeted his customers enthusiastically by name, without bothering to take the sandwich out of his mouth or even stop the biting motion.

"Afternoon Ed, sorry to interrupt your lunch there," Richter smiled.

"What?" Ed pulled out his earphones.

"Your lunch. Sorry to interrupt it."

"Oh don't worry about it," Ed said, fiercely mauling the bread, meat and sauce into one big mush, which was turning over in his open mouth like clothes in a washing machine. "What can I do for you today? A lane? Some specific guns?"

"Just the lane today Ed," Richter said.

"Sure. Why don't you take the number one, right outside," he pointed. "You can pay when you come back. Finish my lunch first."

"Actually, can we take the number ten? I think it's slightly longer?"

"Well yeah, but only by about 25 yards or so," Ed responded, studying his sandwich as if it was an artifact, before taking a big chunk out of the right side. "Besides," he continued with his mouth full again, a piece of meat hanging from the left corner of his mouth, "you're 'oing 'andgun shooting right? Or did you bring your rifle today?"

"No, but I want to try something new and we might need a longer range for that," Richter lied.

"Suit yourself. It's all the way at the end of the range, though. Well, you know that."

Yes he did. That was the point.

Richter nodded. "Okay, see you later Ed, enjoy the rest of your sandwich."

"Bye Ed." Veldman said, following Richter out the door.

The number ten lane was the outermost lane, running parallel to the edge of the forest on its left. It was also about 100 yards from the farmhouse. Junior was usually too busy playing games or watching movies on his phone and rarely bothered keeping an eye on the lanes anyway, but today Richter wanted to make extra sure not to draw the chubby gun fetishist's unexpected attention.

After Veldman had fired about twenty rounds at the cardboard target from ten yards away, all hitting the center of the chest area, Richter got the palm-sized two-shooter from his backpack.

"Here, why don't you try this," he said, more commanding than casual, holding out the small pistol as Veldman was pushing 9mm rounds in one of the empty 17-round magazines.

Veldman looked at the gun and stopped loading the mag. "Wow, what is that!? Is that thing real? It looks so tiny."

"It is tiny, and very real. Here, take it."

The Dutchman put down the magazine and took the derringer in his hand. "It's made of plastic?"

"Yeah."

"Where'd you get it? I mean, you can't buy this at a local gun shop, can you?" Veldman weighed the gun in his hand and turned it around. "Where do you load it?"

"Here, let me show you." Richter took the gun back, pushed down the small lever on the left side of the gun to uncouple the barrel from the extended lower part of the grip, and pulled the double-stacked barrel up, exposing its backend. "See? Okay, so it's a 9mm, like you're used to, but it's not a semi-automatic, which means you have to cock the hammer each time you fire."

Taking two bullets, he put one in the upper and one in the lower barrel, then clicked the double-stacked barrel back in its place.

"Without the hammer being cocked, pulling the trigger won't do anything, see?" Richter pulled the trigger to show him.

"But, if I cock the hammer, like so—best to do it with the joint of your thumb by the way, not the soft pad, because it can be tricky—then aim at the target, and…."

Bang! The bullet went right through the head of the cardboard target.

"Fuck, that was loud!" Veldman cried excitedly.

"I know. It's because of the extremely short barrel, only 2.5".

Bang! Another one through the head.

"So how do you determine which barrel fires?" Veldman asked. "Because I can see only one trigger, one hammer."

"Ah, yes, good question." Richter cocked the hammer back. "You see, the front of the hammer has a firing selector. It rises and drops each time you cock the hammer. If it's up, it will fire the upper barrel. If it's down, it will fire the lower barrel."

Showing the firing selector to Veldman, he continued: "It's best to make sure the hammer is in the lower position for your first shot, because the sight is aligned for the lower barrel. So what you would do, is align front sight and rear sight for the first shot, fire, cock the hammer again, align the sights again and then compensate slightly for the second shot coming from the upper barrel, meaning it will hit slightly higher."

He reloaded the derringer, clicked the barrel back in its place and handed the gun to Veldman. "Obviously, it's not the most accurate gun, but from 10 to 15 yards it's accurate enough, and just as deadly as any other 9mm. Come on, try it."

Veldman adopted the fighting stance, wrapped his right hand around the small rubber grip, his left hand around his right hand and cocked the hammer with his left thumb. He aimed the front sight at the target, aligned it with the rear sight and gently squeezed the trigger while keeping his focus on the front sight.

Bang!

The bullet had completely missed the cardboard target.

Veldman looked up. "Huh? Where'd it go? Did the bullet come out?"

"Oh it came out," Richter responded dryly, "you were just too afraid of the loud bang to keep it steady. Do it again, but this time don't be afraid."

"Don't be afraid. Right," Veldman mumbled under his breath as he aimed the front sight at the center of the chest area again. He cocked the hammer.

"Don't forget to compensate for the upper barrel," Richter said quietly.

"Ok..." he was in fact forgetting that. As he re-aligned his sight, he thought about how light the gun was, couldn't be more than a couple of ounces. Alright, front and rear sight were aligned, compensating for upper barrel, gently... squeezing... the... trigger, focus on the sight—focus on the sight...

Bang!

"Well, at least this time you hit the board," Richter smiled. It had in fact gone through the upper left corner, about five inches from the head.

"Yeah, but I was aiming for the chest."

"Details, details. Come on, try again."

About half an hour and 50 shots later, Veldman had gotten the hang of it and could hit the chest area with both shots from a distance of 10 yards. He was more accurate with the Glock, but even if both bullets would miss the heart, two 9mm bullets in the chest would almost always be lethal.

"I'm beginning to like this gun," Veldman said, as he pushed down the lever and routinely flipped the barrel part open to reload it. "I mean, it's so small and light, I can't believe it. I knew plastic guns existed, I read about that gun that was manufactured with a 3D printer—"

"The Liberator."

"Right, the Liberator. Very impressive of course, but it still looked like a clunky toy gun glued together by a ten-year-old. But this," he aimed the derringer at the cardboard target—now riddled with holes—and cocked the hammer, "this looks and feels awesome!"

Bang! He quickly re-cocked the hammer. Bang!

"It can't be legal, though. I mean, I know it's different for you, being a Secret Service agent, but for normal citizens a gun like this can't be legal. No metal detector could pick it up, it's untraceable and could be completely destroyed in minutes. It's every criminal's wet dream. Not to mention terrorists."

Richter said nothing, he just looked at Veldman.

"So why do you have it? Did you guys confiscate it from someone?"

Richter still said nothing, but kept looking at him.

"What?" Veldman said, sounding confused. "Did I say something wrong?"

Richter walked to one of the tree stumps that passed for chairs at Cahill's shooting range and sat down.

"Few weeks ago, I was on duty on the protection detail of Ronald Drump. We were at some hotel in Pittsburgh—we've been in Pennsylvania a lot, on account of it being an important battleground state. Anyway, that doesn't matter. So we were at this hotel, and his wife decided she wanted to go for a swim in the outdoor pool. In the spur of the moment, Mr. Drump decided he'd join her."

"For a swim?"

"No, he just wanted to see *her* swim. It wasn't the first time, he loves showing her off to whoever is around. Anyway, we had to clear the whole pool area. Mr. Drump said it wasn't necessary, but our SAC—the Special Agent in Charge—insisted it was too risky. So, about 30 minutes later, Amalia was swimming in the pool in a tiny white bikini, Mr. Drump was on the phone and I and three other agents were guarding the pool area."

"Ok…"

"I was standing about 10 yards away from Mr. Drump, when I overheard him say to whoever he was speaking to on the phone that it was 'absolutely possible', that it was 'the only way to fight homegrown, radical Islamic terrorism' and that he already had 'the best legal minds in the country looking into it.'"

"What was?" Veldman asked. "What was 'absolutely possible'?"

"I was wondering the same thing," Richter continued, "so I moved a little closer while looking the other way, pretending I was checking the perimeter. Then I heard him say that Roosevelt had done the same thing, and that extraordinary times asked for extraordinary measures."

"Roosevelt? Which one? Teddy or Franklin? I still don't get it."

"You will. And he meant Franklin, I looked it up later. Anyway, next, he mentioned a couple of states. New Mexico, Montana, Wyoming, North Dakota. At first I thought it was about the election, but then he said something like 'they would easily fit there' and that they would first build all the facilities and then just transport all of them there."

"Who?" Veldman looked confused.

Richter looked him straight in the eye. "Muslims."

"Muslims? What, why? Which Muslims?"

"All of them."

"What? But that's ridiculous, there must be millions of them."

Richter nodded. "2.75 million to be exact. Looked that up as well. And when he mentioned Roosevelt he was probably referring to the internment camps for Japanese citizens during World War II."

"Yeah, but that was different, there was a war on."

"Look, this is what I heard. That he means to relocate all Muslim Americans to internment camps in those four states, presumably to guard and keep them there, or maybe to force them to emigrate, that I don't know."

"Oh my God, I was right…" Veldman whispered to himself. "It's starting all over again."

Richter silently nodded.

"You have to tell someone."

"Who would believe me? I'm just one guy. My career would be over, I mean really over, I'd be lucky to get a job as a security guard at a golf resort. And of course Drump would sue me for every penny I got, which isn't much to begin with. No thank you very much."

"Then we have to stop him," Veldman countered, sounding agitated. "I mean, this is just what we talked about, a chance to kill Hitler before he rose to power. This is exactly that!"

"It is. And that is why I made this gun."

"You made this?"

Richter nodded. "I'm something of a hobbyist when it comes to making guns. I also 3D-printed that Liberator gun a couple of years ago, but designs for plastic guns have enormously improved since then. For this one, I used an existing blueprint for a Bond Arms derringer backup gun and then modified it so it could work as an all-plastic gun. The idea was to take it with me to a rally or something and then shoot Drump in an unguarded moment. Since the bullets would not be coming from my service weapon and the gun is made of plastic, they would likely assume someone had smuggled it in."

"Sounds like a plan."

"Yeah, only these past few days I have never been in a position where I could fire at him unnoticed, or from where it would be viewed as someone shooting from the audience. I mean, there are plenty of moments where I am close enough, really close actually, but 95 percent of the time I'm positioned in a restricted area and the other 5 percent there are always other Secret Service agents around."

Richter sighed. "Bottom line is, even if I got a shot off—which is doubtful—I would never get away with it."

"But you would have saved the country," Veldman said, still reeling from the shocking information he had just heard.

"Yeah," Richter said, sounding resigned and defeated, looking at the ground.

That was the pitch. This was the moment. The next few seconds of silence. All he could do now was wait, like a salesman who has just made his final offer. He waited two, three, five seconds, the longest seconds of his life. He felt a great urge to continue talking, to nudge Veldman closer, rephrase his story, but the rational part of his brain told him to bite his tongue and wait. And that is what he did.

— — —

— — —

— — —

"I'll do it."

Richter looked up. "What do you mean?"

"I mean, I'll do it. I'll kill Drump. At the debate, the day after tomorrow."

"You're out of your mind."

"No, in fact I've never been more sure of anything in my life. I am going to stop him if it's the last thing I do." He sat down on a tree stump across from Richter and leaned forward. "Look, this is a chance most people can only dream of. To actually *do* something about the evil threatening us, instead of looking on helplessly. You know how much I accomplished as the head of the Anti-Fascist League? Nothing. Absolutely nothing. A few counter-demonstrations at some of those pathetic right-wing white-power rallies, a few blog posts denouncing fascist regimes and practices. That's it. Everyone always plays that game of 'what would you do if you met Hitler before 1933', but it's super lame, because fact is he is dead, he did his damage and there is nothing we can do about it now. But this," he pointed to the ground, "we *can* do something about this. And I want to be the one to do it."

Richter scratched his head. "Well, if you're serious... I mean absolutely determined... I suppose I could get the gun inside the Thomas & Mack Center and then hand it off to you there. I could probably also help you get away during the chaos after, even plan an escape route... but no, it's crazy Peter. Let's just forget about it."

But Veldman shook his head. "You know you want me to do this. You didn't show me that gun for nothing."

"Well, I..."

"Don, it's not even important. I want to do this. This is my chance to make everything right in one big blow and I'm going to take it with both hands. You just make sure you get the gun inside the Thomas & Mack Center." He slapped Richter on the shoulder. "We're going to make history together!"

October 19

40

Wednesday, October 19, 2016, 9:30 a.m.,

Criminal Investigative Division Director's

Office, FBI Headquarters, Washington D.C.

"So, where are we?" Claire Longstreet looked at the two special agents sitting in front of her. "How was your tax-funded road trip?"

"We... eh... I mean, I e-mailed you a report yesterday evening?" Underhill said.

"I am well aware of that agent Underhill, don't you think I'm well aware of that?"

—

"Well?"

"Ehm, yes?"

"Yes what?"

"Yes, I think you are well aware of that?"

"Of course I am," she said decidedly. "But I have about 40 other e-mails to plow through before I can get to your little report, so how about you just tell me what you found out?"

"We've narrowed the list of possibles down to four," Berenson said. "Two of them are employed by private military contractors, one owns a ranch in Montana and the fourth is a yoga instructor—of sorts—in Toulouse, France."

"Oh I love France," Longstreet sighed, sounding much softer, almost feminine. "Especially Paris. I love Paris. Where is Toulouse

263

anyway?"

"It's in the south west of France, about 400 miles from Paris."

"Oh." The snarky tone was back instantly. "And why is he still a person of interest?"

"Well, for one, he didn't have an alibi for September 12—"

"None of the four did," Underhill interjected.

"Right," Berenson said.

"Remind me again what happened on September 12?" Longstreet asked.

"That is when the assassin took delivery of the drone and plastic gun in Zurich, from the Swiss gunsmith."

"Right, Herr Bieberman," Longstreet said confidently.

"It's Zimmerman actually, but yes," Underhill corrected her.

"Oh potato potahto. Okay, so no alibi. What else?"

"All four are still in excellent physical condition—something that can't be said of everyone else on the list—while the rancher, Steven Dykman, came off as very guarded and uncooperative—"

"Well, he's a rancher from Montana. Aren't they supposed to be guarded and uncooperative? Frankly, I'm surprised he didn't aim a rifle at you as soon as you stepped on his land."

"Actually, he sort of did."

"Well, there you go," Longstreet gestured. "And the yoga instructor?"

"Joseph Moretti, though he calls himself Shandor these days…"

"As long as it isn't printed on a fake ID he can call himself Krishnamurti for all I care."

"Yes, well, he was also the only one who was visibly startled when we asked him if he knew Dieter Zimmerman."

She looked up. "Hmmm, okay, that *is* interesting. And the other two?"

"Conrad Richter and Martin Hernandez," Berenson said, "They

just both looked and acted very much like mercenary types. Independent, methodical, naturally guarded."

"That's it?"

"That, and the fact that they have no alibi for September 12 and that they qualified to be on the list in the first place."

Longstreet put her hands palms down on the table. "Okay, I think we are sufficiently covered for now. The elections are in less than three weeks anyway. I suggest you do some more background digging into these four persons of interest and maybe revisit the three located here in the U.S. during the next week or so, to see if they're still on the grid. As far as the yoga instructor is concerned, I suggest you reach out to the Legat Office in Paris and ask if they can send someone down to Toulouse to check up on Krishnamurti the Magnificent."

She got up. "Alright, good work gentlemen. Keep me posted."

As Berenson and Underhill left, Longstreet pressed the intercom. "Susan, where is that macchiato you were supposed to get me fifteen minutes ago?"

The two special agents passed Susan's desk on their way out, but it was empty. "Susan!" the intercom blared, "Susan are you there!? Where is my effing macchiato!?"

Ed Cahill Jr. had a problem. A dilemma actually, one asking him to sacrifice his principles for the greater good. That wasn't exactly how he himself would put it, but it was what it came down to. Those who knew him would not likely characterize Ed Jr. as a man of principles, but he did in fact have many principles and rarely, if ever, broke them.

For instance, he strongly believed that people had the duty to defend themselves and others against the 'bad guys' (which is why he would never go anywhere unarmed), that Jesus Christ was his Savior, that the Bible should be taken literally, gay marriage was an abomination, blacks were inherently inferior to whites—actually, all races were inherently inferior to whites—and that the government, especially the federal government, was the root of all evil. And therein, as they say, lies the rub.

Ed Jr. had never been the sharpest tool in the shed, but there were two things he knew a lot about. Guns, and hunting. He loved guns, especially handguns, and being the son of an avid gun collector and owner of a shooting range—where he had worked since dropping out of high school at age sixteen—guns had come as naturally to him as cows did to a kid growing up on a dairy farm.

Ed Jr. knew everything there was to know about handguns. You could name a particular type of gun and he would tell you when it had come in production, which calibers it was chambered for, how many rounds its standard magazine held, what other types of magazines were available for it, what its safety features were, its trigger sensitivity, durability, how it stacked up against comparable types and what he thought of it personally—because he had fired them all. It was almost freakish, really, the breadth of encyclopedic knowledge about handguns this morbidly obese, smelly, racist simpleton commanded. And boy did he love to display that knowledge. It was the one topic he loved to talk about for hours on end, and of which his knowledge was superior to almost everybody else.

So when, two days ago, after he had finished watching *The Godfather* II on his phone and pulled out his noise-canceling earphones, he had heard the loud Bang! of a pistol shot but couldn't immediately make out the type, his attention had been piqued right away. He had listened intently, waiting for another shot, which had come a few seconds later. Bang! Then nothing. He could tell it was coming from one of the outer lanes and it was definitely exceptionally loud. It had reminded him of a Bond Arms derringer, maybe a Snake Slayer, a Ranger II or a Texas Defender, equipped with one of the shorter barrels. 3.5"? 2.5"? Still, something had been off.

Like an oenophile who lets the memory of a single sip of wine linger in his mouth, while patiently dissecting its complex layers of taste and smell, so had Ed Jr. let the memory of that last pistol shot linger in his ears, while patiently dissecting its peculiarities. And when he had finally decided he had never heard that exact sound before, that it couldn't be a Bond Arms derringer even though it was very close, he knew he just had to find out what type of gun it was. So he had grabbed his phone and Sig Sauer P220 Match Elite—his newest and currently favorite gun—gone out the door and plodded the 100 yards of lawn to lane number 10.

It had to be the 10, he had thought, where Don and Peter had gone off to about an hour earlier, to 'try something new', as Don had said. Uh-huh. No, he got it. You had to wake up pretty early in the morning to fool Ed Cahill. Besides, the only two other lanes that had been occupied were the 3 and the 5, and both of them were way too close to be the origin of those two pistol shots.

He hadn't heard any more shots, but when he was at the beginning of lane 9, he had suddenly heard Peter say 'then we have to stop him'. There was something in the way he had said it—serious, agitated—that had made Ed Jr. stop. The next part had been inaudible, but then he'd heard something about 'Hitler rose to power', followed by a clear 'this is exactly that!'.

Sensing it would not be prudent to make his presence known, he had hidden in the shooting station of lane 9. Both the lane separations and shooting stations were constructed from thick oak planks, but he could still easily overhear everything that was being said. When he had heard Peter say he wanted to kill Ronald Drump at the presidential debate, Ed knew he was in real trouble.

After hiding in the shooting station for another minute, his heart racing and straining to breathe silently, he had snuck out and hobbled back to the house as fast he could, while looking over his shoulder about fifteen times and with the butt of the Sig Sauer—stuck under his belt—pushing uncomfortably against his lower back.

After somehow managing to act normal when the two men had returned to the farmhouse to settle their bill, about half an hour later, he had started agonizing over the question whether or not to contact the authorities. That was two days ago.

To the average American citizen, there is no question they would contact law enforcement authorities after accidentally learning of a credible plot to kill a presidential candidate. Most people would likely contact the police or FBI right away, although it is actually the Secret Service that is charged with threats to presidents and presidential candidates, of which there are a lot—even if in most cases the only really serious thing about them is how mentally disturbed those doing the threatening are.

But to someone who is a member of the Pennsylvania Patriots Militia (PPM), which actively trains and prepares for the time federal government encroachment has become so totalitarian and unbearable that a Second (some would say third) American Revolution is the only remedy to 'take America back'—as the founding principles of the PPM state—that question is not so easily answered. Like his father, Ed Cahill Jr. hated the FBI, not least since their militia group had been actively harassed by the Bureau for the last ten years.

On the other hand, he was a huge fan of Ronald Drump, the first presidential candidate he had ever heard who talked some sense. The idea to build a wall to keep the Mexicans out was absolutely genius—why hadn't anybody else ever come up with that—same for the idea to ban the Muslims from coming in. Mr. Drump was rich, successful and he promised to make America respected and admired again. He was exactly the guy America needed, and these assholes were talking of killing him. The more he thought about it, the angrier he got. He should have done something about it himself, but at the time he had just been, well, scared.

Time was running out, though, because they had said they'd do it at the debate, and that was tonight. He had looked it up this morning. It would start at 9:00 p.m. Eastern Time. It was now 3:30 p.m. Eastern Time. If he was going to do anything about this and save Mr. Drump, even if it was with the help of those Federal pig fuckers, he would have to contact them right now.

"Y'ello."

—

Underhill shot up straight. "Yes sir, I mean ma'am, this is Jake Underhill."

—

"No ma'am, I usually say my name."

—

"Yes ma'am, right away."

He hung up and looked at Berenson. "That was Longstreet. She wants us right away, something about the assassination case."

"What?" Berenson said, putting down his sandwich.

"I don't know, she didn't say, only that we have to come over right away." He grabbed his jacket, put it on and stepped into the corridor, with Berenson—sandwich in his mouth, jacket in his hand—just a few steps behind him.

"You can walk right in," Susan waved them on.

Inside, Longstreet was pacing her office. As soon as she saw Berenson and Underhill, she said, without stopping: "Right, I just got off the phone with Eric Johnson from Threat Assessment. He said someone had called the tip desk earlier with information about a plot to kill Ronald Drump, tonight, at the debate, with a plastic gun that looks like a Bond Arms derringer."

The two men looked at each other. "Oh shit, it's him," Underhill said. "Do we have the number of the person that called? We have to get back to them right away."

"Yeah, it's right here," Longstreet said, walking back to her desk. "I was just waiting for you." She took a quick look at the number she had scribbled on her notepad and punched it in, then put the phone on speaker.

ED: "Ed."

LONGSTREET: "Yes, hello, am I speaking to Mr. Ed… Sigsauer?"

ED: "And who might you be?"

LONGSTREET: "My name is Claire Longstreet, Mr. Sigsauer, I'm the head of the FBI's Criminal Investigative Division. I'm calling with regard to the information you gave to our tip desk."

ED: "Uh-huh."

LONGSTREET: "Could you repeat to us what you told them?"

ED: "Us? Who else is there?"

LONGSTREET: "Ah yes, I have special agents Berenson and Underhill here, of the Specialty Weapons Department."

BERENSON: "Good afternoon Mr. Sigsauer."

UNDERHILL: "Afternoon Mr. Sigsauer."

ED: "Yeah, yeah. Look, like I told the other guy, two days ago I had two gentlemen on the range who were firing a weapon I ain't never heard before."

BERENSON: "What were their names?"

ED: "Of the two gentlemen? Jeez, I only know their first names. Don, and the other guy is Peter."

LONGSTREET: "Okay, Don and Peter, please continue Mr. Sigsauer."

ED: "Okay, so I was minding my own business, when suddenly I heard this very loud discharge. I was positive I'd never heard it before. I mean, it sounded a lot like one of those Bond Arms derringers, but not quite like it, you know? I just couldn't stand not knowing, so I went to check it out. But just before I got there, I heard them talking about a plan to kill Ronald Drump, so I stopped and hid myself. I would have arrested them right then and there, 'tis just that I didn't have my gun on me, see? Otherwise I would have stopped them myself, sure as there are tits on a bitch."

BERENSON: "What did they say exactly Mr. Sigsauer?"

ED: "Well, Don was talking about a plastic gun he had made and his plan to shoot Mr. Drump with it, but that the other Secret Service agents were always too close to do it."

LONGSTREET: "I'm sorry, did you say 'other Secret Service agents'?"

ED: "Yeah, from what I understood Don is a Secret Service agent himself as well. Certainly looks like one."

LONGSTREET: "Oh God."

ED: "I'm sorry?"

LONGSTREET: "Nothing Mr. Sigsauer. Please continue."

ED: "Well, then this other guy, Peter, he says that he would do it, that he would kill him at tonight's debate, and then Don said he would smuggle the gun inside for him."

BERENSON: "Do you have a copy of their photo ID?"

ED: "Now why would I have that?"

UNDERHILL: "They are shooting guns at your place aren't they? Are you renting out guns too?"

ED: "Now hold on there Mr. FBI agent, if you're going to be like that I'm hanging up right now. Asking me for photo IDs."

UNDERHILL: "I only—"

BERENSON: "No problem Mr. Sigsauer. But if you'll stand by we'd like to send twelve head shots of persons of interest to your phone, to see if you can identify any one of them."

ED: "You can send all you want mister, but I ain't gonna open any one of them."

BERENSON: "W-what—I don't understand Mr. Sigsauer."

ED: "Look, I know about this, don't think I'm stupid or anything. I know about the worms and the horses and all those computer viruses and shit. You send me an attachment, I open it and before I can say 'hello Dolly' you are spying on me 24/7. No thank you big brother."

UNDERHILL: "Mr. Sigsauer, I assure you we have no interest in spying on you, all we want to know is if you recognize any of the people we think might be involved in this plot."

ED: "Well, you're going to have to come down here then, because I ain't opening anything you send me."

LONGSTREET: "And where are you right now Mr. Sigsauer?"

ED: "Well, don't you know? Aren't you tracing this call?"

BERENSON: ("Shit.")

LONGSTREET: "No Mr. Sigsauer, we are not tracing your call."

ED: "Oh, well, in that case I'm in, ehh… Pittsburgh."

LONGSTREET: "Mr. Sigsauer, I think you are lying."

BERENSON: ("We don't have time for this.") "Alright Mr. Sigsauer, how about you just describe them to us?"

Ed: "Ehm, okay. So Don is, I don't know, tall… about 45, 50 years old… dark-brown hair, in good shape. Peter is in his thirties… also brown hair, average build."

Berenson: "Anything else that you remember? Beard, mustache, glasses, scars, anything like that?"

Ed: "Nope."

Berenson: "Anything at all?"

Ed: "Look, I've told you all I know and I think I've been pretty helpful to you folks. Have to go now, take care."

Klik.

"What the—did he just hung up on us?" Longstreet said. She started to punch the number in again. "That little hillbilly hair-brain redneck mongrel…."

Berenson hit the disconnect button. "There's no point ma'am, he won't tell us more anyway." He looked at his phone. "It is 3:56. We have just five hours until the debate starts. Come on Jake, we have to get to Vegas right away."

41

Even in times of crises, life doles out little pleasures. Because time was of the essence, Longstreet cleared Berenson and Underhill for using one of the helicopters stationed on the roof of the Hoover Building, to take them to Reagan National, a short three miles south of downtown Washington. By car it would have taken them at least fifteen minutes—more if there was heavy traffic on 14 Street Bridge, which, at 4:00 p.m. on a Wednesday, was a virtual guarantee—but the helicopter did it in three.

While they were under way, Longstreet called FBI Director Leavy, briefly explaining the situation and asking him to clear Berenson and Underhill for using the Citation Jet stationed at Reagan National. Leavy said he would be more than happy to, but that a few hours ago he had already given permission to the CTD to use it. Was there another government jet reserved for the DOJ they could use, Longstreet asked. After considering her request for a few moments, Leavy answered they could use one of the two Gulfstream Vs that were normally used to transport the Attorney General and himself, adding he would call ahead right away to arrange for the plane to be relocated from its secret location (because the Gulfstreams are the official transportation for the Attorney General—seventh in line to the presidency—and the FBI Director, they

274

are held in an undisclosed nearby location for security reasons) to Reagan National Airport.

As they waited for the plane to arrive, Berenson and Underhill discussed how the information from the gun range owner fitted with the facts they already had and the conjectures they had distilled from them.

"It can't be a coincidence, it has to be the same gun," Underhill said, leaning against the wall next to the heliport entrance. "Zimmerman wrote the American had specifically asked him to manufacture a plastic version of the Bond Arms Backup derringer and then this guy hears about a plot to kill Drump with a plastic gun that *sounds* like a Bond Arms derringer?" He moved away from the wall, walked a few steps and turned around. "It *has* to be the same gun," he repeated.

Berenson tilted his head a bit. "I agree it certainly looks that way, but that doesn't necessarily make it so. And none of the other elements seem to match."

"What do you mean?"

"For one, we were looking for a single assassin, a professional hit man who we assume has been operating since the mid-1990s. But the gun range owner was talking about two men, one in his mid-thirties—which would make him too young to be our assassin—the other supposedly a Secret Service agent."

"Could be that that guy was lying about being in the Secret Service."

"Yeah, that is certainly a possibility," Berenson agreed, "but the whole thing doesn't exactly come off as thoroughly planned, does it? One guy saying something like 'I'll do it' and the other offering to smuggle the weapon inside, a mere two days before the debate? I don't know, it just doesn't jibe with the experienced, high-value contract killer ordering custom-made weapons from a gunsmith he has worked with for the last twenty years."

"And on top of everything else," Berenson lifted his right index finger in the air like a professor highlighting an important detail, "our assassin didn't just acquire a plastic gun but also a highly sophisticated poisonous drone. Where does that fit in? Where is the drone?"

Underhill sighed in frustration. "I don't know. But you have to admit it's too much of a coincidence that a plastic gun of a specific type is connected to both a gunsmith in Zurich—who delivered such a gun to his long-time client a little over a month ago—and a redneck gun range owner, who says he overheard people talking about killing a presidential candidate with it."

"Okay, so where do we go from here?" Berenson asked, shelving his doubts for the moment.

Underhill started pacing the tarmac. "We have to send some agents to the homes of our remaining four persons of interest ASAP. Because anyone they are able to locate can be scratched off our list."

"You still think one of them is involved in this?"

"I do," Underhill said confidently." I think that older guy, the so-called 'Secret Service agent', could very well be our man. Don't know how the younger man fits in, though..." he mused.

"Alright," Berenson opened his phone and started building a quick to do list. "So, 'get conf on loc of 4 POIs'," he entered. "We should also contact NTAC and make them aware of the situation, so they can escalate it to the protection details of the presidential candidates and the Secret Service detail charged with security at the Thomas & Mack Center itself. I'll do that." He added it to the list.

"And we have to contact the Las Vegas field office," he continued, almost mumbling now, while he added it to his list, "provide them with the ID shots of our four POIs and tell them to start checking the people arriving at the Thomas & Mack Center."

"You think they have facial recognition software running?" Underhill asked, as he was looking up the number of the New York field office.

"What, at the Center? I doubt it. It's a sports arena, not a casino. And we can't use the FBI's Next Generation Identification system either, because it's not our operation. Not sure it would have made much difference in this case anyway, though," Berenson shrugged. "NGI is only accurate 85 percent of the time and that is under optimal conditions, not when it has to recognize a face on the fly out of thousands of people passing a security camera."

Underhill tapped a number on his phone. "Alright, calling the New York field office, see if they can pay Mr. Conrad Richter a visit."

En route to Las Vegas, cruising at 41,000 ft.

"Hold on… ehhh, eh, *attender* please." Underhill put the phone down. "Steve, you speak a little French, don't you?"

Berenson gave him a quizzical look.

"Joseph Moretti?"

Berenson, on hold with NTAC himself, raised his hands to signal his continued confusion.

"Our friend Shandor? In Toulouse?"

"Oh Shandor! Yes of course."

"Help me out here? INTERPOL put me through to the Toulouse

police station but the guy I'm talking to only speaks French and from what I understand his colleagues also only speak French."

"I'm sorry, but I've been on hold with NTAC for the past five minutes and I can't risk losing them. Why don't you call the Legat Office in Paris instead, and ask them to contact the Toulouse police for you?"

"I wanted to do that first, but then I thought calling the French police directly would save time," Underhill said.

They looked at each other and burst out laughing. Ah the French.

A few seconds later, the other side of Berenson's line came alive, and someone introduced himself as Kay Gaylin.

"Yes, Mr. Kaylin, my name is Steve Berenson."

"Gaylin. It's Kay *Gay*lin."

"Mr. Gaylin, okay, pleased to meet you."

"You too Mr. Berenson, you too," Gaylin said, with a voice and accent that reminded Berenson of an exaggerated version of Kinsey Macmaham, the senator from South Carolina.

After Berenson had briefly explained the situation, Gaylin asked a few questions with a soft southern drawl so thick and drawn-out, the FBI agent had a hard time determining if the guy wasn't pulling his leg just to spice up his workday.

"So, these two gentlemen, the males playing with the little gun, what were there names?"

"I only have their first names, Don and Peter."

"Right… and their last names?"

"No, I only have their first names."

"Right…"

"And they were playing with a little plastic gun that this other gentleman, the gun range owner, said sounded like a… what was it again?"

"A Bond Arms derringer."

"And how do you spell that?"

"Bond, B-O-N-D."

"Bond, like in James Bond?"

"Yes."

"Right, please continue."

"eh, Bond Arms, A-R-M-S."

"Like in arms dealer."

"Correct."

"Right…"

"And according to the gun range owner, these two gentlemen talked about shooting Republican presidential candidate Ronald Drump at tonight's presidential debate, at the Thomas & Mack Center in Las Vegas."

"Yes."

"With a toy gun."

"No, not a toy gun, a plastic gun."

"Right….and what was the gun range owner's name again?"

"Mr. Sigsauer."

"Right… Mr. Sig—Sauer," Gaylin said, somehow succeeding in sounding even more sarcastic. "Mr. Berenson, can I ask you something? Are you really with the FBI? It's okay, you can tell me, I won't be mad."

Berenson couldn't believe his ears. "What? What!? I'm sorry, but are you serious!? I'm informing you of a plot to kill the Republican presidential candidate and you are asking me if I'm really with the FBI? I'm calling you on the FBI's liaison number, aren't I!?"

"Calm down Mr. Berenson. There's no reason to get upset now. It's just that the whole story sounds rather fantastic. Two gentlemen—one of whom may or may not be a Secret Service agent—who, according to a Mr. Sigsauer, are plotting to kill a presidential candidate with a plastic gun. I mean 'Sig Sauer', really?"

"So the guy gave us a false name. That doesn't mean he was lying about the rest."

"Doesn't mean he was speaking the truth either Mr. Berenson. Sounds to me like you've been had."

Berenson fought to control himself. "Look, maybe you're right. But if you're not, and Ronald Drump gets killed with a bullet from a plastic gun tonight, it will be on your conscience—and your career, I might add."

He quickly checked the time on his phone. "Look, the debate starts in less than four hours, so I suggest you get to it and contact whoever is in charge of the protection details. And now if you'll excuse me, I have a lot of other things to take care of. Good-day Mr. *Kay*lin." Berenson hung up. "Asshole."

"For the last time, it's *Gay*lin, *Gay*lin!" the NTAC liaison assistant shouted into his mic. But there was no one there anymore.

42

When he was eleven years old, Peter Veldman had seen an unsettling movie about the French Revolution. In one scene, a group of French nobles—the women still dressed in the same expensive silk, lace-trimmed dresses they had been arrested in—were being led up the makeshift, shaky stairs of a scaffold, where a hooded henchman was executing the condemned in a most orderly fashion, aided by the guillotine. First he laid them face down on a wooden plank, resting their head on a tree stump on the other side of the deadly contraption. Next, he made sure their neck was directly beneath the blade, still dripping with the blood of those who had gone before. Meanwhile, soldiers standing in front of the scaffold, dressed in blue uniform with white cross-belt and wearing the *bonnet rouge* and *tricolor cockade*, were beating a drum roll. Finally, after a last quick glance at the position of the head and neck of the condemned, the henchman pulled the cord releasing the blade, and an instant later another head rolled in the wicker basket, to the cheers of the rambunctious crowd. The whole procedure took less than a minute.

But what had terrified young Peter the most was not the blood dripping from the blade or the heads being chopped off and sent tumbling in the brown wicker basket. It was the waiting the condemned nobles had to endure as they slowly climbed the rickety stairs, the horrified look on their faces as they watched their approaching violent death unfold before their eyes, again and again and again.

It was 3:30 p.m. PDT. Veldman was waiting in line for the security check at the entrance to the Thomas & Mack Center. The debate would begin in two and a half hours. If all went well, Don would have given him the gun by then, loaded and ready. But how was he ever going to sit through the entire debate, waiting for that one moment at the end, crawling closer one second at a time, when he had to draw the gun, aim it at Ronald Drump and pull the trigger? He wanted to, he really did, but now that he was here, he doubted he could.

"Over here sir. Your ticket and ID please."

Veldman handed over his ticket and pulled his passport out of his inner jacket pocket.

"You're Dutch?"

"Yes." Was something wrong? Were they already looking for him, for somebody who they knew was from Holland? But how could they know? How could they possibly know? Who could have told them?

"Thank you Mr. Veldman." The man handed back ticket and passport and gestured at the person who was waiting behind him.

Another security guard signaled Veldman to proceed towards him. "Step over there please."

Of course, unlike the French nobles waiting on the stairs, he could still turn around, he could still decide not to go through with it. He could still walk away from killing this man, who planned to bring back institutional discrimination, concentration camps and deportation. But he wouldn't. He really hoped he wouldn't.

"Please take off your belt, empty your pockets and put the contents in the plastic tray."

This chance was a gift. If he backed down now, if he gave in to his fear, knowing he could have prevented history from repeating itself, he would be nothing less than an accomplice to everything President Ronald Drump would do. If he did nothing, knowing what he knew, he would be a collaborator himself.

"Arms wide please." The man searched him swiftly and routinely. "Thank you." Veldman collected his things and entered the secure area.

"Welcome to the Thomas & Mack Center sir. Would you like a program?"

"No thank you," he smiled.

And there was something else. His grandfather. However wrong and despicable his choices and convictions had been, he certainly was no coward. In September 1944, when the Allies attempted to secure the bridges over the Rhine by dropping over 30,000 British and Polish paratroopers in occupied Holland, most Dutch collaborators quickly fled to Germany. But not Henk Veldman. He went *to* the front, with a fighting unit of his own, to help the Germans push back the British paratroopers. A few months later he was killed on his way to another battlefield, when his car was strafed by a Spitfire.

For all his shame and anger about his grandfather's actions, Peter Veldman could not help but also admire his fortitude, loyalty and courage. How could he pretend to be the better man if he turned back now?

Conrad Richter's emotional state as he waited in line, fifteen minutes after he had seen Veldman go in, was far less elevated, even though he was carrying several items that, if discovered, would not only end the entire operation right then and there, but probably also land him in jail for at least a decade.

Of course, unlike the Dutchman, Richter had received extensive training in operating under much more extreme circumstances than waiting in line for a presidential debate. He was also far more experienced in the job at hand. Killing another human being, even someone you hate, is not an easy thing to do, especially when it's premeditated. You can be trained in the methods, but nothing can really prepare you for the moment when the target is no longer a cardboard cutout but a person of flesh and blood just like you. Richter had already past that point of no return a quarter of a century ago. But for Veldman, it was just around the corner.

There was also the question of character. All his life, Conrad Richter had been independent, stable, methodical, a loner, someone who was inherently at peace with the universe and who didn't need religion, purpose or confirmation from others to keep it that way. His life was a never-ending chess game in which plans were conceived, pieces were moved and plays were executed. There was no point in worrying.

5:30 p.m. PDT

"Gentlemen, this is the captain. Just a short update, we will begin our descent in about fifteen minutes and expect to land at McCarran International Airport a few minutes past 6:00 p.m. local time. We have been told a car will be waiting for you at the hangar to take you to your destination right away."

"Shit, the debate will have started already," Underhill said.

"Well, that can't be helped," Berenson responded. "But people from the LV field office are already there and they have the photo IDs of our four persons of interest."

"How are they checking everybody?"

"They're not. The Thomas & Mack Center opened at 3:00 p.m. local time and by the time our people got there and had sorted out jurisdiction issues with the Secret Service, more than half of those invited had already passed security clearance. The Special Agent in Charge, ehm… Randall Dinello, told me he has sent two agents to check the ticket holders still coming in, two to monitor the images from the security cameras and the rest to patrol the center."

"What, like regular beat cops?" Underhill scoffed. "That is unbelievable. So basically we're looking for the proverbial needle in a haystack."

"Yeah," Berenson scratched the bottom of his chin, "that is, if there even is a needle. Plus, the Secret Service so far hasn't given our agents permission to access the restricted area, so if our guy is indeed masquerading as a Secret Service agent—or a journalist, or a member of the support staff or something—our people wouldn't be able the spot him."

"Jesus, what a mess," Underhill sighed.

"Yeah."

"By the way, I just heard back from the Miami field office. They said Martin Hernandez wasn't home. According to his office he left for an assignment in Turkcy three days ago."

"Wasn't he in Turkey last month as well?"

"Could be the same client," Underhill offered.

Berenson nodded. "Anyway, we can't verify it right now, so let's just keep him on the list."

"Agreed."

"Any word on the others?"

"Well, Richter you know already, he wasn't at home either, but they are keeping an eye on his apartment. Nothing yet from the guys who are supposed to pay Mr. Dykman a visit." But they had to come from Helena, which is a little over two hours away from Livingston. Apparently the Resident Agency in Bozeman couldn't spare anyone."

"Yeah, well, tell them to get out of the car veeeeery slowly when they arrive at Dykman's log cabin, unless they want to risk getting shot at by our rancher friend."

"If he's there in the first place," Underhill noted. "Anyway, nothing from the Paris office about the Toulouse police yet either, but it's the middle of the night there now, so I doubt we'll hear anything from them before tomorrow."

"So all four stay on the list." Berenson put his hands on his face for a moment, rubbed his eyes and looked at his phone. 8:30 p.m. Washington time, meaning it was… 2:30 a.m. in Toulouse. He was still tired. Damn jet lag. But there was no room for that now, because in about thirty minutes he would be in the hunt of his life, a race against time to save a presidential candidate he personally wouldn't even elect dog catcher.

An hour and fifteen minutes earlier

4:15 p.m. PDT

"Your ticket and identification please."

286

Richter presented his ticket and passport.

The security guard briefly examined the document. "Mr....Greenwald," he mumbled under his breath as he verified the name on the ticket. "Here you go sir." He handed back ticket and passport.

Richter nodded and proceeded to the official standing next to the metal detector gate. "Please take off your belt, empty your pockets and put the contents in the tray."

Richter removed his belt and put it in the tray, then took out his phone, wallet and keys, put them in the tray as well and stepped through the metal detector gate, where another security guard was waiting to search him.

At the same moment, less than 50 yards away, FBI Special Agent in Charge Randall Dinello and Secret Service SAC Jane Sanders were engaged in a heated discussion. Dinello wanted Sanders to set aside jurisdiction issues and allow his men access to all parts of the Thomas & Mack Center, to help locate the potential assassin. But Sanders viewed allowing FBI agents in the restricted area more as an act of contamination than cooperation. The situation in the small office where Sanders had brought Dinello and his men to was tense, to say the least, with Secret Service agents basically guarding their FBI colleagues, to prevent them from entering the secure zone without their SAC's permission.

It was one of those situations where the person putting procedure before action is often blamed when things go wrong, by those blessed with the benefit of hindsight. And how easy it would be for pundits and politicians to ridicule precisely this moment: a professional assassin, hired to kill Republican presidential candidate Ronald Drump, passing through security while the nation's top security forces were bickering about rules and regulations.

But Jane Sanders didn't have the benefit of hindsight and therefore told Dinello that since the Secret Service was responsible for protecting the presidential candidates, the FBI should have simply informed her of the threat, so she could have taken appropriate counter-measures, instead of barging in on her shortly before it was going down. Dinello, a very dedicated, if not the most even-tempered man, agitatedly responded that the Bureau had indeed notified the Secret Service (at least that was what Berenson had told him), to which Sanders calmly responded that was impossible, otherwise she would have known about it.

NTAC liaison assistant Kay Gaylin should have indeed contacted Jane Sanders, but had somehow completely overlooked the fact that the Thomas & Mack Center had its own Secret Service security detail in place and had called Mike Armstrong, SAC of the Republican candidate's protection detail, instead. Armstrong, for his part, might have thought to ask Gaylin if he had also relayed the information to the Thomas & Mack Center security detail, had he not been facing a temporary crisis of his own, after the candidate had ordered the motorcade to stop on Lincoln Boulevard, en route to LAX, because he had decided not to attend the debate after all (a decision he would reverse just as abruptly fifteen minutes later).

Sanders' icy calmness infuriated Dinello even more. He practically shouted at her it didn't matter who had fucked up, because he could tell her for a fact they had received a credible tip that somebody would try to kill Drump at tonight's debate with a plastic gun. Sanders scoffed at the mention of a plastic gun, but the 4.5" x 3.75" x 1.2" weapon had at that moment in fact already passed security. By the time Dinello had calmed down and Sanders had agreed to allow the FBI access to the Center, with the exception of the restricted area, Richter had locked himself in a bathroom stall. It was 4:30 p.m.

Meanwhile, Veldman was wandering around aimlessly, looking anxious and ill-at-ease. He bought a pizza slice to kill the time, walked around with it for a while, then threw it away without having taken a single bite. At a campaign stand he bought a red baseball cap with the slogan 'Make America Amazing Again!' printed on it and a white T-shirt saying 'USA #1!', figuring he could use some camouflage. Two college girls cheerfully shouted "Drump is Dumb!" in his ear as they passed him. One of them had the words 'Stronger Together' printed on her well-proportioned behind, one word on each butt cheek.

He thought about leaving every second of every slow-crawling minute, the way a smoker yearns for a cigarette at the end of a long international flight. But at the same time he was also determined to see it through. Two paths, each leading to an intolerable outcome. Doing nothing would forever destroy his self-respect—and what is that but the very soul of existence?—while going through with it would likely destroy his life but redeem his soul. It was an impossible choice, and yet also a very easy one.

Inside the bathroom stall, Richter carefully removed the double-stacked 2.5" barrel, plastic screw, 4" Allen wrench and a syringe from the heel of his right boot, placing them on the toilet roll holder, then retrieved the grip and trigger part from the heel of his left boot. He put the barrel in his lap, aligned the screw opening sitting on top with the ones on top of the grip, picked up the small screw with his free hand and placed it on the opening, then slowly reached for the Allen wrench, fixed it on the screw's head and turned it until the screw had been driven in completely. Lastly, he pushed the barrel into the groove that extended from the grip until he heard a plastic-sounding click. After confirming the barrel was solidly fixed, he pushed down the lever between the trigger and grip and swung the barrel open again. Richter smiled. What a wonderful little gun this was. He was almost sorry he had to part with it.

He got out his key chain and carefully screwed off the head of the jolly-looking small teddybear, holding it face up. When the head was loose, he took the furry pink body and shook the two 9mm bullets into his lap, then screwed the body back on the head. He picked up the bullets, loaded the gun and pushed the barrel back into the groove until he heard the click. Satisfied, he tucked the gun in the left inner pocket of his jacket and looked at his phone. 5:25. Almost time to meet Veldman. He picked up the syringe and checked the cap on the needle.

5:30 p.m. PDT

Around the same time Berenson was rubbing his eyes and cursing his jet lag at 41,000 feet, Richter looked out for Veldman at the Snack Attack immediately to the right of the South-West entrance, their agreed meeting place. Almost subconsciously, he pulled the red 'Make America Amazing Again!' cap a little deeper over his eyes. He had never liked crowds like this. Being surrounded on all sides, the yelling, the shrieks of laughter, the pushing, the sheer chaos of it all. He preferred people to be dispersed and in front of him, so he could keep tabs on everyone.

But there was something else going on that made him feel uncomfortable, only he couldn't quite place it. Was it the adrenaline talking, being so close to the culmination of months of planning for the biggest hit of his life? Was he still spooked by the visit from those FBI agents? Had they returned, maybe even with a warrant?

290

But even if they had, though, there was nothing in his apartment that could lead them here. The same held for Zimmerman, who only knew about the how, not about the who, when and where.

And yet all of a sudden there it was, this strain of anxiousness running through his mind, something he normally never felt in connection to a job. Of course he normally never worked with amateurs either, so maybe that was the source of his uneasiness, the remote possibility that Veldman had somehow betrayed him. But no, even if the Dutchman had decided not to go through with it, he would never go to the police, he'd sooner hope 'Secret Service agent Don Jensen' would take the shot himself after all.

Just when his attention shifted to two men in dark-blue suits who were acting like they were looking for someone, seemingly alternating between studying faces and checking their phones as they slowly walked in his direction, Veldman stepped in front of him.

"You're here," Richter said, genuinely surprised.

"You didn't think I'd show up, did you?"

"The thought had crossed my mind. But you're here now and that's what's important." He pulled at his baseball cap again and looked over Veldman's shoulder at the two suits, who were about 40 yards away and closing. "Listen, we don't have much time. I have to be back soon." He moved a little closer to Veldman, reached into his jacket and pulled out the gun. "Take it. It's loaded."

Veldman hesitated.

"Look Peter, there is no time for fucking around anymore, either you do it or you don't do it, but in 15 seconds I'm gone."

For the past two days Veldman had fantasized about being the hero assassin, the young Dutchman who stopped fascism from rearing its ugly head in the United States—not unlike the little Dutch boy who plugged the dike with his finger. But during the past two hours he had found it increasingly difficult to hold on to that fantasy. And now time was up. Had it all been driven by make-believe? Was that all he had been after, *imagining* what it would be like? But if that were true, then where exactly did the pretending stop and reality begin?

He took the gun and put it in his own pocket.

Richter nodded. "Wait until after the debate, when he is shaking hands with the audience and posing for selfies. That will be your best chance. Drop the gun as soon as you've fired the second shot and then make your way to an exit. There are thousands of people in the audience and they'll all want to get out. The chaos should give you at least a short window before they close all the exits. As soon as you're outside, make your way to the rendezvous point I showed you. I'll be there as soon as I can."

He saw the two suits looking in his direction. They were maybe 25 yards away.

The Dutchman looked him straight in the eye. "Yeah sure," he said matter-of-factly. "Well, see you on the other side."

"Good luck," Richter said. The suits were at 20 yards now. Something didn't feel right here. He needed to go, but there was still one more thing to do.

Veldman turned around to walk away.

It was now or never.

"Peter, wait, you have a wasp or something on your back."

Veldman tried to look over his shoulder but couldn't see anything. "Can you get it off?"

"Yeah, hold on," Richter said, the syringe already in his right hand.

He quickly took off the needle cover with his other hand, inserted the needle in Veldman's back at a 90 degree angle and pushed the plunger down.

"Ouch! Shit I think it got me!" Veldman exclaimed, frantically trying to look over his shoulder again.

"Sorry about that. He's gone now, though."

"Fucking bugs." Veldman rubbed the place where had felt the sting, then exhaled loudly to shake it off. "Okay, I'm gone."

As he walked away in the direction of the two suits, he turned around with a smile and said: "*Sic semper tyrannis.*"

But Richter was already gone.

6:04 p.m. PDT

The turbofan of the Gulfstream V was still winding down when Berenson and Underhill raced down the airstair and into the black Suburban. As the car sped towards the Thomas & Mack Center via Paradise Road, Berenson called Las Vegas SAC Randall Dinello.

"Randall, Steve Berenson here. We are three minutes out. Any updates?"

—

"Okay, I understand. Has the debate started already?"

—

"No, it works to our advantage. It means the audience is now concentrated in the arena. If our guy is there, it might be easier to spot him."

—

"Oh come on, there must be a thousand cameras in there."

—

"Well how about the kiss cam? They can use that one can't they?"

—

"Yeah, alright. And please tell agent Sanders we're almost there."

—

"You too."

The candidates had just finished their opening statements and Chris Anderson was about to read the first question.

Richter was standing inside the arena, on the upper section, immediately to the right of the portal entrance to sections 217 and 218, from where lower sections 111 and 112 could also be reached. He knew Veldman's seat was close to the front of section 111—from where it would be easier to reach the stage after the debate had ended—but he couldn't see him. His own seat was on the last row of section 217, but for what he was about to do he needed some room. Leaning against the wall, he carefully unscrewed the teddybear's head again—this time to get the drone out of the head—as Anderson asked the first question.

"Nevada has one of the fastest growing Latino populations in the country. In 1970, only about 5 percent of the state's population was Hispanic or Latino—in 2016, it is close to 30 percent. Mr. Drump, you are a strong advocate of curtailing illegal immigration from Mexico by building a wall along the border. However, more than five million Mexicans are currently already residing illegally in the U.S, together with six million illegal immigrants from other countries. What is your plan for these eleven million people and what policies would you put in place to realize it?"

Richter switched on the drone and put it in the palm of his hand. With his free hand, he pulled out his phone and tapped the drone app icon. Tapping the green square brought the drone's camera view online. He had practiced endlessly for this next part, but never in an arena filled with people and watched by the Secret

Service. He checked to see if anyone was looking at him. The first seconds would be the most vulnerable. But all eyes were directed at the debate stage.

"The plan is very simple Chris, I'm going to deport them all. It's very simple. They have no right to be here and they're costing us a huge amount of money, I mean, it's so much, you wouldn't believe it."

Richter tapped the green-striped rectangular take off button on the right bottom of the app. The drone's piezoelectric actuators kicked in right away and started flapping the wings at 120 times per second. As soon as the artificial bug was in the air, Richter took the phone in both hands and hit the upward pointing arrows at the center of the transparent circle on the right, to accelerate the drone's lift off.

"And can you tell us what specific policies you would implement to achieve that goal?" Anderson asked.

Richter's first objective was for the drone to reach the big cube with the four projection screens, hanging from the ceiling at the center of the arena. He would land the drone on top of the cube and then plan the last part of the trip.

"Look, Mr. Berenson, not to disrespect you or the Bureau, but I find it all a bit confusing," Jane Sanders opened the ad hoc conference with Berenson, Underhill, Randal Dinello, Mike Armstrong and his counterpart—responsible for Clayton's security detail—Brenda Feelgood. They were in the same small office where she and Dinello had had their heated argument about two hours earlier.

"You received a tip from a gun range owner about two men planning to assassinate Ronald Drump with a plastic gun, one of them supposedly a member of the Secret Service. But you've also gathered intel about a professional killer who wants to eliminate the candidate with a poisonous drone—and this killer may or may not be one of the four persons of interest your men are looking for right now."

"I have to say, I find it highly unlikely that a member of the Secret Service would participate in such a plot in the first place," Armstrong said, "even more so when it's all based on the say-so of some hillbilly gun range owner who wouldn't even confirm the identity of the supposed plotters. I don't know, sounds like a hoax to me."

"I have to agree with Mike here," Sanders said.

"Look," Berenson began, forcing himself to remain calm, "the Swiss gunsmith who was picked up a month ago had just sold a custom-made plastic gun *and* a modified military reconnaissance drone the size of a housefly, armed with a remote controlled syringe, to a customer he had been doing business with for over twenty years."

"So? Could just be a gun nut. Not like we don't have plenty of them here at home," Armstrong shrugged.

"This customer paid 40,000 euros for them."

"So he's a rich gun nut."

"Now, according to the gun range owner, the plastic gun he heard sounded almost exactly like a Bond Arms derringer," Berenson continued, looking at Sanders.

"Oh I love those little things," Armstrong chuckled, "I have one in my car, one in my other car, one in the shed, one—"

"Yes, well, apparently the 'rich gun nut' likes them too," Berenson interjected, "because he had specifically asked the Swiss gunsmith for an all-plastic version of exactly that type of gun."

"Uh-oh," Armstrong uttered.

"And you think the man who bought the drone and gun is one

of these four people?" Sanders pointed at the creased ID printouts of Richter, Hernandez, Dykman and Moretti, a.k.a. Shandor.

"Yes."

Sanders was sold. "Okay, let's issue a high-level threat among all Secret Service agents present here right away, together with the ID shots of the four persons of interest. The debate is already underway and there will be no breaks, which means we can't communicate with the candidates until the debate is finished, at 7:30 p.m."

"Any chance the candidates will agree to forgo the usual handshaking pleasantries after the debate is over?" Berenson asked.

Armstrong scoffed. "I can't speak for Senator Clayton but as far as Mr. Drump is concerned: none."

"How many cameras can we point at the audience?"

"We have two at the moment," Dinello said. "Two of my guys are monitoring them in the control room."

"I'll ask the Center's manager if we can get some more cameras pointing at the stands," Sanders said.

"Jake, why don't you go to the control room as well," Berenson suggested, wanting someone up there he trusted and whom he knew had actually seen all the people on the list himself. "By the way, do you guys have any snipers at the upper level of the restricted area, behind the debate stage?"

"We don't normally at an indoor event like this, but you're right, I'll arrange for two teams to take position right away."

"Alright, let's get this fucker!" Armstrong shouted, as he slammed his fist into his hand, forgetting for a moment his days as quarterback at Notre Dame were long behind him.

"Love your enthusiasm," Underhill grinned as he walked out.

Still leaning against the wall at the back of upper level sector 217, Richter reactivated the drone and had it take off from the top of the cube. He had practiced this last part dozens of times, but this was for all the marbles and he would be lying to himself if he pretended this flight would be the same as all the others.

"Okay, Steve, I'm in the control room," Underhill said, putting his phone on speaker. "We have two cameras zoomed in on the audience, scanning it sector by sector. Nothing yet so far."

High above Chris Anderson, sitting behind his desk, and Valery Clayton and Ronald Drump, standing behind their glass lecterns, the drone flew towards the back of the debate stage.

"You should release the speeches you gave to those big Wall Street banks," Drump said, disregarding the rule not to directly engage the other candidate. "How much you got for them, $250,000 a piece? Tell you what, I'll double that if you release them right now, today, because it's just sad that you won't release them, very sad."

"I will publish my speeches if you publish your tax records," Clayton, smiling confidently, shot back her standard response.

Richter had the drone descend until it was just a few inches above the ground.

"Oh God, I think that's him," Underhill said.

"What, who!? Where!?" Berenson's voice shouted through the speaker.

"That guy, the New Yorker, ehm, Richter, Conrad Richter."

"Where? Where!?"

Underhill pushed the comm button for camera 2. "Go back, go back, I think we just spotted our target."

Richter had maneuvered the drone behind Drump, hovering about ten feet away, at the height of his ankles. He tapped the forward thrust button.

"Oh that's just a bunch of baloney," Clayton said, to loud cheers of her supporters. "Even the IRS says it's okay to release your tax data while you're being audited."

"There!" Jake said, looking intently at the screen, together with the others. "Sector 217. The guy standing at the back."

"Well, is it him!?" Berenson shouted, agitated to the point of explosion.

"Eh…"

"Come on Jake, it's a simple question, is it him!?"

"Eh…, he's wearing a baseball cap… he's looking down at his phone… he's doing something on his phone. It's hard to tell, but yes I think it's him."

"You *think*? I can't give them the go ahead on an assumption. You tell me you *know*, Jake. Because if we blow this man's brains out and it's *not* him, it's all over."

The dark-blue pant legs were growing bigger and bigger on Richter's phone. It was just a couple more feet now.

"Jake! Is it him?"

Underhill desperately wanted to be sure. "Ahhhhhh… I don't know. I can't say for sure without him looking up."

"Goddammit!" Berenson exclaimed in frustration. Then, to Sanders: "Tell the director to go to commercial so we can pick him up."

"There's not supposed to be any commercials," Sanders said.

"Look, we can't take the risk. Either we drop this guy right now, or we make the candidates leave and pick him up. I'm sure DNN can conjure up a commercial block at a moment's notice."

Sanders quickly changed the channel on her comms and told

the agent at the broadcast booth to tell the director to go to commercial immediately.

Three feet.

Two feet.

Just a few inches now. Richter swiped his index finger downward, decreasing the drone's speed to a crawl, then swiped the semicircle button in a clockwise direction, so it would land vertically .

"Last week, you said—"

"I'm sorry to have to interrupt you there Mr. Drump," Anderson interjected, "but I'm told we have to go to commercial first. We'll be right back."

Richter heard Anderson say they were going to commercial, but the drone was too close to abort now. It was just two inches away… almost there… and gotcha… it was latched onto Drump's right pant leg.

Suddenly the drone's camera image began to move violently. Richter looked up and saw that both candidates were already leaving the stage, with Drump moving at a particularly brisk pace.

He looked down on the phone again and moved his finger to the red button that would push the syringe forward, force the needle through Drump's pants and skin and press the plunger down.

He tapped it.

But at the same moment Drump went through the exit to the right of the stage and disappeared, preventing Richter from seeing any physical reaction.

Richter allowed another one… two… three seconds to go by, then tapped the red button again—to retract the needle—and swiped the semicircle counter-clockwise, to unlatch the drone from the pant leg.

Did it work? Had the ricin been delivered and the drone been released? Was it lying on the floor somewhere? The camera image was just as dark as a moment before. At any rate, it was time to get out.

Just as he stepped away from the wall, two men came through the portal entrance on his left.

"Excuse me, sir." Richter saw a tall, bold man, left hand along his side, right hand behind his back, an athletic figure filling out a dark-blue suit, beige tie, light blue shirt. Secret Service.

"There seems to be something wrong with your allotted seating number. Would you please follow me?"

Richter smiled.

"This way please sir," the man said, sounding polite but adamant as he stepped aside and gestured him to go through the exit, where other dark-blue suits would no doubt be waiting. He knew somewhere up there, behind the battery of bright stage lights, sniper rifles were already trained on him. That's where he would be.

43

"He's clean," Jane Sanders said, standing outside the small office. Inside, Richter was sitting handcuffed to his chair.

"No he's not, I'm holding his fake passport right here." Berenson waved the document they had just taken from Richter.

"I mean no plastic gun, no drone, nothing. If this man really was a threat, I think it's safe to say he's been neutralized."

"What do you mean 'if he was a threat'?" Berenson's eyes widened. "He's our guy. He was on our list of suspects, we talked to him just three weeks ago and now he shows up at the same place where according to an anonymous source an assassination attempt was going to take place?"

"I agree it's suspect, but that doesn't make it true. Could still be a coincidence. It's also not my concern. My concern is the security of this location and, ultimately, the security of the two principals. With your man in our custody, I consider this threat neutralized."

Berenson threw his hands in the air and opened his mouth to say something, then reconsidered. "Mind if I talk to him?"

Sanders grinned. "Have at it. I'm going to update Armstrong and Feelgood."

"Brought you some coffee. You drink coffee, right?" Berenson put two cups on the desk.

"Sure."

Berenson sat down. "So… Mr. Greenwald, huh?"

An arrogant little smile curled up in the corner of Richter's mouth.

"You can smile all you like Mr. Richter, but I already have you on using a forged passport."

"Good for you."

"You don't seem worried." Berenson took a sip from his coffee, leaned forward and lowered his voice a bit. "But you should be."

"Really?"

"Title 18, Section 1543. 'Whoever willfully and knowingly uses a forged passport, shall be imprisoned for up to 10 years, in the case of the first or second such offense'. Well, I'm paraphrasing, but that's the gist of it."

Richter scoffed. "You seem to enjoy knowing that stuff. Maybe you should have been a lawyer. Pays a hell of a lot better than being an FBI agent, I can tell you that. And while we're on the subject, I think I'd like to speak to a lawyer myself."

"Where's the drone, Richter?" Berenson said. "Where's the plastic gun Zimmerman manufactured for you?"

"No idea what or who you are talking about. Zimmerman? Sounds German."

"Where's your buddy? Is he still in the audience?"

This was new information for Richter and for just a tiny speck of a second he showed a hint of surprise.

Berenson didn't miss it.

"Yeah, yeah, we know all about him and the two of you practicing at the gun range with that plastic Bond Arms derringer."

The gun range. Cahill. He must have overheard them and called the Feds. Motherfucker.

"Yeah, you didn't know about that, did you?" Berenson smiled.

"Look, if he's still in the audience, and he succeeds, you'll be tried as his co-conspirator…" He paused for a moment, to let it sink in. "And Nevada still has the death penalty. Did you know that? Yeah… that means you'll fry, or get injected, or gassed, or whatever the hell it is they do down here."

Richter kept looking at him with the same cold blue eyes and the same arrogant little smile.

"But if you tell us where he is, you might still walk out a free man some time before your 80th birthday."

Richter kept looking at Berenson.

"I'd like to see a lawyer now."

Outside, Berenson came across Underhill, who had lingered at the control booth after ID'ing Richter.

"You talked to him?" Underhill said.

"Yeah, just now."

"What's the matter, you look worried. We got him, right?"

But Berenson wagged his finger. "No, no. No. I got a bad feeling about this. This is not over. Come on, let's go."

"Where?"

"Back stage."

"Sorry sir, this is a restricted area." The Secret Service agent briefly lifted his right hand.

Berenson showed him his badge. "I'm agent Berenson, this is agent Underhill. We've been working with your boss and we need to speak to her right away."

"I'm sorry sir, but you have no jurisdiction here and you know it. Can't let you through."

Berenson sighed in frustration. "Then contact her, contact agent Sanders and tell her we have important information."

"Mr. Drump, your closing statement please," Chris Anderson said.

"Thank you." The Republican candidate looked squarely into the camera. "I've known politicians all my life. They're all talk, but nothing gets done. Take a look at our country. All these politicians, they're in the pockets of special interests, they give speeches to banks for a quarter million dollars and then tell you they're going to break up the banks, but they're not going to break up the banks, because they're *paid* by the banks, they need the banks. But I'm in nobody's pocket. I will make us win again, against China and Mexico, because I will build that wall and stop the tidal wave of Mexicans crossing our border illegally. And I will defeat ISIS, instead of sitting around a table and talk about them. Politicians get nothing done but I will get it done. I will make America Amazing again!"

"Thank you Mr. Drump. And that concludes the third and final presidential debate. I want to thank the candidates and the Thomas & Mack Center here at the University of Las Vegas, Nevada, for hosting us, and of course you, our audience, for watching. Thank you very much and good night."

Berenson, Underhill and Sanders were standing to the right side of the stage, close to the entrance the candidates had taken during the unexpected commercial break, and which they would be taking again in a few minutes. Ronald Drump was about 15 yards away from them, waving, as he was walking to the edge of the stage to shake hands with his fans and sign a few baseball caps and T-shirts.

"You have to get them out of there now! Berenson shouted over the music. "That guy, the second guy, he is still there!"

"You don't know that agent Berenson, we don't even know that the guy we apprehended had any intention of attacking one of the candidates."

"He had a fake ID."

"So does my 16-year-old daughter," Mike Armstrong said, coming up from behind.

"Not like this," Berenson shook his head. "This was done very professionally. You can't get this from a guy selling fake IDs to teenage kids looking to buy a beer."

"So he's a rich criminal and he likes weird, exotic weapons," Armstrong shrugged. "Besides, we've got him, I really don't see the problem."

The Dutchman had elbowed himself to the edge of the stage. Drump was less than five yards away, signing a college girl's copy of 'The Art of the Steal'.

He slowly pulled the gun from his pocket, cocked the hammer, and, fully extending his right arm, aimed it at the Republican presidential candidate.

"Drump, you son of a bitch!" Peter Veldman exclaimed.

Epilogue

An hour later, Alan Barker put down his phone and leaned back into the heavy leather chair behind the mahogany desk, his hands cupping the desk's soft round edge, his fingers drumming its surface. As he reflected on the news, he allowed his eyes to wander. Past the sparse light shining through the green shade of the bankers lamp, along the patient rows of books and the library ladder, leaning against the towering bookcase, until resting on the colonial era chairs in the middle of the den, where Paul Skovack, Chris Mathers and he had sat that Sunday night, less than three months ago, and set in motion the events that had abruptly reached their apotheosis tonight.

The house was quiet. Bunny had long gone to bed, she hadn't been feeling well. Suddenly, the space around him felt dark and cold. Barker looked at his watch. A few minutes to midnight. He nodded to himself. He would talk to Skovack and Mathers in the morning. He leaned forward, flicked off the switch on the bankers lamp and rose in the dark. He didn't need the light to find his way out.

The day was done.

Dear reader,

Thank you for buying *The Dog and its Day*. I hope you enjoyed reading it as much as I did writing it.

I would also like to thank Merijn de Haen for creating another beautiful layout and helping to improve the book through sharp and meticulous editing. Same goes for my wife, who pointed out a few darlings that still needed to be killed, and Teddi Black, for designing a powerful cover.

I hope to meet you again on the pages of my next book. Until then, find me on jellepeters.com or shoot me an email at info@jellepeters.com.

Lastly, if you have a moment, I would of course appreciate it if you could write a short review on Amazon, letting me and others know what you thought of *The Dog and its Day*.

All the best,
J.C. Peters